Drive Me Wild

Books by P.J. Mellor

PLEASURE BEACH

GIVE ME MORE

MAKE ME SCREAM

DRIVE ME WILD

THE COWBOY
(with Vonna Harper, Nelissa Donovan, and Nikki Alton)

THE FIREFIGHTER
(with Susan Lyons and Alyssa Brooks)

NAUGHTY, NAUGHTY
(with Melissa MacNeal and Valerie Martinez)

ONLY WITH A COWBOY
(with Melissa MacNeal and Vonna Harper)

Published by Kensington Publishing Corp.

Drive Me Wild

P.J. MELLOR

APHRODISIA

KENSINGTON BOOKS

http://www.kensingtonbooks.com

APHRODISIA BOOKS are published by

Kensington Publishing Corp.
850 Third Avenue
New York, NY 10022

ISBN-13: 978-0-7582-2024-0
ISBN-10: 0-7582-2024-3

First Kensington Trade Paperback Printing: January 2009

10 9 8 7 6 5 4 3 2 1

Printed in the United States of America

To Peggy Hamilton-Swire, with much love and gratitude.
I couldn't have done it without you, Peg!

Acknowledgments

Special thanks to John Scognamiglio—we make a great team! I look forward to working with you for many years to come.

Contents

DOUBLE TROUBLE

1

"No way in hell." Ryan Wright squinted in the late afternoon sun at his twin brother, Braedon, and wondered what kind of mess his sibling had gotten himself into this time.

"Please." Braedon cleared his throat, and took a draw from the sweating longneck before setting it back on the sun-bleached wood table between them. He glanced nervously around the deck of the deserted ice house before zeroing in on his brother again. "You loved the *twin trick* when we were kids."

"We're not kids now. We weren't kids the last few times, in fact."

"I wouldn't ask if I had any other choice. I'll never ask you for another thing. I swear."

"You swore last time." Ryan stood and threw some bills on the table, trying to ignore the way the hairs on the back of his neck stood on alert whenever he was near his twin brother. "Not only did it cost me several thousand, it damn near wrecked my life."

Braedon's hand on his arm halted Ryan's exit. "Please. Don't you think you're the very last person I'd ask for a favor?" He gave a bark of laughter. "Unfortunately, you're the only one I *can* ask. The only one who will do. What do you want me to do? Beg? I'll beg. Hell, I'll do whatever it takes to get you to help me, to agree to do this just one more time." He raked a hand through his short blond hair. "This is my life we're talking about here," he added in a strangled voice.

"My God, what kind of trouble are you in?" Ryan sank back into his chair and gauged his brother's expression. In his experience, Braedon's face told him more than his mouth. And right now it was telling Ryan his brother was scared shitless.

"I made some, uh, less than solid investments, took some chances that didn't pan out." He held up his hand. "I know, we all do that occasionally. But I thought I could fix it. I took out a loan. Then another. And another."

Dread clawed at Ryan's stomach. "I get the feeling these loans weren't from a bank."

Braedon scrubbed at his face and shook his head.

"How much?" Despite his firm resolution to not aid his irresponsible brother again, he reached into his open sport coat for his checkbook. When Braedon remained silent, Ryan looked up, pen poised.

"More than you can float me, this time," Braedon said in a choked voice.

"How much?" Ryan asked again.

"Eight hundred would get them off my back for a while."

"Only eight hundred dollars? Sorry, bro, but I don't understand how you can be so bent out of shape over eight hundred dollars."

"That's eight hundred *thousand* dollars . . . *bro.* And, like I said, it's only a payment."

Ryan stopped writing.

"I can't help you this time," he said, closing the checkbook and slipping it back into his coat.

"Ah, but that's where you're wrong, big brother. Like I said, you're the only one who can. And it won't cost you anything except a few days out of your life."

Ryan wrestled with the pros and cons. He'd told Braedon he was finished with him and his stupid get-rich-quick schemes and shell games, that he was tired of bailing him out every time he turned around. He paused, swallowing the dread. Then again, he did have some vacation time coming. He had no plans. And Braedon did look desperate. And he was his brother.

His shoulders slumped in defeat. "Okay, I'll do it. I'll pretend to be you. Just one more time." At Braedon's triumphant smile, he gripped his younger brother's shirt and drew him closer until their noses touched. Eye to eye, he said, "But I swear to God, this is the last time I'm bailing your sorry ass out. And there have to be some ground rules."

Braedon's blue eyes took on the cool turquoise Ryan had come to recognize as cocky arrogance. He tugged his wifebeater T-shirt from his brother's fists and stepped back with a satisfied smile. "Thanks. I knew you wouldn't let me down." His gaze scanned Ryan head to toe. "You'll need to lose the pretty-boy haircut. No one will believe my hair grew overnight."

"What about your job? I don't even know where you work these days."

"No problemo. I'm currently on permanent hiatus. I plan to find a better job, anyway." He dug in the pockets of his jeans. "Here's my license, and the keys to my car and my apartment. And my cell. Now give me yours. Then we'll switch clothes and shoes."

"Wait. You haven't heard my stipulations."

Braedon heaved a sigh and shifted his booted feet on the deck. "Go on."

"You will not contact anyone in my address book, either on the cell or my computer. I have some vacation time coming, so you don't have to worry about going into the office. You are not to touch or even look at my stock portfolio. I mean it. No selling or trading, no matter how great of a deal you think it is. And I expect you to treat my home and my belongings, including my clothes, with respect. Is that clear?"

"Man, I told you the fire was an accident."

"Is that clear? Because if it's not, I'm not doing this."

"Yeah, okay, it's clear."

"And one last thing."

Braedon arched his brow.

"Don't sleep with anyone I know this time."

"That wasn't my fault—"

"I don't care. Swear to me you won't sleep with anyone I know. Swear, or I call the whole thing off."

"I don't care if you sleep with anyone *I* know." Braedon held up his hands. "Okay, I swear. I swear." He looked across the parking lot at the highway. "Not that I'd be attracted to the skanks you date anyway."

Ryan took a deep breath in an effort to relieve the tension radiating into his shoulders. This was such a bad idea on all levels. But he'd do it. Just one more time.

2

Ryan watched his brother leave the parking lot with a squeal of the brand new tires he'd had installed on his Lexus SC430 the previous day, then glanced down at the keys in his hand.

A long time ago, he'd been an only child for a little over five blissful minutes. Then Braedon had put in his appearance, complaining all the way out of the womb, and had not stopped whining since.

Whenever he'd bailed Braedon out as kids, their grandmother always reminded him no good deed went unpunished. He thought of that as he walked to the back of the parking lot, not at all sure what he'd find, absently scratching along the neck of his brother's T-shirt.

What he saw made him blink.

A bright red Aston Martin Vantage convertible sat alone under the streetlight.

Just to be sure, he thumbed the keypad. The car elicited a blip, and the taillights blinked at him.

"No wonder he's drowning in debt," he murmured, sliding

into the glove-soft leather driver's seat. He'd just read about the car in *Car and Driver* magazine. It ran an easy hundred and twenty-six thousand dollars. He ran his hand along the shift box, and caressed the leather covered steering wheel.

The motor purred so smoothly it almost gave him a hard-on.

Anxious to try out the *Sportshift* he'd read about, he lowered the top and took off after pushing the navigation system for home, and did his best to relax and enjoy the ride.

He grinned when the sexy computerized voice told him to take the next exit. Oh, yeah, he could definitely get used to driving a car like this.

Penny Harding sniffed and wiped her drippy nose. Braedon would be back. He always came back. She twisted the engagement ring on her finger, thinking about the fight they'd had, and wondered if his return would be a good or a bad thing.

Braedon Wright was gorgeous. She'd been thrilled when he'd sought her out at their company party. Breathless when he'd first kissed her. And positively orgasmic when he'd taken her, that first time, standing up against his sexy red car, along the side of the road by the beach.

In hindsight, she couldn't help but wonder if part of the earth-shattering orgasm wasn't due to the thrill of being with a bad boy, the possibility of being caught, literally, with their pants down beside a public road. The sex afterwards sure hadn't come close to that first mind-blowing time.

Her stomach hurt, just thinking about the hateful, awful things he'd said to her earlier. She walked to the fridge and pulled out a Coke, popping the top and chugging down half the can. Her burp practically rattled the glasses in the cherrywood cupboards. She looked guiltily around the abandoned apartment, then slowly walked to stare out the sidelight by the door. Where was he?

What had Braedon seen in her that no one else had ever seen? Had their last argument chased him away for good? Why was she so hesitant about setting a wedding date? Anyone in their right mind would beat feet to the altar. She knew he could certainly do better. Her blah brown hair and pale green eyes were nothing to write home about. Allergies prevented her from wearing much makeup. Not that she'd ever been any good at applying it, anyway. She glanced at her less than impressive chest. Maybe she should ask her father to pay for augmentations for her birthday.

Braedon had his flaws, but he was handsome and would make pretty babies. And in all probability, he was her last shot at marriage. Heck, to be honest, he was her only shot in her whole twenty-nine years. She would not blow it. When he came home—and he would come home eventually, he always did—she was going to be waiting for him. She would prove she wasn't pathetic and needy, prove her sexuality. The thought of Braedon having sex with anyone else tore at her, and she made a vow to be sexier, to be the aggressor, like he was always telling her to be. Who knew? Maybe she'd discover she liked being sexier, and it would push her into making that final step in her commitment to Braedon.

Ryan turned the car into the covered space with the apartment number above it and sat for a moment. He closed his eyes, listening to the distant sound of waves in the Gulf of Mexico breaking on the shore, and took a deep breath.

Braedon's apartment was just across a short expanse of grass. Ryan snorted. His brother had no respect for money. He'd left all the lights on.

It took a second to fit the key into the lock, but the tumblers eventually fell into place and the door swung open.

The first thing he noticed was a trail of yellow rose petals leading from the tiled foyer down a hardwood hallway. Tossing his keys on the small table by the door, he followed the petals.

Light flickered on the walls of the hall, causing him to wonder if there was a fire.

The door to the right stood open. He nudged it with his toe, his breath catching.

A goddess stood by the door on the other side of the room. Totally naked, her smooth skin glistened in the candlelight, burnishing her chin-length hair. She walked to him, a small smile on her glossed lips.

"Braedon," she purred, stopping just short of rubbing the tips of her tits against his skimpy shirt. "I was getting worried. It's not like you to be gone so long. Where have you been?" Her pale eyes widened. "I-I'm not quizzing you, honey. I was just worried." She stroked his erection, then slipped her hand into his jeans to hold him. "And horny." She smiled up at him. "You, too, I see." She reached for the top button of his fly. "Let's see if we can do something about that."

"Ah, I need a shower." Who the hell was she, and why was she in his brother's apartment? "I'm sweaty. Drove with the top down, then stopped and got a haircut, so I need to rinse off."

She frowned. "I thought you got a haircut yesterday."

Shit. "Yeah, well, I had to go back and have it redone."

"Are you okay?"

"Sure . . . why?"

She shrugged, causing him to force his gaze from her well oiled chest. "Your voice sounds odd. Like maybe you're coming down with something."

He coughed for effect. "Probably from the night air."

She nodded absently and he slipped into the bathroom, closing and locking the door. He dug in his pocket and pulled out Braedon's BlackBerry. "C'mon, pick up!"

When his own voice came on the line, he hung up and twisted on the shower controls, cursing his brother for forgetting such an important detail, like the woman standing naked on the other side of the door.

Rather than clear his mind, the steam of the shower wove around him, stroking his sudden erection, making him impossibly harder.

He jumped when the shower door opened and cool air surrounded him. Before he could find his voice, the woman stepped in. How had she gotten in?

"I locked the door!" *Smooth, Ryan, real smooth.* It was a safe bet those would not have been Braedon's first words.

She smiled and placed her cool hands on his chest. "Why'd you do that? You know that lock hasn't worked since you moved in." The steam activated the warm, sultry scent of her perfume to waft around him, making his mouth water. She took the soap in her hand and began lathering him. All over.

No working lock. *Great, Braedon, another thing you neglected to mention.*

He reached down to push her away and somehow ended up with his hands full of breasts. Slippery, warm breasts with pebbled nipples.

She stepped closer, evidently thinking he wanted to play. Given the circumstances, not a stretch of the imagination. Her tan hand, with short unpolished nails, dragged over and around his pectorals. Then that same hand stroked the quivering muscles of his abdomen, gliding lower to travel to the part leaping to attention. When she gently fisted his length, he closed his eyes, shuddering as he tried to dredge up thoughts of baseball.

Unfortunately, all he could see behind his lids was the woman in front of him with nothing on except umpire padding.

He groaned.

She must have taken that as a sign because she climbed on his body and took his mouth. Her kiss was teasing, innocent yet sexy. Before he realized what he was doing, his arms held her high against his chest, while his mouth devoured hers.

Stop, his mind screamed. *You don't even know her name. You're standing in a shower at your brother's house. The naked woman in your arms has probably fucked your brother in ways that are illegal in most states.*

She shifted position, breaking mouth contact to push down on his shoulders, bringing her breasts in line with his mouth, her warm, wet pussy branding his abs.

He'd stop. His tongue ringed a plump nipple before drawing it into his mouth. Soon. Just a few more seconds of luxuriating in the tactile pleasure surrounding him, in the smooth sexiness of the woman softly moaning in his arms. He would stop very soon. In a minute, at the most.

She bent to whisper in his ear, her boobs temporarily cutting off his air supply. Not that he minded. Her panting breath in his ear sent shivers down his spine.

"I'm so sorry, Brae, so very sorry," she whispered, nipping at his ear. He wasn't sure exactly how it happened, but her breast had once again insinuated itself into his mouth. Had that not happened, he was sure he would have stopped her.

"I hate it when we fight." She reached down and drew his hand up, guiding him until he stroked the smooth hairless skin between her legs. "Feel that? I had it done, just for you. It wasn't as unpleasant as I thought it would be. Maybe because I kept thinking about how much you would like it, imagining you licking me and kissing me *there.*" She pushed his hand down farther. "Feel how much I want you, how much I need you." She shoved his fingers inside her wetness and gasped. "I don't know if I can wait until we get dried off."

The next few minutes passed in a sexual haze. Before he realized what either of them was doing, his dick was buried deep within her heat.

It liked it there.

* * *

Gasping for air, he waited for his muscles to stop vibrating. He'd never come so violently, so completely. And he could not do it again. He firmly set her on her feet, then turned off the shower, hoping she would take a hint.

His spine stiffened at the warm feel of female anatomy against his back. Evidently he'd have to hint harder.

Gently disengaging her roving hands from his chest, he stepped away and grabbed two towels from the heated rack just outside the glass door, and handed her one. The fact that the rack was heated—yet another frivolous way his brother spent his money—distracted him for a second. When he glanced back, she was gone.

Just as well. Maybe she went home. The thought should have been a good one, yet he couldn't help feeling a tad bereft. She could have at least said good-bye, great fuck or something.

He took his time refolding and hanging his towel, then strode into his brother's bedroom to see if he could find any decent underwear.

What he found took thoughts of underwear completely out of his mind.

3

Candles cast the room in a warm glow. In fact, the room was so dark, it took a second for him to see her lying on the bed. But once he did, he couldn't tear his eyes away.

Candlelight flickered and danced along the smooth skin surrounding her sex. She spread her legs in invitation, moisture glistening on her swollen folds. Swollen from their recent encounter in the shower.

His cock made an instant recovery.

"If you still want to tie me to the bed, I don't mind." She pointed with her toe to a pair of fur covered handcuffs hanging from the post at the foot of the bed.

Despite her words, now that his eyes adjusted to the dark, he could see the doubt on her face. What had his sack of shit brother done to this poor woman to make her so anxious to please?

He walked to the lamp on the nightstand. Before he could turn it on, her hand clamped around his now rampant erection.

"Don't," she whispered, "Please. Let's just use the candles tonight." Her thumb moved up and down his erection. "I need you," she said in a plaintive voice. "I need you now. I want you to, um, to, ah, fuck me," she finally choked out.

He'd heard about guys being led around by their dick, but had never experienced the phenomenon until now.

Leaning closer to see her face, he attempted to force words around the constriction in his throat. Damn, he hated lying. Hated lying to anyone, but for some reason, especially to the woman before him.

Strains of "Born To Be Wild" sounded from the bathroom.

Their gazes met.

"I should get that," Ryan said, edging toward the open door. "It might be important." Stepping onto the damp tile, he closed the door and lunged for the phone.

The Caller ID said Dick-Head. Since the incoming number was his cell, he knew how Braedon had his number programmed into his cell. "Jerk." He pushed the talk button. "Want to tell me what the hell's going on, little brother?" he asked in a fierce whisper.

"I was just calling you back, but I don't have to take verbal abuse—"

"Wait! Don't hang up!" Too late. Hands shaking with anger, he dialed his cell number. "Pick up, damn it!" Of course, he didn't.

Resisting the urge to throw the phone, he laid it on the counter and scrubbed his face. Who was the woman he'd just taken a shower with, and why did she seem to feel obligated to show him a good time? For that matter, why was she even in his brother's apartment? And why did he make that idiotic promise to Braedon? The woman on the king-size bed in the other room had not asked to be lied to, or used. Yet, by having sex with her and not revealing his true identity, that was exactly what he'd done.

He glanced at the phone, then picked it up and hit redial, growling when his voice message came on.

A promise was a promise, but if the woman insisted on continuing what they'd started, and kept calling him *Brae* in her soft, sexy little voice, he would not be responsible for what he said or did. Well, okay, he'd still be technically responsible, but he wasn't a total idiot. He knew exactly where it would lead.

And, God help him, he wanted to go there.

Wrapping a towel around his hips, he walked into the bedroom, averting his gaze from the woman still spread on the bed, and dug in the first drawer he reached, hoping to find a pair of boxers.

What he found barely qualified as underwear. Maneuvering around the towel, he finally got the strings up onto his hips and his boys somewhat accommodated by the skimpy patch of fabric. The joining strap cut into his crack, separating his cheeks. How did Braedon stand to wear stuff like that?

"Braedon?" The woman was sitting on her knees on the bed, the corner of the sheet pulled to cover her still partially exposed breasts. "Come back to bed, baby. Let me make everything better."

He hesitated. Sex with her was the best he'd experienced. Ever.

But it was wrong. He needed to remember that.

"Brae?" She dropped the sheet and raised to her knees, running the tips of her fingers over her mound and between her legs. "Don't you want to come play? I'll let you do anything you want. Just don't shut me out anymore. Please?"

He blinked. Before he could censor himself, he'd stalked to the edge of the bed. "What is wrong with you, lady? Don't you have any self-respect?"

Her eyes widened. For a second, he worried he'd given himself away. Then a slow smile curled her lips. She leaned forward and stroked her hand up his leg, under the towel.

"Okay, we can play it any way you want." She crawled to

the edge of the bed, and rubbed the tips of her nipples against his abs.

He felt it in the pit of his stomach.

"I know I've been a bad girl," she cooed, stroking him ever higher. "Are you going to spank me?" She released him and turned her sweet ass to him, arching her back to give him a better view, and looked back over her shoulder. A look of what could only be called apprehension clouded her face for a moment before she flashed a shy smile. "I don't mind, as long as you don't leave a mark again. Maybe if you used something lighter, like a fly swatter, this time?"

What had his brother done to this woman?

Without thinking, he bent and kissed first one smooth cheek then another, hooking his arm around her hips and pulling her closer while he kissed his way up her spine.

She stiffened, then allowed him to pull her to him.

When he got to her neck, he kissed his way up, then ran the tip of his tongue around the shell of her ear.

She moaned and wiggled against his erection.

Gently taking her face in his hand, he turned her enough to trail kisses to her mouth. As his lips claimed hers, he turned her fully, pulling her against him, her breasts flattened against his chest, and followed her down to the mattress.

Penny returned Braedon's gentle kisses with equal parts relief and abandoned joy. She'd been so worried he was still mad at her.

His kiss turned hungry. Deep and wet, it awakened a long dormant need in her. It reminded her of their first kiss, so long ago.

His hands caressed her from her waist to her neck. Gentle hands kneaded her breasts, rubbing her nipples to aching peaks of need instead of raw pain.

She moaned and arched her back, offering her nipples.

He took them greedily, sucking deep, as though he couldn't get enough. It was just like old times . . .

No, it wasn't. It was better.

Her heart fluttered in her chest. Thrills ran to her extremities. Something about Braedon had changed during the short time he'd been gone, mellowed. She liked it. No, she loved it, and needed more. She reached for his towel, not stopping until it fell from his lean hips. Laughter bubbled at the sight.

He leaned back, his eyes feverish with his lust. "What? What's so funny?"

"Wh-why—" Laughter overtook her again. She wiped a tear from her eye and struggled for composure. "Why are you w-wearing my panties?"

4

Braedon leaned back, naked in his brother's hot tub, and sighed. He stretched to toss the cell onto the patio table. Ryan had called him so many times, he'd lost count. Not answering was the best thing he could do for his brother. Ryan needed to know what it was like to walk in his twin's shoes.

All of their lives, Ryan had been the golden boy, the good twin who could do no wrong. Well, that was about to change. Braedon could get used to living his brother's life. What harm would it do to drag things out a while longer than absolutely necessary?

He took a sip of his longneck and closed his eyes while the jets jostled his cock. The only thing better would be to have some female company. He thought of his promise to Ryan. Would Ryan be doing Penny by now?

He sank down lower in the hot bubbling water. Nah, Penny was so uptight, she'd probably be pissed off for the next week. And even if she wasn't, she'd pretend to be, to avoid sex.

Poor Ryan. Braedon chuckled. "Better him than me." What had he been thinking? After he'd found out who her father was, it seemed like a brilliant plan to cozy up to her at the Christmas party. She'd been more than eager to spread her legs for him that night. And Charley Harding had been more than willing to loan him any amount of money if it kept his little girl happy.

Then, helpless as he sank deeper and deeper in debt, Braedon had allowed Penny to railroad him into an engagement. Well, to be honest, that and fear about what her daddy would do had forced him to pop the question. Lucky for him, Penny's marriage train had been derailed after a few heated arguments. It wasn't until Daddy Dearest had began putting pressure on him that Braedon had pushed to set a date. He'd thought it would buy him some time.

Didn't happen. He rubbed his still sore abs and wondered how long the bruising would last.

For whatever reason, his *lucky Penny* had balked when it came time to actually choose a wedding date. Maybe she wasn't as much in love with him as she claimed.

Closing his eyes, he slid lower in the churning water. Regardless of the reason, he had a reprieve. He prayed his brother would distract Penny until the current situation had been resolved. Then they could both ride into the sunset and go their separate ways.

No harm, no foul.

The warm water caused his sore abdominal muscles to contract, sending pain shooting through his trunk. Gingerly probing his ribs, he wondered if Charley's goons had broken anything when they'd had their little "talk" the day before.

The lame-ass ringtone of his brother's phone broke into his thoughts. Didn't take a rocket scientist to figure out who was calling. Evidently Penny wasn't impressing Ryan, either.

With a sigh, Braedon stretched to reach the phone. "Yeah?"

"Yeah?" His brother's strident whisper echoed in his ear. "Is that how you were taught to answer a phone? Did you even check the Caller ID? You had no idea who was calling."

"Bullshit. I knew exactly who was calling. The same person who has called at least ten times in the last few minutes. The *only* person who has called. Man, don't you have a life?"

"Yes, I have a life! And I want it back! I knew this was a piss-poor idea—"

"And yet you agreed to it. What does that say about your judgment, big brother?"

"Unless you tell me what the hell is going on, the deal is off, Braedon. I'll tell your girlfriend everything. I swear, I will."

"Chill." He stood and reached for the towel he'd thrown over the patio chair. "I told you. I made some poor financial deals, took a few too many risks. Before I knew it, I was in way over my head. The guy who bankrolled me was getting pissy about repayment. I needed a way to lay low for a while. Then, out of the blue, you called and asked me to lunch." He stepped onto the sun-warmed patio and toweled his legs. "It was a god-damned sign."

"Define pissy."

"Bodily damage, among other things." Braedon reached into the fridge under the outdoor kitchen counter his goody-two-shoes brother had designed, and popped the top on another beer.

"Real or implied?"

"Both, if you want to know the truth."

"And you want me to pretend to be you? What if they come after me?"

He took a swig. "How's Penny?"

"What? Who?"

"Penny. Short, brown hair, light eyes. Never can remember if they're green or blue." He paused. "We share a bed. Is any of this ringing any bells?"

"She lives here?" Ryan practically shouted. He lowered his voice to a harsh whisper. "How did you manage to forget that little detail when we exchanged identities? I asked if you were telling me everything. You said yes."

"No, I think my exact words were *sort of*. So . . . have you done her yet? She's not much on sex, but if you get her primed just right, she's a fair ride."

Silence.

"I take it that's a no? Don't hold back on my account, big brother."

"What's wrong with you? You don't care if I screw you girl-friend?"

"She's not my girlfriend."

"She lives here, you sleep together. If she's not your girl-friend, who is she?"

"Technically, my fiancée."

5

Ryan's stomach lurched. Clutching Braedon's phone to his ear, he sank to sit on the closed toilet. "What did you say?" he finally managed to choke out.

Braedon's chuckle sounded malevolent as it floated through space to the earphone. "You heard me. But don't worry about it. It's not like it's serious or anything."

"Are you a total moron? Of course it means something! Women don't accept marriage proposals if they don't think you're serious about marrying them. What were you thinking?"

"You know, Ry, that was exactly my thought not ten minutes ago. I guess I panicked. That, combined with the world class blow job she'd just given me, well, I guess all the blood was in the wrong head, if you know what I mean. All I can say is it seemed like a good idea at the time."

"She needs to be told."

"Tell her what, Ryan? What should I say? How about 'Oh, hi, Penny. Guess what? My twin brother and I switched places. That's right, he's the one who's been porking you.' How do you think that will go over? I know you've been fucking her. That's why you're so outraged." He laughed. "After all these years, you still have that knight-in-shining-armor complex. Hey, I don't care. As far as I'm concerned, you can do her all night, every night. Hell, it'd save me the trouble. Sometimes she can be such a needy bitch."

"You're talking about your fiancée." A headache wove its way from his clenched jaw up between his eyes.

"Ha! Only until I get this mess cleared up. Then I'm outta here."

"What was her name? Penny? What about Penny?"

"What about her?"

"She deserves an explanation. After all, you did propose to her."

"What she deserves, big brother, is a gigantic, mind-blowing orgasm to loosen her up. I never did do it for her. Maybe you can."

"You're a real asshole." Ryan ground out. "She deserves to know the truth. If you have no plans to marry her, you need to tell her. If you don't, I will."

"Ah, I don't recommend that, big brother. Leastways, not right now."

"Why?"

"You know the guy I told you about? The one I owe all that money to, who wants to take it out on my kneecaps, among other things?"

That didn't sound good. Taking a deep breath, Ryan asked, "What about him?"

"He's Penny's daddy."

Ryan sat with the cell phone still at his ear long after his brother had hung up. Great. He'd not only just slept with his brother's fiancée, she was also the daughter of a loan shark. A loan shark who thought he was Braedon.

He dropped the phone to the fuzzy throw rug and hung his head. What kind of hell had he gotten himself into?

One thing was for sure. If he survived this mess, he was going to have to kill his brother.

Penny wrapped her silk robe tighter, padded to the closed bathroom door, and tapped softly.

"Braedon? Honey, I didn't mean to embarrass you." She swallowed another laugh. "I was just surprised. Um, I actually think you look kind of . . . sexy in my underwear."

No answer.

She tapped again. "Come back to bed. Please?"

The door flew open. Braedon stood bathed in the light from the bathroom, with a towel once again wrapped around his lean hips.

Her mouth went dry. Her hormones must be active. She'd never been so turned on by the sight of his naked chest—or naked anything, truthfully. Very strange. Not that she was complaining. Lusting after your future husband was a good thing.

She hooked her finger in the towel and tugged. It fell to the floor.

Oh, yeah, a very good thing . . .

Ryan stood rooted to the spot. She needed to be told the truth. He needed to tell her. Braedon sure as hell didn't plan on doing it.

He swallowed, but before he could open his mouth, she dropped the silky robe to stand before him in all her naked glory.

His cock sprang to attention.

She looked at it and smiled.

It was the smile that got to him. It was a secret, sensual smile. The smile a woman gets when she's confident in her sexuality, knows she's aroused her mate. Did he want to be the cause of the smile going away?

Images of potentially very hot sex on the rumpled bed flashed through his mind like an X-rated video, making him harder. Sex with her was unlike anything he'd ever experienced.

He wanted to experience it again. Technically, she was single. He'd tell her the truth . . . later.

She reached toward his erection, stroking him in a whispering, circular motion that had him vibrating with need.

Tomorrow would be soon enough to end things . . .

6

Daylight barely peeked through the drapes, while Ryan kissed his way down Penny's slumbering body as he slid out of bed.

Today he would tell her the truth. He just needed some time to gather his thoughts. A run always did that for him, so after a quick shower, he donned a pair of running shorts he'd found on the shelf of the closet. On his knees, he strained his eyes to find a pair of running shoes.

All through college, he'd run to sort through things. Although Braedon scoffed, he'd dragged himself out of bed most mornings to join his brother.

Biting back a triumphant exclamation, he grabbed the Nikes he'd given Braedon for Christmas last year, with the three pack of running socks still tucked inside. Evidently, his brother wasn't into running these days.

Ryan made his way through the apartment, pausing on his way to the patio door to absorb the high-end furnishings. From the looks of things, Braedon had hired a professional decorator. Chalk up one more thing to his brother's frivolous spending habits.

While he appreciated fine furniture and granite countertops as much as the next guy, his brother was over the top. A twinge of—what? Envy?—swept through him at the disparity of his own sparse accommodations, compared to those of his twin's.

Once the patio door was closed, he began stretching, trying to clear his mind. Although he and Braedon were identical in appearance, that was where the resemblance ended. While he, Ryan, at thirty-two, was a self-made millionaire, thanks to wise investments and frugal habits, his brother, despite his accounting degree, was lucky to make it from paycheck to paycheck. Night and day. He took off at a fast pace.

Still, though, Braedon had some classy digs. Maybe once he got back home and into his routine, he'd contact someone about decorating his place, or at least his beach house. Yeah, that would probably be better, he thought, waiting for the light on Ocean Drive to change while he jogged in place.

He'd try out whichever decorator he decided on with the beach house in Pleasure Beach first, then move on to his condo in Houston.

Meanwhile, he needed to figure out a way to break the news to Penny that she'd been sleeping with the wrong brother. Half a block later, near the beach access, he came to a stop. Damn. He couldn't tell Penny anything. For now, anyway. He'd promised Braedon.

"I'm coming, sugar, hold on!" Braedon gnashed his teeth at the high-pitched exclamation, and gripped the tiny waist of Ryan's next-door neighbor while thrusting deeply, her back hitting the wall with a satisfying thump-thump-thump.

She gave a little squeal of excitement and shimmied, her augmented tits dragging across his chest, their hardened nipples setting off zings of excitement zipping clear down to his pecker.

Her hot slippery canal caressed him like wet silk. The inner clenching began, milking him of his staying power. Every muscle in his body trembled with the effort to control his release.

Finally, she let loose a scream that would wake the dead. He was probably deaf in his left ear now.

Crushing her to him, he gave one final thrust, slamming her against the wall.

The air conditioning clicked on, blowing blessed cool air against his sweating back. Other than the distant hum of the compressor, no sound filled the condo except for their labored breathing.

Now what? He didn't even know her name. Did Ryan? Doubtful, given the way she'd timidly knocked on his door earlier. He racked his brain in an effort to remember if she'd introduced herself. Her cleavage had had him so distracted, he couldn't recall. He did remember she seemed genuinely surprised when he'd asked her in for a drink. Since he'd promised not to have sex with anyone Ryan knew, he rationalized it would be okay. His brother may know her, but probably not in the biblical sense.

She must've had the hots for Ryan because from there, things had progressed at the speed of lust.

Guilt reared its ugly head. What the hell was he thinking?

He lifted her from his diminishing erection and smoothed her miniskirt over her hips while he glanced around for the thong he'd all but ripped from her body a few minutes earlier.

Not seeing it, he pulled his swim trunks up and stepped back. She followed, her hand reaching tentatively toward his bare chest.

Shit! Go home, he wanted to yell.

Weak sunlight slanted across the foyer, illuminating the blue streak in her unnaturally light blond hair.

She pursed her collagen-enhanced lips—well, as much as they would allow anyway. "Wanna come to my place? I have some weed."

Weed. Great. Just what he didn't need in his life at this point.

"Ah, no thanks. I'm trying to quit." In reality, it had to have been a good decade since he'd stopped, but she nodded as though she were totally impressed by that fact, so he let it ride. "Listen. I had fun, but, um, now I have some stuff I have to do. Alone-type stuff." Take a hint.

She nodded absently and wandered into the living room, dragging her hand along the back of what Penny would call an oatmeal colored sectional sofa. Personally, he thought of it as blah beige. That was Ryan, all right. Blah.

He spotted her thong hanging on the fake tree by the door and snagged it on his way into the living room.

"Thanks," she said when he handed her panties to her. Pausing with her leg lifted to put them on, she grinned, evidently noticing where his eyes were trained. "Should I leave them off a little while longer? If you want to fuck again, I wouldn't mind."

Maybe not, but I sure as hell would. The thought gave him pause. Since when did he turn down sex? Must be the vibes from Ryan rubbing off on him. "Ah, thanks, but I have stuff to do. Maybe some other time."

Standing, she made a big production of sliding the string up her legs, hiking her skirt to her waist and pushing her tight little ass at him while she adjusted the thong. Talk about obvious.

Finally, she turned to face him. For the first time, he noticed she was still topless. Damn. There was a time he'd have spotted that right away. If he looked closely, the sunshine streaming in through the patio door touched the razor thin white scars running along the edge of her nipples. Why do women put their bodies through that? While he appreciated a gigantic rack as much as the next guy, when it came to playing with them, even he preferred the real thing to the water balloons with hard, plastic-feeling nipples in front of him.

"Put your top on. Please," he added at her startled look. "Then I need to take off, so you have to leave."

"Fine." She shimmied into her minuscule tank top, her nipples jutting against the thin material. "At least now I know."

"Now you know what?" He held the door open, wanting nothing more than for her to walk through it.

"I've wondered about you ever since you moved in. I thought you were so handsome, smooth, and sophisticated." She shook her head. "But you're not any different than the others. Permanent booty call."

He shrugged. What could he say to defend his brother's honor? For that matter, why would he want to?

Pausing with her hand on the door to prevent him from closing it, she gave her parting shot. "And the worst part is, you weren't nearly as impressive as I'd thought you'd be. In fact, you're a lousy lay. Sorry to have bothered you. Don't bother walking me home. I never want to see you again."

Stunned, he watched her sashay down the hall, then leaned out and yelled, "I am not a lousy lay!"

A door across the hallway cracked open.

"I'm not!" he yelled at whoever peeked through the crack, then stomped back into his brother's condo, and slammed the door for good measure.

Ryan shook the sand from his running shoes while sitting on the sun-warmed beach, and looked out over the clear blue water of the Gulf of Mexico. He was so exhausted, he'd have to rest before heading back to his brother's apartment. And Penny.

Forty-five minutes of hard running had brought him no closer to an answer as to what to do about her. It was wrong to deceive her. Even more wrong to continue sleeping with her without revealing his identity.

His cock stirred at the thought of what they'd shared the night before. If he said he didn't want a repeat performance, he would be lying. Again. Still.

"Damn." He flopped back on the sand, eyes clenched against the bright morning sun. The sound of the surf should have relaxed him. Instead it reminded him of the minutes and hours ticking past. Minutes and hours with Penny. Minutes and hours he would never have again.

Did he really want to spend that time agonizing over something he could do nothing about? He'd made a solemn promise to his brother. Sure, he knew Brae would have no problem breaking a promise. But promises meant something to him, and despite his brother being a screw-up, he intended to honor that promise.

At least for a while. And that meant he had to continue deceiving Penny. But he would tell her. Eventually.

With a sigh, he got to his feet and jogged toward the beach access.

Maybe he was no better than Braedon. He wanted nothing more than to lock himself away with Penny, making love, and learning all he could about her. No matter what spin he put on it, the bottom line was he would still be lying to her by omission.

He paused on the patio and bent at the waist, taking deep, cleansing breaths. He didn't know what to wish for: that the mess with Braedon be cleared up soon so they could both resume their lives, or that it continue indefinitely to allow him more time with Penny.

Penny rolled to her side at the sound of Braedon's voice.

"Hey, kiddo, you planning to sleep all day?" He elbowed the bedroom door open wider and stepped into view, carrying a lap tray. "I've already gone for a run and showered." He hefted the tray and smiled. "Hungry?"

Yawning, she nodded and sat up, scooting over to make room for him to sit beside her. "What's all this?"

"I thought that was obvious." He winked and handed her a napkin. "It's breakfast."

"There's only one plate. Are we sharing?"

"Nope." He brushed a kiss across the surprised O of her mouth and stood. "I already ate." He wiggled his eyebrows. "Maybe we can share breakfast in bed tomorrow."

The heated gaze he sent her way had thoughts of food leaving her mind. "What's wrong with sharing it today?"

He leaned to lave her nipples, then kissed each one before

pulling the sheet up and tucking it beneath her armpits. "I already ate." He smiled. "But I'll definitely take a rain check." He grabbed her toe through the sheet on his way out. "Get a move on! We're burning daylight. We have things to do, places to see."

She swallowed a bite of toast and washed it down with a quick sip of orange juice. "Where are we going?"

"It's a surprise. Wear something casual, and comfortable shoes. We're going to be doing a lot of walking."

"Okay, but again, where are we going?"

"The aquarium," he said, closing the door.

"The aquarium," she muttered under her breath. "Great. I've finally found my sex drive and he wants to go look at fish with a bunch of schoolkids."

She finished the scrambled eggs in record time and chugged the rest of the orange juice. Holding a piece of wheat toast between her teeth, she picked up her coffee mug and carried it into the bathroom with her.

She'd just been complaining to Braedon the other day that he never took her anywhere. Evidently, he'd listened. Even though the aquarium wasn't at the top of her to-do list, Braedon was, so it looked as though she was going to the aquarium.

"I heard about this place on the news," Penny told Ryan as they walked through the turnstile, "It hasn't been open very long." She took a deep breath and smiled up at him. "I love the way the ocean smells."

He swallowed and tamped down the guilt he felt at the trusting smile she gave him. Instead, he leaned to nuzzle the side of her flowery smelling neck. "I love the way *you* smell," he said, his nose buried in the fragrant hair by her ear.

She giggled and hugged his arm close, her breast pushing against his tense muscle. Stopping, she pointed. "Look! I read about that. It's the dolphin habitat. There's an observation cave where you can watch them swim underwater."

"Okay, let's start there." Dolphins were a safe thing. There would probably be a bunch of schoolkids around.

The cave was noticeably cool and smelled of humidity, fish, and stale popcorn. Once his eyes adjusted, he saw they were alone in the semidarkness with nothing but the blue glow from the dolphin tank to light their way.

So much for children acting as a buffer to his baser instincts.

Penny snuggled closer, so close he could feel her rigid nipple against his arm.

"Brr!" She did a delicate little shiver that made his body clench. "It's cold in here. Oh, look!" Yanking on his arm, she dragged him deeper into the darkness. "Look how fast they swim!"

She moved in front of him, wrapping his arms securely around her, the weight of her breasts against his forearms.

He stood ramrod straight, willing his traitorous body not to react to her closeness. It wasn't listening.

He swallowed a groan when she twisted to look up at him, the action causing her sweet bottom to rub in a very disturbing way against him.

"Thank you for thinking of this," she half-whispered. "I was beginning to feel as though you didn't want to be seen in public with me." At his frown, she hurried on. "We never go anywhere anymore. I didn't want to fight about it, but I appreciate you taking the initiative and planning this." She brushed a kiss on the tip of his chin, the sensation zinging through to his extremities. "I love you."

He swallowed and forced his gaze to the tank, and watched the cavorting dolphins. Anything was better than looking at the expectation in her green eyes. He wasn't stupid. He knew she was expecting him to return the declaration of love. Although he was already a liar by omission, he could not force the verbal lie past his lips. Damn Braedon for putting him in such an awkward predicament.

"I do, you know." She snuggled back against him. Was she deliberately rubbing his erection? "I also know you love me, too." Her laugh seemed sad. "I know you told me you wouldn't have proposed if you didn't love me, but sometimes it's nice to actually hear the words, you know?" Her eyes wide, she glanced back at him. "Not that I'm trying to force you to say anything you're not ready to say. I understand. And I can wait until you feel comfortable enough to say the words. No matter how long it takes." Her cool lips brushed against his chin again. "I know you don't like to hear me say it too much, but I do love you."

Okay, that settled it. His brother was a total asshole. He had a hot woman who loved him completely, unconditionally, and he'd made her feel guilty to even tell him she loved him. Un-fucking-believable.

Penny rubbed her head against his chest, occasionally pressing her bottom suggestively against his rock hard erection.

While he stood, trying to process her body language, she tucked one of his hands under her tank top, pushing on his wrist until his fingers closed around her bare breast. How could he have not noticed she was braless? His cock surged with excitement.

Gradually, they backed deeper into the shadows. To the side of the tank, the rough faux rock jutted out to form a small bench. When the back of his knees touched it, he sat, pulling Penny onto his lap.

As soon as he confirmed they were still alone, he took her mouth, his kiss revealing his pent-up desire, his hands beneath her top, kneading her breasts in time to the movement of his tongue.

She moaned and wiggled closer, opening for him.

His turgid flesh pressed against the teeth of his zipper in a desperate plea to seek release.

With shaking hands, Penny reached between his legs to free him, her cool hand closing around his heat.

"Make love to me," she demanded in a breathless whisper. "Right here, right now. I need you inside me."

Before he could respond, she shimmied out of her panties, sticking them in the pocket of his jeans before settling onto his lap, her back to his chest, his sex nestled against her warmth.

All it took was a few slight adjustments. He lifted her and flexed his hips, impaling her.

She glanced around, a secret smile on her well-kissed lips, then smoothed her skirt around them, hiding their joined bodies from prying eyes.

"We're going to get caught, you know," he whispered against her ear, while beneath her top he tweaked her nipples.

"Not if we take it—ah!" She arched her back, shoving her hardened nipples into his palms, pulling him deeper into her wet heat. "Not if we take it slow and easy, and don't get too carried away. No one is here and even if someone comes in, they won't see us, won't know what we're doing."

"Slow—and—easy?" He thrust with each word. "After the way we did it the last time, do you really think that's possible?"

Eyes closed, she licked her lips and nodded. Buried deep within her, his dick twitched at the sight.

He rotated his hips in slow, lazy circles, pushing higher with each grinding motion. "As I recall," he said on a breath against her ear, "you were a screamer." He squeezed her nipples and ground his hips, his penis probing. "What if I make you scream again?"

"Then we'd both be caught with our pants down." She wiggled for a closer, deeper penetration. "I don't think you'd want to be, um, exposed like that. Would you?"

He growled. "Hell, if you keep doing that, I don't care if the whole world sees us fucking."

At his graphic words, her sex gave up more lubrication, making it slippery, and difficult to keep her seated on his lap for the entire act.

"Easy, baby," he breathed against her ear. "If you keep that up, I'll have to lay you down on this bench and have my way with you. I wouldn't care who saw us." He chuckled at her obvious excitement at the suggestion, pounding into her with hard, pulsing thrusts. "I wouldn't mind, but we might shock the dolphins."

Penny opened languorous eyes and followed his line of vision. At the observation window, a gray bottlenose dolphin bumped the glass, its fishy face grinning at them. Before she could decide if she was embarrassed, the dolphin swam away.

The edges of Braedon's zipper gently nipped and abraded her backside, but his fullness buried snugly inside her made the little discomfort worth it. His warmth drove away the damp coldness she'd felt when they'd first entered the cave. Just as she thought she could stay like that forever, her climax washed through her, stiffening her back. Braedon's fingers squeezed her nipples, heightening her inner contractions, making her so slippery with her climax, it was difficult to stay on his shaft.

"Stay with me, baby, don't move," he said in a guttural voice against her neck. Powerful arms tightened around her, clamping her down hard against his hips while he pumped into her with quick, hard thrusts. Once, twice, three times, then he squeezed her so tightly, she could barely breathe as he emptied himself, spurting hot cum inside her.

Tears burned her eyes. Braedon loved her. She knew he did. Why wouldn't he say the words?

8

Penny opened her eyes and gasped.

A little girl walked toward them, her thumb in her mouth, a rag doll hanging from the crook of her scrawny little arm. Not blinking, she raised her other hand and scratched the bridge of her freckled nose.

Penny casually let her hand drop to her side and nudged Braedon. She knew the moment he saw the girl by the way his posture stiffened beneath her.

"Hi," he said, his voice still sounding a bit husky. "Are you having fun watching the dolphins?"

The little girl nodded, her brown pigtails bobbing with the action. Still staring, she shifted from one pink sneaker clad foot to the other.

"Are you here with your school?" He slowly slid his hands from beneath Penny's top then slipped his arms around her, anchoring her to his lap.

The girl removed her thumb long enough to answer, "Nope," then popped it back in.

Penny decided to try. "Are you with your mommy and daddy?"

The girl nodded.

Encouraged, Penny continued, "Well, you should probably go find them. I'm sure they're very worried about you."

The little girl nodded, her gaze riveted to something by their feet.

Penny's face flamed when she followed the girl's line of vision and saw the thong panties she'd tucked into Braedon's pocket earlier.

With a saucy grin around her thumb, the little girl turned and skipped from the cave.

Penny collapsed against Braedon's chest. "I'm so embarrassed! Do you think she'll say anything to her parents?"

His chuckled vibrated her back. "Nah, she seemed like a pretty smart kid. She won't want to let on to her parents that she'd wandered away, much less that she was around strangers." He eased her from his lap. "But we should probably get out of here, just in case. Are you hungry? I saw a little restaurant by the duck pond."

She moved back into the shadows to pull on her panties, all the while casting furtive glances at the entrance of the cave.

"Ah, Penny?"

She paused in the act of stepping into her thong and glanced up. "What?"

Instead of answering, he gestured, looking down. The front of his jeans was definitely a shade darker than the rest. "I don't know if that's from you or me, but we definitely have a problem."

"Won't it dry in the sun?" She looked around the trash can, hoping to find some papers or something to help dry his pants.

"Eventually, but I can't go out like this."

"Here." She shoved her satchel toward him. "Carry this in

front of you and then while we're eating lunch, the sun can dry you."

He hopped back. "I'm not carrying a purse!"

"Don't be so picky! And it's not a purse, it's a carryall. Men carry them, too."

"Not with flowers on them."

He had a point.

"Well, what choice do we have? Do you have a better idea?" She bit back a smile watching him fan his hands in front of the damp spot. "How about if you take off your shirt and tie it around your waist?"

It wouldn't tie around his waist, but didn't look too weird hanging in front of his pants, and over the offending spot like a plaid loin cloth.

Of course, the sight of his broad chest, clad in only his muscle shirt, brought on another whole set of problems for Penny. How was she going to eat her lunch without doing the other things that were popping into her mind? Things like ripping the thin barrier from him and licking his chest.

"We can just go back home, if you want," she said as they made their way toward the concession stand.

"No, I'm okay. It's not totally soaked. The sun should dry it while we eat lunch. Besides, I'm starving." He leaned close and whispered, "Sex always makes me hungry."

Funny, she didn't remember that. Maybe she hadn't been as in tune with Braedon as she'd assumed.

A few minutes later they tucked into their hot dogs and chili cheese fries, eating in companionable silence.

Ryan set his Coke on the table and leaned back, his face to the sun. "Damn, that was good. I can't remember the last time I ate junk food."

She took another napkin from the pile and wiped the sticky cheese from her mouth. "You can't? What's the matter, getting short-term memory loss?" she teased. "Brae, you know you always eat this stuff. It's irritating how you can eat it and never gain an ounce." She took a sip from her Diet Coke, then ran her fingers over the condensation on the plastic cup to clean the remaining goop off them. At his silence, she paused from drying her hands on another napkin. "What's wrong? You look weird."

Damn, why hadn't he remembered his brother's affinity for fat laden food? He tossed his cup in the trash, buying time. "Ha. I'm kidding. Of course, I remember." He stretched out along the picnic bench. "Do you mind if we stay here a little while longer? I'm almost dry."

"Sure, no problem. I'll just get a refill on my soda. Be right back." She made her way to the bank of fountain drinks and refilled her cup, grinning. Braedon had really changed. Until recently, he never asked her opinion about anything. Maybe there was hope for them yet.

"So," she said, settling back on the bench by his feet. Did she dare broach the subject? "I thought of something the other day."

He squinted against the sun, raising his head to look at her. "Oh, yeah? Anything in particular?"

It took a moment to reply, since her attention was distracted by his rippling abs. How had she never noticed how defined her fiancé was? "Hmm? Oh, I just realized I don't know anything about your family. Funny, huh? We're engaged, and yet you've never talked about them."

He regarded her for a second, then lowered his head, eyes shutting again. "What do you want to know?"

Could it really be that easy? All this time, she'd agonized over possibly getting into a fight, and all she'd had to do was ask. Go figure. "Um, do you have any brothers or sisters?"

"A brother."

"Older?"

Just when she thought he was not going to answer, he muttered, "Younger."

"Are you close?"

He snickered. Rising to his elbows, he smiled at her. "You have no idea." He heaved a sigh and sat up, causing his stomach muscles to contract and show off again. "That wasn't really an answer. My brother is, well, hard to be close to. But yeah, I guess you could say we're close. Closer sometimes than others."

He reached out to twirl a strand of her hair around his index finger. "What about you?"

"What about me?" She knew she should be paying closer attention to their conversation, but lately when he touched her, it seemed to short circuit her thought processes. Maybe she was ovulating.

"Any brothers or sisters?"

Was he kidding? She heaved an inward sigh. No, typically Braedon, he obviously hadn't listened to much of what she told him. "I'm an only child, remember?"

He dropped her hair. "Oh, yeah. Guess I forgot." He picked up her soda and took a sip, surprising her further since he'd always maintained he had a thing about sharing straws. "So your parents live around here?"

Had he never heard a word she said? She did a quick mental ten-count. "My mother died when I was a little girl. My dad still lives in their house on Ocean Drive. The place where you go to fish off the dock. Any of this ringing any bells?"

He closed his eyes briefly, then pulled her to him for a kiss. "I'm sorry, babe. I guess I'm just more tired than I thought."

From doing what? "It's okay," she said, leaning into his loose embrace. "We should probably be going. I told Gram we'd be there by five."

"For what?" He helped her up from the picnic bench.

"Ah, dinner? At my grandparents' house? You said it was

okay when they called last week." She raised on tiptoe to place her palm on his forehead. "Are you feeling all right?"

His warm hand circled her wrist and brought her hand to his lips, where he kissed the tips of her fingers. "Yeah, I'm fine. Just a little tired. In fact, why don't you drive to your grandparents' house?"

"Are you kidding?"

No doubt his brother always refused to allow Penny to drive his sexy car. Well, that was about to change. He drew the tip of his finger across the seam of her lips while he shook his head.

"Braedon," she said in an exasperated voice, "they live next door."

9

Ryan took a last look in the mirror before opening the door for Penny. He couldn't afford any more slipups. Of course, it would have been good if his brother had remembered to tell him about all the stuff he'd been blundering through.

Damn, she looked hot tonight. Decked out in a red dress with a neckline designed to torment. It was going to be difficult to keep his mind on dinner and conversation with her sitting in the same room. But he'd do it, or die trying. His jackass brother had let her down enough—she didn't need him adding to it.

"Precious baby!" the short, frail looking, white-haired woman exclaimed upon opening the door to their knock. She grabbed Penny, pulling her into a hug, then nodded politely at him. "Braedon."

"Where's Gramps?" Penny looked around a living room that resembled theirs only in the terms of having an identical floor plan. Every surface was covered in doilies and knickknacks.

Her grandmother shook her head and chuckled. "Still doing his hair, I assume." She gave a wink. "We're having adventures in hairstyling today. Keith!" she yelled in the direction of the hallway. "Get out here! Your favorite granddaughter is here."

"I'm his only granddaughter."

"Yeah, I know, but I like to mess with him sometimes." She made a shooing motion. "Sit. Sit. Dinner is almost ready."

At that moment, a scrawny gentleman toddled into the room. He wore mismatched socks with his brown corduroy slippers, gray dress pants hiked up to his nipples by a pair of bright red suspenders, and what looked suspiciously like a pajama top. Behind his trifocals, blue eyes twinkled. A big smile creased his weathered half-shaven cheeks. Steel gray hair, parted somewhat crookedly in the middle, was gelled to within an inch of its life, sticking straight up.

He stopped and glared at Ryan. "Who are you?"

"Gramps!" Penny stepped forward and looped her arm through Ryan's. "You remember Braedon. We're engaged, remember?"

"I've never seen this fella before in my life."

"C'mon, you old fart! Supper's getting cold." Penny's grandmother ushered everyone into the dining room.

Throughout the evening, Ryan caught Penny's grandfather staring at him.

Finally, it was time to leave. Penny's grandmother insisted they take home leftovers, and the women went into the kitchen to pack them up.

Gramps sat in his recliner, staring at Ryan. "I don't know what you're pulling, but you and I both know you ain't that idiot Braedon." A wan smile creased his face. "But anything's an improvement. Just don't hurt my granddaughter, or you'll have to answer to me. I may be old, but I'm wiry."

"Yes, sir." Ryan bit back a smile.

He stood as Penny reentered the room, a shopping bag hanging from one arm. "Ready to go?" she asked, kissing her grandfather's cheek.

DOUBLE TROUBLE / 47

After thanking her grandparents for the meal, they headed home.

"I'm sorry Gramps didn't recognize you," Penny said a few minutes later as she stored the food in their refrigerator.

"Don't worry about it." He slid his arms around her waist and nuzzled her neck. Her grandfather was right, but thankfully, no one would believe him.

She turned in his arms, linking her hands behind his neck. "I guess I want my family to love you as much as I do, and it bothers me that my grandfather didn't even know you."

"Shh." He brushed her lips with his. He didn't want to hear how much she loved his brother. "It's okay. I understand."

"But I don't want you to not like him—"

"Hey, he's your family. How could I not like him?"

"Have I told you lately how much I love you?"

Dropping his arms, he reached around her to get a beer from the fridge. "I believe you mentioned it a time or two."

With a sigh, she sank to the kitchen chair and leaned on her elbow on the oak table, watching him drink his beer. "What's your brother like?"

The swallow of beer lodged in his throat, sending him into a coughing spasm. "Why do you want to know?" he finally gasped out.

"Are you okay?" She pounded his back.

He nodded and waved her away, then made a rolling motion with his hand to continue.

"Well," she said, sitting again. "I never had any brothers or sisters, and always wanted some. At least one, anyway." She grinned. "I used to watch the movie, *The Parent Trap*, over and over again, and wished I would find a secret twin sister."

She laughed and his stomach twisted. If only she knew having a twin wasn't all it was cracked up to be.

"Don't you think it would be cool to be a twin?"

"Um, I don't know." Stalling for time, he tossed the empty bottle in the trash. "Not really."

"That's because you have a brother. Trust me. To an only child, the idea of having a twin—better yet, an identical twin—is intriguing." She fished his bottle out of the trash and walked to a narrow cupboard. "I've told you a thousand times, we're recycling. Throw your bottles in the blue bin in here." She tossed in the bottle and closed the door. "Please. I know you think it's stupid, but it's important to me."

"Recycling isn't stupid. It's sensible, and the right thing to do." Noticing her stunned look, he grinned, pulling her into his arms and bumping her with his hips. "It turns me on."

She laughed and pulled away. "What's going on with you? Lately, *everything* I do turns you on."

"What's wrong with that?" He closed his mouth over her earlobe and gently sucked, biting back a grin when she shivered in response.

"Stop trying to distract me." She stepped back. "I want to talk and I can't when you keep doing stuff like that."

He tugged on her hand as he walked toward the bedroom. "We can talk in bed."

"No, we can't." Her steps lagged, pulling against his momentum. "Well, regardless, we won't."

Turning toward her, he cupped her shoulders, sliding the neckline of her dress down her arms until he'd bared her to the waist. Running the tip of his index finger along the top of her breast where it swelled over the low-cut red bra, he smiled at the catch in her breath. "We can talk while we're naked."

"I'm serious!"

"So am I!" He tried to tug her into his arms, but she stiffened her posture and resisted.

"Brae, we haven't talked the way we did today in, well, forever. We never talk. All we do is cohabit and sleep together. Until yesterday, we didn't even have sex all that much." Her eyes narrowed. "What's going on?" The smile slid from her face. "That wasn't break-up sex, was it?"

He forced a laugh and pulled up her dress until she was once again covered. "No, it was not break-up sex. C'mon. If you want to talk, let's sit in the living room where we can at least be comfortable."

Her eyes rounded. "Really? You're actually agreeing to talk?"

"Is that so hard to believe?"

"Well, you never wanted to talk before—"

"I can change my mind." He tugged her to sit next to him on the sectional. "Nice," he said, smoothing his hand over the suede-like upholstery.

Frowning, she put her hand to his forehead. "Are you sure you're feeling all right? You're acting like you've never seen your own furniture before. You were with me when we picked it out."

He nodded. "I know. I guess I just never felt it before. Didn't realize how soft it was since I don't come in here all that often."

She shot him an exasperated look and picked up a remote. Never blinking, she pushed a button. A soft whir filled the room, and the pastoral picture above the mantle rolled back to reveal a flat-screen TV. "Sweetie, I don't know what's going on, but you're the original couch potato. Lately, you're on the couch when I leave for work, and are still here, surrounded by trash, when I come home." She leaned close. "What's going on? Is something bothering you? Talk to me."

He took a deep breath, promising to kill his brother if he survived this mess. "I guess I've been a little stressed, is all. Seeing you go to work every day while I lay on the couch doesn't help." His lazy, good for nothing brother needed to get his ass off the couch and get a job. No self-respecting man would allow his woman to support him.

"Oh, baby, I'm sorry. I didn't mean to make you feel guilty."

He clenched his teeth. Great, now she was apologizing. "Forget it. You wanted to talk." He leaned back and drew her close, his arm thrown across her shoulder while his fingers played with her hair. Whatever they discussed, he knew he'd feel better if he was touching her.

"I want to meet your family. I especially want to meet your brother. I can't believe you never told me you had a brother. What does he look like?"

"Look like?" He shrugged. "Average, I guess. I'm a guy. Guys don't notice other guys."

Laughing, she gave him a playful punch. "Sure they do, they just don't admit it. So, what's your brother's name?"

"Braedon." Her eyes widened at the same time he realized what had fallen out of his mouth. "Ha! Joking. Ryan. His name is Ryan."

"How much younger is he?"

"Could we talk about something else?" At her puzzled look, he hurried on, "I mean, there really isn't anything to say. We aren't all that close anymore."

"Does he look like you?"

Baby, you wouldn't believe how much we look alike. "Sort of, I guess." He dipped his finger inside her neckline and petted her nipple. "But I'm sexier." He leaned to kiss her. "And better looking," he said against her mouth.

Brushing aside her gaping dress, he flicked open the front closure of her red bra, then took her nipple deeply into his mouth. Initiating sex may be devious, but it was the only way to ensure she didn't pursue her line of questioning about his "brother."

It was stupid to be jealous of himself, but there it was.

10

"Wait!" Penny broke away, her breath coming in shallow pants that heaved her naked breasts in a most interesting manner. "I forgot to put the Jell-O salad in the fridge."

"Forget the salad," he said, reaching for her.

"I can't." She stepped back, out of reach. "It will make a big sticky mess if it melts."

Groaning, he flopped his head back on the sofa, watching her hurry from the room through half-closed eyelids. Damn, she had a fine ass.

And he wanted it. Now.

With a slight adjustment, he stood and made his way through the highly polished swinging door into the kitchen.

Penny stood in front of the stainless steel refrigerator, both of the French doors open, its light bathing her in a sexy glow.

Stepping close, he bumped her with his erection, grinning at her exclamation.

He walked his fingers up the outside of each smooth thigh, bunching the skirt of her dress as he went. Pressed close to her buttocks, he ran his hand down the slick red satin of her thong.

She moaned and leaned back, grinding her softness against him.

Cool air bathed her heated skin. Braedon wasted no time in slipping the bodice of her dress to her elbows, and releasing the closure of her bra. Her nipples puckered at the sudden change in temperature, making her arch her back, and squirm against his hardness.

Hormones, technique, proximity . . . whichever was at work, she didn't care. All she knew was that she wanted her fiancé with a deep, burning desire she'd never felt before. He was a constant itch she needed to scratch. Whatever switch he'd managed to turn on within her, she prayed he never turned it off.

His hot fingers slipped beneath her damp panties to stroke her moisture, spreading it, causing her hips to flex.

Against her ear, he chuckled, a low sexy sound that vibrated in her ear, sending goose bumps to her extremities and moisture between her legs. Her nipples tightened to hard, almost painful points. After sucking gently on her earlobe, he whispered, "You like that, huh?"

She nodded, bumping her hips against his, rubbing her bottom along the hard ridge of his zipper, shamelessly offering herself. In case he had any doubt, she licked her lips and finally managed to say through a half groan, "Oh, yes!"

He applied pressure to her inner thighs by spreading his fingers. "Open for me, sweetheart."

He didn't have to ask twice. Heck, she'd do a horizontal split, if he wanted.

On his knees now, he slipped between her and the open doors. "Keep holding onto the doors," he instructed as he pushed aside the scrap of silk and then dragged his tongue over her sensitive flesh.

With a whimper, she locked her knees to remain upright, her fingers in a white-knuckled grip on the steel handles.

Between her spread legs, his tongue speared her opening. She cried out her pleasure. She may have even told him to never stop. She certainly thought it.

He chuckled against her, setting off ripples of release. His fingers joined the party.

If she were not from a line of strong females, she might have swooned.

More, she needed more. Much more.

Beep! Beep! Beep! A high-pitched sound vied with their heavy breathing.

Braedon stopped, mid-swipe.

Her breath hitched, her heart slamming against her ribcage.

Beep! Beep! Beep!

He sat back on his haunches, still holding her splayed, the cool air bathing her overheated genitals. It wasn't unpleasant.

"What the hell is that?" Face flushed, he looked up at her.

Beep. Beep. Beep.

Reality dawned. "Oh!" She laughed and tried to close her legs and not fall in a whimpering heap of need on top of him. "It's the refrigerator alarm. It's telling me the doors are open."

With a growl, he stood, scooping her up and over his shoulder. "Then let's shut them and go to bed."

She smiled against the warm fabric of his shirt. The man was a genius.

Ryan rolled onto his back, pulling Penny close, her head resting on his heart, and listened to her breathing slow as she drifted.

Meanwhile, his heart was trying to rip through his chest. And it wasn't from sexual exertion.

He recognized an impending panic attack when he felt it.

Deep breath. In. Out. Relax.

He began to doze, only to be jerked awake again, sweat beading his brow. His heartbeat echoed in his ears. How had he allowed Braedon to get him into this mess? More important, how was he going to get out of it?

Penny made a soft sound and snuggled closer.

Penny. What he felt for her was unlike anything he'd ever experienced. It might even possibly be love.

Shit. Just his luck. He finally falls in love, and it's with Braedon's fiancée. Worse, it's with a woman who is in love with his brother. And when she finds out she's been lied to and used for sexual gratification by a virtual stranger, she will run right back into her unworthy fiancé's arms.

With a shaking hand, he brushed a strand of hair from her face. Now that he'd found her, how would he survive without her?

What a mess.

He willed his muscles to relax, but to no avail. Tormented, every muscle in his body clenched, he held the love of his life while she blissfully slept.

If this was all the time he had with her, he would have to take it, hold it close, and savor it. Lord knew, it would all come tumbling down on him soon enough.

On the nightstand, his cell phone—rather, Braedon's cell phone—chirped. Great. A message. Since it was most likely from his brother, he needed to get it and delete it before Penny woke up.

His outstretched arm couldn't quite reach the BlackBerry.

Inch by inch, he scooted, pulling Penny along with him, until he closed his fingers around the cool pearl black square. It wouldn't do to have Penny see a message from Braedon.

Turning as much as possible, he scrolled to the message and frowned. *What the hell?*

Wright, your time is up. Pay up.

The sender was not someone he recognized, but he knew the last name: Harding. It had to be Penny's father.

Ryan heaved a silent sigh. Just what he needed. Beneath Penny's head, his heart clenched. Were it not for shortening his time with her, a heart attack might be a viable way out of the situation. Nothing fatal, mind you, just serious enough to buy him some time to think.

While he stared at the glowing screen, it chirped again as another message came in from the same sender.

I'm waiting. Tomorrow morning. Ten o'clock. Don't be late. It makes me cranky.

With his thumb, he laboriously typed out:

Where?

A few seconds later, the phone chirped again.

Don't play stupid.

"I'm not playing," he grumbled, tucking the phone under the spare pillow. He needed to call his brother and find out what all the cloak and dagger stuff meant. A glance at the clock on the nightstand confirmed the early hour. No doubt Braedon was still out.

Easing away from Penny, he inched his way to the edge of the mattress, grabbed the phone, then stood. A glance back confirmed she was still sleeping.

Cautious steps took him through the living room into the kitchen, where he waited to turn on the light until the door had swung shut.

He wasted no time, hitting the speed dial button, then paced the cool tile while he waited.

"Now what?" Braedon's voice vibrated his ear.

Ryan walked to the far corner of the kitchen before he spoke in a low whisper, "You had a message."

"So? Take care of it."

"I'm trying!" He glanced at the still-closed door and lowered his voice. "But it was cryptic."

"Cryptic? What the hell does that mean?"

"A text message saying to meet the sender tomorrow. At ten. With money . . . sound familiar?"

Braedon's sigh heaved through the air waves. "What else did he say?"

"That's it. To meet at ten tomorrow morning. Do you know where that would be? 'Cause when I asked where, he said not to play stupid."

"I've met them a few places. He give any clue?"

"Brae, I wasn't about to play twenty questions."

"There's an abandoned golf course, about half a mile down the road from my place. Try the caddy shack there. It's on the Gulf side of the parking lot."

"Okay, but . . . How much do I need to give him?" When his brother quoted the price, Ryan winced. "Will he take a check?"

Braedon's laughter vibrated the cell phone, then he hung up.

Ryan stood for a while, trying to formulate a plan. He could notify the police. But if he did that, he'd also implicate his brother, as well as possibly alienate Penny by having her father arrested. Assuming her father actually showed up at that type of meeting in person. Regardless, she would still be affected.

The idea of parting with such a large sum of money made him physically ill. There had to be a better way of handling it.

He'd talk to whomever he met. Most people were not unreasonable. Surely they could reach a compromise.

11

"Compromise?" The thug slammed his fist into Ryan's solar plexus again, knocking the air from his lungs. "Sure we can make a compromise." He flashed green teeth as he dragged Ryan up by his shirt collar. "How about this? You pay us the money and we won't kill you. How's that?"

"Sounds fair." He spit out some blood, and hoped a tooth didn't tag along.

"So where is it?" Green Teeth gave him a little shake.

He wiped blood from his mouth with the back of his hand. "I didn't bring it. I don't suppose you'd take a check?"

"You suppose right." Green Teeth turned to his partner, a bald man with no neck. "He didn't bring it. What should we do?"

"You could always wait while I go get the money." Ryan's breath whooshed out with the punch Green Teeth rounded on him.

"I'll call the boss," No Neck said, striding from the shack.

Ryan pulled up his shirttail and wiped more blood away. He

paused mid-wipe to find Green Teeth staring. "What? You weren't finished beating me?"

After a beat, Green Teeth said, "Naw, I'm done. For now, anyway. You look . . . different."

"Probably because I'm covered in my own blood." Giving up, he pulled his polo shirt over his head and mopped his face with it.

The other man shook his head. "No, that's not it. I can't put my finger on it." He shrugged. "Maybe it's the haircut."

"Yeah, that's probably it." Warily, Ryan tugged the shirt back on.

"Your voice sounds different, too, like you're getting a cold or something," the man persisted.

"Blood running down the back of your throat will do that," Ryan pointed out.

No Neck stepped back into the gloom. "He said you've got twenty-four hours to get the cash and bring it back here to us."

"That's it?" Where the hell was he going to get his hands on that much cash in such a short amount of time? But if they were willing to give him twenty-four hours, he'd take it. Maybe he could formulate a plan by then.

"He said to tell you one more thing," No Neck said as he backed Ryan against the wall by the door opening.

"What's that?" Ryan edged toward the door, but No Neck grabbed him to hold him in place.

"Don't fuck up."

Penny hummed as she turned the pancakes on the griddle, then smiled when she heard the front door open and close.

Switching off the heat and moving the griddle, she wiped her hands on her apron and hurried into the living room. "Hi, honey, where have you—oh, my gosh! What happened to you?" She hurried to his side and helped him to the sofa. "Are you okay? Do you need a doctor?"

Braedon winced as he settled onto the cushions but shook his head, brushing away her hands. "I'm fine."

"No, you are *not* fine! What happened?" *Was that blood on his shirt?*

"I decided to skateboard and had a little accident." He chuckled and grimaced. "Guess I'm out of practice."

"Since when do you skateboard? Here, raise up so I can put this pillow behind you."

He complied, but she could tell he was in pain.

"I used to skateboard a lot, but I haven't done it since college. I'm not as good as I used to be." He chuckled and winced again.

"College! That was a good ten years ago. What were you thinking?"

He sighed and closed his eyes. "Trust me, I wondered the same thing a little while ago."

"I made pancakes for breakfast." Obviously he didn't want to discuss his accident. "Would you like me to bring you a plate on a tray?"

He shook his head and mumbled something that sounded like "I don't eat pancakes." But that couldn't be right. Pancakes were Braedon's favorite.

While Braedon showered, Penny made her obligatory Sunday phone call to her father. After some chitchat, he asked if they were still coming for dinner. Darn. She'd totally forgotten she'd accepted the invitation earlier in the week. And she'd neglected to mention it to Brae. Well, when he found out why she'd been preoccupied, he'd forgive her.

"Sure, Daddy. I remember. We'll see you about five." She couldn't wait to tell her father she'd finally decided to set a wedding date. She knew she should probably tell Braedon first, but she wanted to get the plans rolling before she sprung it on him. He'd been putting so much pressure on her lately, he'd probably be ecstatic.

Of course, she wanted it to be special when she told him her decision. Lunch. She'd take him to the boardwalk café where he'd proposed. It would be the perfect place to declare her intentions.

She couldn't wait.

Faking a running injury was low, even for the man he'd become of late, but it was the only way Ryan could think of to get Penny to drive to her father's house. He couldn't afford to make any more stupid mistakes by revealing yet another lack of memory. As soon as he could contact his brother, he'd tell him the deal was off. He was in love with Penny and wanted to spend his life with her—and *not* as his twin brother. It was past time to tell her the truth. If her actions of late were any indication, there shouldn't be a problem with her accepting him and his love.

Penny flipped on the signal, turned right, and stopped at a closed gate with a big star of Texas in the middle. "Brae? What are you waiting for? Push the button."

Button? What button? He scanned the dash and console. Shifting in the bucket seat, he gasped and grabbed his thigh. "Damn, I must have moved wrong again."

"Poor baby! Are you sure you're up to this?" She reached past him to push a button hidden on the far side of the console and the gates parted. "I can always tell Daddy we need to reschedule."

He rubbed his leg for effect. "No, no, I'm okay. We said we'd come, so we need to stay. At least for a while."

The smile she flashed him made it all worthwhile.

Ryan tried to relax while he took in the palm tree–lined curving drive. No point in making it obvious he'd never been there.

They rolled to a stop under a porte cochere and got out of the low slung car. He glanced up—way up—at the illuminated three stories of windows. Penny gave his hand a squeeze and began walking toward the massive double doors. Gas coach lights on either side of the entrance cast a warm glow.

Penny rang the bell with several sharp punches, then opened the door. "Woo-hoo! We're here! Hello?"

"Woo-hoo!" came an answering singsong female voice, an instant before a full figured woman, who looked old enough to be Penny's mother, bustled into the cavernous foyer. "I thought you'd never get here! Gimme some sugar!"

The woman grabbed Penny, enveloping her in her purple silk clad arms, a cloud of sweet smelling perfume fogging over to tickle Ryan's nose.

"Aunt Doreen, you're smothering me!" Penny laughed, kissing the heavily made-up cheek of the older woman.

Aunt Doreen. Ryan made a mental note.

Penny stepped back. "Look who I brought."

The smile slid from Doreen's face. Her mouth drew down, frown lines bracketing her red glossed lips. "Braedon." She gave a curt nod. "Found a job yet?"

"Aunt Doreen!" Color seeped into Penny's cheeks. "She doesn't know what she's saying," she said in a low voice.

"I heard that, young lady. I'm not deaf, and I'm certainly not senile." Doreen shot him a withering look, then took Penny's face in her bejeweled hand, light reflecting from the blood red nail polish. "I said it before and I'll say it again, you're marrying beneath you."

"Crissakes, Doreen, can't you give it a rest?" a male voice boomed from the other side of the foyer.

Penny shot the man a grateful look and a small smile. "Hello, Daddy."

"Hi, shortcake." He walked to her and pulled her into a hug, kissing the top of her head. After a moment, he released her and nodded at Ryan. "Wright."

Whatever Ryan had expected Penny's father to look like, Charley Harding wasn't it. Short, with sparse sandy color hair, his horn-rimmed glasses, dress pants, shirt, tie, and vest gave him the appearance of an accountant. A very successful accountant, Ryan amended, taking in the shoes that were very likely custom-made.

"Doreen," Charley said, "why don't you and Penny go see how dinner is progressing? Braedon, let's go in my study. I have something I want to show you."

"Daddy . . ." The look Penny shot her father made even Ryan want to squirm. "Be nice."

"I'm always nice, shortcake. Now you go on and let us men have some peace and quiet for a while."

She stared at her father for a second, then rose on tiptoe to kiss Ryan's cheek. "Don't let him bully you," she whispered, then followed her aunt through the swinging door at the far end of the hall.

Charley motioned for him to proceed to the left. Since Ryan had no earthly idea where the study was, he made a slight bow, "After you, sir."

Penny's father frowned slightly, but then walked to the second door and stepped in, Ryan right behind him.

"Have a seat, Wright." Charley sat in the burgundy leather executive chair behind a massive carved dark wood desk, indicating with a wave of his hand that Ryan should take a seat in one of the high-backed matching chairs grouped in front of the desk. "May as well get right down to business. Did you bring it?"

Ryan didn't pretend to misunderstand. "No, sir. I was told I had twenty-four hours."

Charley made a disgusted sound and shook his head before pinning him with his green gaze.

Even knowing Charley was Penny's dad, it was odd to realize they had the same color eyes.

"Do you have anything to say for yourself, son?" He picked up a pen and rolled it between his fingers. "Lord knows why, but my baby loves you. She insists on marrying you." He leaned closer, his eyes much colder than Penny's. "Give me a reason why I shouldn't arrange for you to permanently disappear."

Ryan swallowed around a lump of fear and took a deep breath before answering. "You said it yourself," he drawled in what he hoped sounded like his brother's careless arrogance, "Penny loves me. If I were to disappear, she'd be devastated." He leaned closer, determined not to let the man intimidate him. "I wouldn't recommend it."

They stared for a moment, then Charley broke eye contact, throwing back his head and laughing. "You've got balls, I'll give you that, Wright." He wiped tears of mirth from his eyes, then leveled his gaze again. "Your time is almost up. I strongly suggest you find a way to make your payment." He stood, indicating their meeting was at an end. "As for Penny being devastated . . ." He shrugged. "As her daddy, of course, I'd stand by her in her grief. And time heals all wounds. She's a woman. Eventually, she'd find another lost soul to nurture. Do we understand each other?"

"Yes, sir."

After a meal of gigantic proportions, of which Ryan tasted only fear, Charley and Penny went for their *traditional* walk. Since Ryan got the impression it was a private ritual, he offered to keep Doreen company.

In the formal living room, he perched on an uncomfortable brocade wingback chair and watched Penny's aunt sip her cognac, her gaze never wavering from him.

"What's different?" she asked in a slow drawl. "There's something different about you tonight. I can't put my finger on it, and it's driving me plumb crazy."

Schooling his expression, he shrugged. "Nope. Same old me."

She leaned back, kicking off her ridiculous parrot green high heels, and crossed her stocking-clad feet on the coffee table. "I don't think so . . . who the hell are you?"

"Maybe you *are* getting senile, Doreen." Damn, he hated treating his elder like that, but it would definitely be the attitude Braedon would take. With a grin he was far from feeling, he leaned closer, extending his hand. "Braedon Wright."

She swatted it away. "Bullshit. You may have my niece fooled, but I know different. At first glance, you look like him, but as soon as you opened your mouth, I knew you weren't that imbecile Braedon." She swirled her liquor, watching the oily residue on the side of the goblet, then looked up, her blue gaze cool. "Obviously you're related. A twin?" She nodded, smiling at her obvious cleverness. "Of course! The creep would be just the type to never mention he had a twin brother."

At his stunned silence, she grinned, red lipstick on her front tooth. With a sultry look, she flicked open the bright buttons on her silk top until she was almost exposed.

"You do realize," she said in a sweet voice, drawing an index finger along her ample cleavage, "despite my aversion to duplicity, I find you immensely attractive." Their gazes met. "I never told anyone what your brother and I did in the boat house, hot stuff. But I don't know if I can keep something juicy like this to myself." She leaned closer, tugging until she'd exposed the dark circle of one nipple. "Convince me to take a vow of silence, lover."

12

Convince her? Convince her how? Sweat popped out on his forehead and trickled down his temple. In horror, he watched her play with her exposed nipple. His dinner threatened to make a reappearance. Good Lord, had his reprobate brother really diddled that woman? He'd always known Braedon led a depraved life, but the thought was a stretch, even for his low standards.

"Well?" she asked, plucking the nipple until it stood erect. "I'm waiting."

That's it. He was definitely going to kill his brother. Assuming he lived long enough to find him.

"Wh—" he cleared his throat. "What would it take to convince you?"

She chuckled and looked down at her now totally exposed breast. "You strike me as a smart boy. I think you can figure it out."

"I don't want any misunderstandings." He met her gaze. "Tell me exactly what you want me to do."

She patted the sofa next to her rounded hip. "First off, come closer." At his hesitance, she chuckled. "I won't bite." She flashed a smile. "Unless you ask real sweet."

On stiff legs, he walked to her, hesitated, then sat down.

"Give me your hand." Without waiting, she grasped his wrist and tugged until his palm rested on the heat of her breast. "Feel that, lover? It could all be yours." She giggled. "Well, for a little while, anyway." Pushing down, she wiggled until his hand was situated under her black skirt between her now spread legs, her damp heat moistening his fingers. "Pet me," she demanded, in a growling whisper.

He glanced at the closed pocket doors, then forced his fingers to stroke the repugnant dampness once before withdrawing his hand. "I can't."

"Sure you can." She pulled on his arm again, but he locked his elbow, keeping his hand as far away as possible. "Dag-nabit, I knew you weren't going to be as easy as your brother." He was shocked to see tears in her eyes. "Please. I need you. Just one more time. No one has to find out."

"We've never done anything. You're confusing me with someone else. I should go."

With lightning fast movement, she straddled him, her dampness pressing into him. "At least help me a little, lover." She reached down and pulled her top and bra down lower, exposing both of her breasts. "Like 'em? I had 'em built just for you. After you told me it was like sucking on deflated balloons, I went to see a surgeon the very next day. Touch them. Go ahead."

Tentatively, he reached up and gave a gentle squeeze, then swallowed. "Very nice."

"Suck them." She rubbed her nipple against his mouth. "Suck them hard."

Busy flailing his head back and forth to avoid contact, he didn't hear the doors slide open.

"Damnit, Doreen! You've been told a hundred times they look real! Now put them back in your bra and get off Penny's fiancé." Charley hurried to his sister, and helped her up from Ryan's lap. "Sorry about that, Braedon." He gently tucked Doreen's bosom into her bra cup and rebuttoned her top. "Sis, have you taken your medicine today? Why don't I walk you upstairs and you can take it?" Never taking his eyes from his task, he said to Penny, "Shortcake, I have to take care of her. Thanks for coming. I'll give you a call tomorrow and we can finish our discussion."

As the two walked from the room, Ryan spotted Penny's horrified face.

Rushing to her side, he reached for her. "I can explain."

With a sad smile, she shook her head. "Sweetie, there's nothing to explain. You should know that. Doreen's obviously off her meds. When that happens, she tries to screw anything that moves." She hugged him, her hair tickling his nose. "I'm sorry. I didn't realize, or I'd have never left you alone with her. Are you okay?"

Relief made his knees weak. Penny didn't blame him. And it was very possible, given the talk of medication, even if Doreen did blab about him not being Braedon, no one would believe her. He smiled and pressed a kiss to her forehead. "I'm fine. No worries. Let's go home."

"Pick up, pick up!" Ryan paced the bathroom the next morning, naked after his post-run shower.

"Hmm? What d'ya want?" Braedon yawned into the phone. "Wha' time zit?"

"Almost eleven. Are you sleeping?" No doubt about it, his brother was a slug.

"Evidently not." Braedon sounded louder but awake. "What's up?"

"What's up? Let's see. I was beaten by some goons who thought I was you. You didn't tell me you missed a payment."

"Must have slipped my mind."

"I want out." Ryan balanced the cell while he stepped into a pair of boxers.

Braedon's sigh filled his ear. "I know. Just give me a little more time. I have an appointment at a bank this morning to see about a loan."

"A loan!" He swiped deodorant under each arm. "Who in their right mind would give you loan?"

"No one. But they're lined up to give you one."

He stilled. "You wouldn't dare. Even you aren't that low."

"I'm desperate. I thought you knew that."

"Listen. Penny and I are going to lunch. Some place that's supposed to be special to you two. Meet us there. We'll figure something out."

"Jacques? She's taking you to Jacques? I can't believe she'd take you there. She was always yammering about it being *our* place."

"It *is* your place, you idiot. She still thinks I'm you, remember?" He pulled a polo shirt over his head and automatically checked his hair, then remembered he didn't have any.

"Oh, yeah. Sorry. I forgot. Is she totally freaking you out yet?"

He sighed and sat on the closed toilet seat. "No. Brae, she's everything I ever wanted. Does that bother you?"

His brother laughed. "Are you kidding? Hell, no! It's a relief. So . . . you're serious? You really like her?"

"I more than like her. I love her. I know Jacques is supposed to be your and Penny's place, but I'd like to tell her how I feel while we're there. I get the impression she thinks it's a romantic place. Since I don't know much about Jacques, I thought it was a good place to tell her—and pop the question."

"Pop the question?"

"I want to marry her. Assuming it's okay with you."

He held the phone away from his ear at his brother's whoop. "That's a yes, then?"

"Hell, yes! But there is one prob, big brother."

"What's that?"

"We're still engaged."

13

Ryan's heart stumbled. "What?"

"You heard me. I'm still Penny's fiancé. You can't propose or you'll blow everything."

"Damn it, Braedon! It's been two weeks. Enough. I'm going to tell her the truth, and beg her forgiveness."

"But, Charley—"

"Screw Charley! I don't care about Charley. And, little brother, in the grand scheme of things, I guess I don't really care about you, either. I love Penny. I want to spend my life with her."

"Like you said, it's only been two weeks! How can you tell if it's real? All I'm asking is for a little more time. You owe me."

Temper flared. "I don't owe you a damn thing! We're twins. There's nothing either of us can do to change that. It's not my fault I was born first, any more than it's yours that you were born second. It was a cruel act of fate. Accept it, and go on. Get over it!"

"That's the problem. I can't get over it. You stole my identity—"

"Bullshit! I was first!"

"Exactly! You were first. You were always first."

"Oh, let's not get into that whole Mom-liked-you-best crap."

"Well, she did. But that's not what I meant. Because you were first, everything I did was second. Second best. You were born first. You walked and talked first. You shaved first. All I ever had in my entire life was had first by you. Even my face. You have no idea what it's like to look in a mirror and see your brother. It's like I don't even exist."

Ryan sighed and ran his hand over his hair. "Did you ever think I see *you* when I look in the mirror?"

"No. Because you don't. You see the same thing I do. You. That's why you owe me."

"And that's why I agreed to this hairbrained scheme in the first place! All our lives, you've whined about how I owe you some kind of restitution for being born first. Like it was my fault! Well, no more, little brother. It's time you cleaned up your own messes. I'm going to go to lunch with Penny, and tell her the truth. Then I'm going to tell her how I feel, and beg her forgiveness."

Penny smiled at the waiter and took a seat on the patio of the restaurant. Across from her, Braedon fidgeted, an anxious look on his face. She really couldn't blame him. She'd put him off long enough. Too long. As her dad said, it was time to fish or cut bait.

Something had changed over the past couple of weeks. After their last argument, her fiancé had changed. Finally grown up.

She was ready to set a wedding date.

Smiling, she reached across the table for his hands. *Give me a sign. Something, anything to let me know I'm not the only one head over heels in love.*

Braedon smiled at her, his thumbs caressing the top of her hands. "I love you, you know."

Yes! She wanted to jump up and down for joy. Finally, finally, he'd said the words she'd been waiting to hear. Around a suddenly tight throat, she said, "I know. I love you, too. That's why I—"

"I don't think you understand. *I* love you. And because *I* love you, I—"

"Hi, how's my lucky Penny?" A familiar low voice said.

She looked from Braedon's struck face to . . . Braedon?

"Wh-what . . . ?" She blinked, but they were still there.

"Surprise," Braedon-standing-by-the-table said, spreading his arms. "We're twins. Pen, meet my brother, Ryan."

She wanted to kill. She wanted to scream. She wanted to cry. She jumped to her feet, sloshing the wine from her glass.

And promptly fainted.

14

"Penny? Baby, can you hear me?" Braedon's voice floated through the cotton filling her head. Wait. It sounded different somehow. Braedon's brother? What was his name? "Penny? Are you okay? It's me, Ryan."

Eyes still closed, she relaxed, cushioned against his firm chest, his strong arms surrounding her. She sighed. Yes, Ryan. No! Ryan was a rat. He and Braedon had deceived her.

Memories of how different her fiancé had seemed over the last couple of weeks flew through her mind. Lower voice. Sexier. Better ripped body. No apparent memory of anything they'd recently shared. She swallowed a groan. How could she have been so stupid? Humiliation washed through her at the memories, the many and varied ways she'd shared her body with . . . a stranger.

"Get away from me!" She opened her eyes, hardening her heart at the sight of his beloved face. Wait, was it him or his brother she loved? It didn't matter. Obviously, neither gave a hoot about her or they'd never have played such a heinous trick.

She scooted away from him, only to bump into his clone and scamper in the other direction.

"Penny, please. I love you. Let me explain—"

"Explain? Explain what? That you lied to me? Deceived me? Pretended to care for me? How can you explain that?" She looked from one man to the other. "How can either of you possibly explain that?"

"Penny—" Braedon number two reached toward her.

She held out her arm, holding him back. "Don't touch me. Either of you. Ever again. You're sick. Sick and twisted, and I don't ever want to see either one of you again!"

"Don't tell your father," Braedon number two said, then winced when she turned what she was sure were wild eyes on him. "Please."

She blinked back tears, then narrowed her eyes at him. "You never really knew me at all, did you?" Turning on her heels, she made her way out of the restaurant with as much dignity as she could muster, considering her heart was broken.

Ryan pushed the hands-free symbol on his navigation screen when he recognized his brother's number. "Any luck?" He signaled and merged onto I59.

"No. She's gone. By the time I got back to the apartment, she'd packed up and left." His laugh seemed less than jovial. "She left the key and her engagement ring on the table."

"After what we did, I'm surprised she didn't flush it." He adjusted his lumbar support and pushed cruise control. "Do you have any idea where she went?"

"I called Charley, but he hadn't heard from her. I just told him we'd had a misunderstanding, and if she called, to tell her to call me."

"Ha. Well, don't hold your breath on that one. I got the impression you weren't one of her dad's favorite people."

"Yeah, well, that's an understatement. I think I survived this long only because his daughter liked me. And, regardless of Charley's other faults, he does love his baby girl."

"I'm going to go out and talk to him."

"No! I don't have his money yet—"

"We already talked about this, Brae. I have to tell him. Maybe he'll take pity on you. On us. Regardless, if I want his help, I have to level with him. Did you contact the therapist yet?"

"Yeah, she said I not only have a gambling addiction, I'm possibly a sex addict, too. Stir in commitment and honesty issues, and I'm one fucked up guy." He gave a bark of laughter. "I have an appointment at the rehab place tomorrow."

"I'm proud of you, Braedon. Admitting you have a problem is a big step."

"Easy for you to say, big brother."

Ryan laughed. There might be hope for their relationship after all. "True."

"Ry?"

"Hmm?" He signaled, and braked on the exit ramp.

"I, um, appreciate everything you did, man. Putting your life on hold, involving yourself in my crap. And even after possibly losing the first woman you ever really loved, you agreed to cosign for that loan. Thanks," he finished in a whisper.

"One more thing, bro. Go on. Say it!"

"I owe you. Butt-head."

"That's what I'm talkin' about! Woo-hoo! I'm feeling the love!"

"Shut up. And Ry?"

"Yeah?"

"I hope you and Penny can work it out."

"Thanks."

Ocean Drive didn't have as many houses fitting the description in Ryan's head as he'd feared. After only one misstep, he turned into the gated drive. In his own Lexus, he had no controller.

Buzzing down his window, he pushed the button on the silver post.

"Yes?" a disembodied male voice said.

"I'm Ryan Wright. I'm here to see Mr. Harding."

The wrought iron gate slowly opened.

"Mr. Harding is expecting you," the maid said, stepping back when he entered. "He's in the living room."

Swallowing his revulsion at entering the room of his recent sexual harassment, he took a deep breath and walked in, only flinching a little when he heard the pocket doors close behind him.

Charley stood by the mantle, unsmiling. "I don't think we've been properly introduced. I understand you're Ryan Wright, the idiot Braedon's brother?"

"Yes, sir." It was probably best to ignore the slur on his brother's character.

"And you were the one who came here with my daughter last time?"

"Yes, sir."

"And you think you love her?"

Surprised, he finally met the man's sharp green gaze. "Yes, sir, I know I do. More than you can imagine. Do you know where I can find her? I want to try to explain."

Charley chuckled and shook his head. "You've got a hell of a lot of explaining to do, kiddo. That was a pretty harebrained scheme you and your brother pulled off."

"Yes, sir."

Charley shook his head again, flecks of gray in his hair glinting in the can lights over the mantle. "I must be losing my edge. I should have made you right off. For one thing, the hairs on the back of my neck didn't stand up like they do whenever I'm around your brother." He chuckled. "I tell you, it's a relief to know she's not in love with that guy."

"Um, sir? I've only known Penny for the last two weeks. Braedon is the one she fell for."

"Well, he's not the one she's crying for now."

"She's crying?" He never meant to hurt her.

"Every time she thinks about you, it seems. I was so sick of the waterworks, I sent her to the beach house."

"Beach house? Where is it?"

"I'll tell you in a minute. Right now, we have some business to discuss." He gestured to the couch. "Have a seat."

"No, thanks, I'll stand . . . if you don't mind."

"Oh, sorry. Forgot about the Doreen incident." He took a sip of his wine. "We still have a problem, Wright. Your brother owes me a shitload of money. I'd have never let him get in so deep if he wasn't living with my baby girl. Now, I'm a business man. Money is my business and this makes me look bad." He looked over the rim of his glass before taking another sip. "I hate to look bad."

"Yes, sir."

"Doggone it, Wright, what I'm trying to say is: Do you want to marry my daughter?"

"More than anything, sir."

"Okay. Your brother told my men you agreed to cosign for a loan to repay me. That right?" At Ryan's nod, he continued. "I don't want my daughter saddled with Braedon's debt. Everyone deserves a fresh start when they get married. Here's my plan. If you can get Penny to marry you, as a wedding present, I'll strike off half the amount your brother owes. Oh, and I promised her I'd stop the threats." He stuck out a slender hand. "Deal?"

"Deal. Now, where is the beach house?"

Penny swiped at her red, leaking eyes and blew her nose. Who knew she had so much bodily fluid? She'd been crying and blowing her nose pretty much twenty-four-seven for the last three days, with no relief in sight.

A knock sounded on the glass patio door. Frowning, she tossed her used tissue into the overflowing waste basket and grabbed another from the dispenser on her way to the door.

"Hi." Ryan stood on the deck, the sunset glinting from the blond spikes of his hair.

"Ryan?" When he nodded, she shot him her best withering look and said, "Just making sure."

Before she could close the door again, he grabbed it, stopping her momentum. "How are you?"

"Peachy keen." Her eyes welled. "How do you think I am? For two weeks I had the best sex of my life with a total stranger." Sniff.

"The best sex of your life, huh?" Hands in the pockets of his khaki cargo shorts, he grinned, bending his knees to look her in the eyes.

She nodded and sniffed again. "Wipe the stupid grin off your face. It wasn't a compliment."

"It was the best time I ever had, too," he said in a low voice. Wait, his voice *was* low. Lower than Braedon's. Dang, the twin thing was confusing.

"Yeah, well, you had an odd way of showing it. How's Braedon?"

"Do you really care?"

She shrugged. "Only in the sense that I care about all human beings. It's a stretch, but I think Braedon still qualifies."

"He's in rehab. And he's paying off his debts." He paused and looked down at his running shoes. "He said to tell you how sorry he is about everything."

"What about you, Ryan? Are you sorry?"

He was quiet for so long, she began to think he wouldn't answer. That was when she realized how much she needed to hear his voice, hear him say he was sorry, say she meant something to him. Say he'd missed her even half as much as she'd missed him.

"About pretending to be my brother? Yes. Sorry about getting to know you, experiencing the *best sex of my life,* and falling in love with you? Never."

Dabbing at a fresh batch of tears, she countered, "If you're so sorry—did you say you fell in love with me?"

He pulled her into his arms, walking her back into the house. "Absolutely, unconditionally, and forever."

She'd played the scene a million times in her mind since she'd stormed out of the restaurant, but now that it was actually happening, she was paralyzed, torn. Could she get past what Ryan and Braedon had done to her?

Ryan chose that moment to trail kisses up her neck, weakening her resolve. She really did love him. The depth of her feelings for him, compared to the shallow superficial attraction she'd had for Braedon, was astronomical.

She'd made some monumental mistakes in her life. Getting involved with Braedon topped the list. But she couldn't even fault that because it brought her Ryan. Yes, she'd made some colossal mistakes, but instantly she knew cutting him out of her life would be the biggest.

Snuggling against him, she arched her neck for better access. "Maybe we should go up to my bedroom and discuss this further."

He abruptly stopped and stepped back. "No. I don't think that's a good idea."

"What? You're not attracted to me anymore?" She ran her hand over the evidence to the contrary.

"I made the mistake of having sex with you the day I met you. It was so mind-blowing, it clouded my judgment. If you're honest with yourself, I bet it did yours, too." He took her limp hands in his and kissed each knuckle. "I love you too much to settle. I don't want just hot sex. I want to make love to you.

Passionate love. For the rest of our lives. And I'm willing to wait until you're ready to make that kind of commitment to me."

He pulled her to him for a kiss that very likely made steam come out of her ears. Her knees were definitely weak. Every nerve ending tingled.

She wanted more.

His finger on her lips stopped her declaration. "Think about it. I'm not going anywhere. I'll be right here. Well, as soon as I go pick up a sleeping bag. Good-night, Penny. I love you."

Penny sat in her tub, up to her neck in the hot, churning water, but it didn't relax her. She'd heard Ryan's car door an hour ago, then all was quiet. She knew he was out there. Waiting.

What was she going to do about it? What could she do about it?

For one thing, she could stop allowing life to happen to her. She'd drifted into a relationship with Braedon based on one fast, hot sexual encounter, and look where that had gone.

But it was different with Ryan, even when she thought he was Braedon. Closing her eyes, she tasted his kiss, felt his unique touch. How in the heck had she possibly thought he was Braedon?

She'd been willing to make the final commitment to him when she'd thought him to be Braedon. Why should now be any different?

Shoring her resolve, she pushed the button to quiet the jets and climbed out of the tub.

She was going hunting.

Manhunting.

15

Ryan swam toward wakefulness, dimly aware of the distant sound of surf rolling to the shore. Where was he? Oh, yeah, on the deck at Penny's beach house.

He turned on the sleeping bag, aware again of the hard planks beneath him, and opened his eyes.

All around him, candles glowed. Penny stood before him, a naked goddess, the candlelight reflecting from her oiled skin.

Did he have the strength to deny her again?

"Shh," she said, lowering to her knees until she was beside him on the sleeping bag. "I love you, Ryan. My soul knew you even if my eyes refused to see." She brushed her lips over his.

A breeze blew from the Gulf, bringing with it the slight scent of coconut oil, cooling his lust-flushed skin. "Where are my shorts?"

Her grin showed white in the darkness. "You sure are a sound sleeper. I unzipped the sleeping bag and pulled your underwear off without waking you up."

Placing his hands behind his head, he grinned. "What were you planning to do to me?"

"Oh, this," she said, dribbling warm oil onto his chest and stroking it ever so slowly around his chest, and then downwards until it reached the spoke leaping to attention. "Or this." She rolled until her breasts slipped along the oil on his chest. "Or this." She slipped lower until her breath fanned the engorged head of his penis.

His breath hitched when her hot mouth closed over him, licking and sucking, ratcheting up his passion.

Penny squirmed, loving the feel of Ryan's hard flesh in her mouth, running her tongue up and down and around, smiling when his hips bucked.

His hands closed around her ankles, then well-oiled fingers slid up her legs to find her wet and needy.

In and out his fingers slid, teasing, promising elusive satisfaction.

When she began to vibrate, poised on the brink, he withdrew, causing her to mewl her disapproval.

Limp, she allowed him to turn her, move her to his satisfaction.

Spread-eagle on the open sleeping bag, she watched as Ryan poured a fine stream of oil between her breasts, then thoroughly massaged it in.

His hot mouth closed over her nipple, sucking deeply while his fingers probed her eager flesh.

The roar of blood in her ears vied with the roar of the surf. In a heartbeat, her orgasm washed over her, drowning her in its intensity.

Limp, she lay gasping for air while he dribbled more oil, rubbing, leaving no pinpoint of skin un-oiled.

Placing a totally relaxed leg on each of his shoulders, he tilted her hips, thoroughly lubing her genitals, then bathed her with his tongue until her hips convulsed against his mouth, begging for more. Begging for release.

He grinned up at her, the edges of his teeth flashing white in the moonlight. "I'm becoming addicted to coconut." He took her nub between his teeth and sucked.

The effect was instantaneous. Sparks shot to every nerve ending. She screamed as another climax rushed over her, pulling her under in its sensual tow. Behind her clenched eyelids, a myriad of fireworks exploded. She couldn't drag enough air into her deprived lungs.

"Now," she finally gasped, "Make love to me now. I want . . . you inside me. Now!"

He climbed on her body, the head of his penis probing her, teasing her with what she was missing. Desperate, she arched her hips, only to have him shy away.

He kissed her then. It was a primal kiss. A kiss to claim her as his. A kiss to claim him as hers.

"Tell me," he said, nibbling at her lower lip.

"I love you," she cried out, trying to pull him into her sex-starved body.

"I love you, too, but that's not what I want to hear. I want to hear you say my name. Tell me you love me, only me." He probed her once, just sticking the very tip of his penis in, then pulling back out. "Marry me?"

"Yes. Do it! Now!"

"Not until I hear you say the words." Again, the head went in and out. "Say them."

"I love you." In. Out. "Ryan! Yes, I'll marry you. Ryan. Only and always. Only you."

He plunged into her, her wetness combined with the oil, making them so slippery it was hard to control their movements.

Frustrated, she grasped his hips with her knees, pushing until she'd flipped their positions.

Her orgasm roared through her, draining her. Ryan's quickly followed, his body going rigid, his fingers digging into her hips.

She collapsed on his chest, their rapid heartbeats slamming into each other. His hand stroked her hair.

"Are you sure?" he asked, still panting.

"I've never been more sure of anything in my life." She placed nibbling kisses along his jaw.

"And you're okay with Braedon being your brother-in-law?"

She thought for a few seconds, then wiggled against his recovering erection. "I can live with it."

He hugged her close, covering her face with kisses. "I don't care, as long as you live with *me*."

DOUBLE THE PLEASURE

1

"I'm not picky," Suzanne Hartley argued, motioning to the bartender to set up another tequila shot while she salted the back of her hand. "All I'm looking for is a guy who'll do what I want, when I want, for as long as I want, then go away. Is that too much to ask?" She licked her hand, threw back the shot, and quickly sucked on the lime before continuing. "Or maybe he could wait around, you know, like a DustBuster, charged up and ready when needed."

"As I recall," Megan Hartley told her twin, "you already have what you're describing . . . a vibrator?" She picked up her Bellini and took a sip.

Her sister motioned to the bartender, and salted her hand again in preparation for her next shot. "The vibrator is okay, but I prefer the feel of hot sweat-slicked male skin rubbing against mine."

"Could you keep your voice down? The guy at the other end of the bar looks ready to pounce."

They both looked at the gentleman in question, who flashed a drunken smile. They quickly averted their gazes.

"Have you packed for the reunion?" Megan took another sip of her drink and smoothed out the paper cocktail napkin.

"Nah. Plenty of time." Suzanne slammed down another shot, wincing as she sucked the lime.

"How many of those have you had?" She shook her head at the bartender hovering nearby, then put her hand over her glass to make sure he understood.

"Not nearly enough. You're still here."

"That was rude. Not to mention uncalled for. I'll leave when I'm good and ready. We agreed to meet here to talk about the reunion."

"So talk."

"Suz." She touched her sister's arm, then withdrew when Suzanne looked down at her hand and then back up at her. "Sorry. I forgot you don't like it when I touch you. Have you ever wondered why?"

In response, her sister glared at her.

"Okay, then. Moving right along. You were the one who called me to discuss some mysterious *strategy* for the reunion."

"Oh, yeah, payback is going to be delicious," Suzanne murmured as she took another shot.

"Suz! That's not the reason we're going to the reunion," she argued. "Well, not the only reason, anyway." She closed her eyes while she savored the last sip of her drink, then opened them to stare at her sister. "Promise me you won't go nuts or cause a scene while we're there."

"Don't get all preachy on me, little sister. I wasn't the one who put a dead roach in your salad or used condoms in your purse. The girls were plain mean to us, and the guys only thought of us as potential duel conquests. Don't you have any desire to turn the table on our former classmates? Or do you have some other reason to go to the reunion?" After getting yet another shot, she licked and salted her hand. "I have no idea why, but I know you're hot to jump Jake Stanton's bones. Assuming he even shows up."

Megan licked her lips, biting back the smile that blossomed whenever Jake's name was mentioned. "Oh, he's going to be there."

Suzanne put down her lime. "And you know this how?"

"I went to the reunion site. Remember? I sent you the web address. Didn't you preregister?"

"Maybe."

"I couldn't help b-but notice," the guy from the end of the bar, who was now standing next to Suzanne, said, his speech slurred. "You two look a lot alike. Are you s-sisters?"

Megan and Suzanne exchanged looks.

Suzanne turned back to her drink. "I have no idea what you're talking about."

His face fell. "Really? 'Cause you two look enough alike to be . . . twins. Hey, do y'think maybe you were separated at birth and are really twins? You know, like in that movie?"

"You're drunk," Suzanne pointed out. "It screws up your perception. I'm sitting here alone. Obviously you're seeing double."

He stood there for a moment, swaying slightly, then nodded and walked back to the other end of the bar.

"Amazing. He didn't even notice we were wearing different clothes." Megan giggled. "You're so bad."

Her sister smiled for the first time since Meg had walked into the bar and stood, hefting her voluminous tan leather hobo bag onto her shoulder. "Stick with me, kiddo. Next weekend, we're going to show everyone a whole new meaning of bad."

2

Megan rolled to her side and batted at the alarm. Groaning, she fell back onto the pillow, clutching her head.

"I should have known better than to let Suz drink so much." She moaned into the pillow. Tequila headaches were the worst. Sharing her looks with her sister wasn't the worst part about being a twin. The sharing of every emotion and feeling was definitely a benefit she could do without.

She sat up, willing her stomach to stop roiling. At least she could be thankful her sister wasn't in a romantic relationship or, worse, hadn't picked up someone last night. Shared orgasms were humiliating enough without the added misery of a killer hangover.

She'd just staggered into the bathroom and turned on the shower when her nipples started tingling. The feeling of being suckled immediately followed. She closed her eyes and concentrated all her negative thoughts toward her sister. It had never worked before, but maybe she'd get lucky.

Clutching her stomach with one hand, she scrubbed at her

nipples with the other in an effort to alleviate the sensations zipping through her.

Evidently she'd been wrong about Suzanne picking up another one-night stand.

Stepping into the shower, she jumped, almost losing her footing, when something intrusive invaded her body. Her hips bucked, tossing her against the water-slicked tile.

She could only hope her sister's current bed partner was quick.

Her hands trembled, forcing her to hold the shampoo bottle in a death grip as she squeezed the herbal goo into her hand. Carefully setting the bottle on the edge of the shower seat, she began to lather her hair while clenching and unclenching her thighs, in an effort to banish the sensations racing through her.

Her sister's climax hit her just as she rinsed the last of the shampoo out of her hair, causing her back to arch, almost choking her with the shower spray running into her open mouth.

She had nothing against orgasms, per se. It was when she was not present during the act, and they snuck up on her that was really annoying. Her sister, while not necessarily promiscuous, was far from being celibate. Suzanne's latest penchant for picking up men in bars and taking them home was the worst for shared intimacies since they'd been in college five years ago.

No doubt about it, Ron Daniels had really done a number on Suzanne. He'd pursued her hot and heavy their senior year of high school, then again their freshman year at the University of Texas. The night he'd taken Suzanne's virginity was the reason Megan had been evicted from her study group. To this day, she suspected everyone thought Walt Whitman made her go into an orgasmic swoon. If it wasn't so embarrassing, even all these years later, it would be funny.

The worst was when Ron dumped Suzanne, causing Megan to burst into tears at the most inconvenient moments.

What was really sad, she thought, rinsing soap from her quaking body, was the fact she and Suzanne were not even close. Making almost duplicate career choices in real estate was a real fluke. In fact, had they not been sisters, she doubted Suz would even acknowledge her existence.

Another orgasm raced through her, slamming her against the shower door, the glass cool against her heated, sensitized skin. The heated flush was immediately followed by goose bumps. Her nipples stood in hard, erect points, aching, needy.

Gasping for breath and willing her snack from the night before not to make another appearance, she stepped from the shower and reached for a towel.

The terry cloth gently abraded her skin, filling her with a deep, yearning ache for fulfillment. Not the kind her sister so often indulged in, but a committed, lasting kind of fulfillment.

The kind she knew she could have with someone. Someone like Jake Stanton.

All through high school, she'd worshiped Jake from afar. But he hadn't known she existed. After graduation, they'd gone to different colleges. She'd heard about him over the years through her fellow classmates and, more recently, on the alumni site. She knew he was still single. She also knew he'd recently completed his residency in obstetrics and was planning to return to Houston to start private practice.

And he planned to attend the ten-year reunion.

Did she have the courage to act on the lust she'd had simmering for him over the last ten years? She'd most likely never have another opportunity.

It was now or never.

Friday morning dawned with Megan packed and waiting for Suzanne and the taxi to take them to the Hyatt Regency downtown. Unwrapping her first Peppermint Pattie of the day, she glanced at her watch, then to the grandfather clock in the tiled entryway of her Champions Forest high-rise condo. The smooth combination of dark chocolate and peppermint melted on her tongue. Where was Suzanne? She'd promised to be prompt.

Megan covered her yawn. Judging by her tiredness, Suzanne had had another wild roll in the hay last night. Yawning again, she flipped open her cell phone to see if she'd missed Suzanne's call. She hadn't.

Crickets chirping, denoting a call from her sister, filled the tiled entry. Glancing at the clock, Megan flipped open her cell. "Are you downstairs?"

"Good morning to you, too, Sunshine," Suzanne's droll voice echoed in her ear. "I'm on Louetta Road, just past SH249. Is the cab there yet?"

"You're not in it? Suz, you said you'd call them. I thought you'd ride over in it—"

"I did call them! They said they'd be there by noon. I should be, too. Bye!"

She stared at the glowing screen for a second, then flipped the phone shut.

Maybe she should wait downstairs.

Next to her elbow, the house phone rang, causing her to jump. "Hello? Thank you. Tell him I'll be right down."

She made a quick scan of the room, checked her luggage to make sure she remembered to pack a couple extra bags of Peppermint Patties, then made a quick pass through her home to make sure everything was picked up and turned off.

If the weekend went like she hoped it would, she would not be returning home alone.

She wanted to make a good first impression on Jake Stanton.

"Why do I have to come up to your room with you?" Suzanne lagged behind Megan on their way to the elevator.

"Because we agreed to go to the opening cocktail reception together. Remember? As soon as I get my things put away and change, we can go to your room and I'll wait for you."

"Oh, goody."

The elevator deposited them on the sixteenth floor, Suzanne shuffling behind her all the way down the hall.

Her sister shifted from one flip-flop shod foot to the other, breathing in huffy little sighs, while Megan swiped her card key in the door in an effort to gain the green light. Three times.

"Well, shit." Suzanne reached around her. "Give it to me. At this rate, we'll be standing here all night."

"I think the card is defective."

"You always think the cards are defective." Suzanne swiped the card, immediately getting a green light and a distinctive click, then pushed the door open. "Okay, princess, here's your castle for the next two nights and three days. See you later."

"Wait!" She grabbed the edge of the door before her sister could step out and make her getaway. "Why can't you just wait? I'll hurry. We said we'd go to the reception together."

Suzanne's shoulders slumped beneath her baggy sweatshirt before she met her gaze. "For one thing, the damn cocktail party isn't for another two hours. For another, why do we have to go together? My God, it's not like we're joined at the hip."

Megan popped a Peppermint Pattie into her mouth and chewed. She would not rise to Suz's bait. They would get along and be the close sisters the entire population of Champions High thought them to be for the last ten years. Even if she had to tie Suz to a chair to do it.

3

"Would it have killed you to wear a cocktail dress?" Megan smoothed her own pale blue chiffon and sequined dress, and checked to make sure her toenail polish had not chipped on the ride down to the ballroom.

"What's wrong with the way I'm dressed?" Suzanne made a production of bending over to look at the expanse of leg revealed by her skintight black leather miniskirt, tottering on black spike-heeled sandals. "I think I look hot."

Megan snorted. "Most likely you'll be cold. There's not enough leather to cover much more than the necessities."

Her sister looked at her cleavage, threatening to spill from the low cut red satin bustier. "If things go like I planned, I won't be wearing anything for too much longer."

"Suz, face reality. Ron Daniels is history. He most likely won't show. It's his MO. In fact, while I waited for you this morning, I went to the alumni site and checked. His name wasn't on the list of attendees." Of course, neither was her sister's, but she wasn't going to get into that again.

"Doesn't mean anything," Suzanne said, scanning the crowd

wandering through the open doors of the ballroom. "I didn't respond, yet here I am."

That was because she'd sent a check for both of their reservations. Sometimes being the responsible twin was a pain. But someone had to do it.

"I just don't want you to get your hopes up. I mean, even if he's here, it doesn't necessarily mean he's available. Suz, are you listening to me?"

"Hmm? Oh, yeah. Hey, is that Debbie What's-her-name by the bar, the one who screwed Ronnie after the homecoming game our junior year? It is! Wow, has she ever piled on the weight. Look! There's Sue." Smiling, she nodded at the redhead. "You vicious bitch," she said in a low voice through her teeth.

"Are you going to do a running commentary on everyone you see tonight?" Megan tugged on the plunging neckline of her dress. "What's wrong with just relaxing and having a good time? After all, that's why we're here, right?"

Her sister turned a blank stare on her, then grabbed her elbow and dragged her behind a potted palm. "We agreed. We came to set the record straight. Remember? We want them to know we're not a matched set. We're individuals, not just *the twins*. Doesn't it bother you that your precious Jake Stanton never knew you existed? And the one time you worked up the nerve to talk to him at lunch, he thought you were me?"

Sure it had bothered her. A lot. Especially when, after introducing herself, he still couldn't remember her name. The remembered humiliation washed through her again. Suzanne was right. They were on a mission.

"But what if Jake's changed? What if he's grown up and finally sees me as myself?" *Please, Lord, let that happen.*

"Yeah, and what if he hasn't? Meg, we already decided this. We're going to make sure everyone sees us as individuals, not half of a pair. Given the opportunity, we will divide and conquer. Got it?"

She nodded. "Divide and conquer."

"That's right. And if we hook up with Jake or Ron or any of the guys who lumped us together, what are we going to do?" She grasped her sister's shoulders and gave her a little shake. "Meg! What are we going to do? Remember?"

"Have fun." Her sister nodded in approval. "Take no prisoners. Love 'em and leave 'em. No regrets."

"Abso-damn-lutely. Now, I think I see that worm Jake Stanton. Over there. About two o'clock, by the bar." She shoved Megan forward. "Go get him," she whispered in her ear, then said louder as Megan walked away, "Fuck his brains out and leave him in the dust, baby sister."

"Is that your plan for the weekend, too, Suz?" a deep voice said from behind her.

She whirled to find the one that got away. The ex-love of her life, Ron Daniels. The real, secret reason she'd agreed to come to the lame reunion. Of course, she planned to use him and leave him crying for more. But there was no reason she couldn't enjoy herself in the process.

He stood, drink in hand, looking just as cocky as she remembered. The bastard hadn't aged a bit. Still tan, broad shouldered, blond, and gorgeous. Everyone had thought they looked like Barbie and Ken dolls.

He arched one perfect brow and took a sip of the amber liquid in his highball glass, obviously waiting for her answer.

Was it? Did she have the guts to ride him hard, slake her lust, and then walk away without a backward glance, like he'd done all those years ago?

Forcing a smile she hoped was seductive, she stepped close and cupped his erection through his suit pants, trying not to read anything into his obvious arousal. Ron Daniels would hump anything that breathed. She needed to remember that fact.

She slowly released him, dragging her hand up his torso to

cup his chiseled jaw and give it a pat. "I don't know yet, Ron, I haven't finished looking at all the candidates."

With more bravado than she felt, she turned, silently ordering her stiff legs to walk away from the one man she could never resist.

"Hi, Jake," Megan said with a smile, hoping she didn't have lipstick on her teeth, and extended her hand. "I don't know if you remember me or not, but I'm Megan Hartley. We had biology together our junior year."

He turned a brilliant smile on her, revealing straight white teeth and the hint of dimples. His warm hand enveloped her ice cold one, pulling her closer to his yummy scented warmth. "And we were also in the same French class for three years. Of course I remember you. How have you been, Megan?" He glanced around. "Is there a *Mr. Megan* around?"

She grinned, reminding herself to breathe. "No. I'm still single. How about you?" Yeah, right, like she didn't already know the answer to that one.

"Nope, I'm single, too." He wiggled his eyebrows and grinned down at her. "Which is why I'm going to do something I only dreamt about all through high school."

Before she could ask what that might be, he pulled her into his arms and covered her mouth with his.

Megan felt herself melting into his kiss and locked her knees to remain upright. But . . . dang! The guy could kiss.

He coaxed her lips apart. The smooth warmth of his mint flavored tongue explored her mouth, which was no doubt gaping in sensual surprise.

As he started to straighten out of the kiss, her mind engaged. *Kiss him back!* What if it was the only kiss she ever had from him? She locked her arms around his neck and dragged him back down to her now starving mouth.

Across the room, Suzanne watched her sister all but devour

Jake Stanton. The bane of their sibling relationship reared its ugly head. Damn. Why did Megan pick here and now to get turned on? Suzanne clamped her legs together as discreetly as possible and dropped into the nearest chair, her nipples tingling.

"Hi, Meg," Sue said, sliding onto the chair next to her, then squinting. "It's Megan, right?"

Trying not to squirm, she took a deep breath and unlocked her jaw enough to say, "No, Sue, I'm Suzanne." She inclined her head. "That's Meg over there. With Jake Stanton," she added, like there might be another person who looked just like her at the reunion. Dumb. Okay, so maybe she wanted to rub Sue's nose in the fact that her sister was all but sucking Jake's face off. The woman beside her had basically been the class whore. But, Suzanne had it on good authority that Jake had never succumbed to Sue's dubious charms.

She bit back a smile as she watched the shock register on Sue's face. Revenge, even secondhand, was indeed sweet.

4

It was a choice of either stripping them both and having her wicked way with Jake Stanton in the middle of the Hyatt Regency ballroom in front of everybody, or breaking the kiss.

Megan reluctantly broke the kiss.

Both were experiencing labored breathing.

The light reflected from his upper lip.

She reached up to wipe the telltale smudge of lip gloss with the pad of her thumb.

Something flared in his deep blue eyes. He turned his head, capturing her hand with his, kissing and tonguing her palm.

Clenching her thighs together, trying to ignore the moisture, she glanced frantically around to find her sister. Suz would know what to do.

Suzanne sat with her legs tightly crossed, glaring at her, next to an oblivious Sue. Megan swallowed a chuckle. *Payback time, sis.* How many times had she suffered through her sister's orgasms?

Jake's tongue tickling her palm drew her attention again.

He pulled her close, close enough to feel her effect on him.

"We don't have to stay for the dinner. I have a room. We can order up." He rubbed suggestively against her. "Get to know each other again."

It was the last sentence that did it for her.

She pulled back, shoring up her defenses. Standing before her was the epitome of everything she'd ever wanted. The standard by which she'd measured every other man she'd dated, only to have them fall short. He hadn't remembered her name in high school, and now he wanted her to go to his hotel room to get "reacquainted." What was wrong with that picture?

Wetting her suddenly dry lips with her tongue, she was flattered to see him follow the movement. Flattered, but determined not to be just another notch on his bedpost. Or a used condom in his trash. And, if and when she did succumb, she dang well wanted him to know her name. If she went up with him now, she seriously doubted that would happen. Jake might not turn out to be her Mr. Right, but she'd be darned if she'd settle for him being Mr. Right Now. She'd waited too long to settle for less.

Taking a deep breath, she let it out and popped a Peppermint Pattie into her mouth. After she'd chewed and swallowed, she said, "As tempting as that sounds, I'm going to have to take a raincheck." When he didn't immediately turn and walk away, she hurried on. "I came with my sister and made a big deal about her not leaving me alone to go off with someone. I can't do that to her."

"I understand. I know how close you and . . . *Megan* always were."

Cold, hard reality slapped her square in the face. "Her name is Suzanne. *I'm* Megan." *The one you were just playing tonsil hockey with, remember?* She heaved a mental sigh. He'd just proved she'd made the absolute right decision. Darn.

"I'm sorry!" He swallowed. "I knew that. I don't know what I was thinking." He moved close again and tried to take her hand. "Let me buy you a drink and try to make it up to you. Please?"

Suzanne relaxed against the padded leather chair and zoned back in on Sue's yammering.

"—always was a player. Fancied himself a stud." She leaned closer and lowered her voice. "I did him once." She shrugged and took another swig of the fruity smelling drink in her hand. "Let's just say I was not impressed." She held up her hand, forefinger and thumb barely separated, and shook her head in mock sadness.

Suzanne laughed. "Bullshit. We both know you never hooked up with Jake Stanton." No one did.

"Jake?" Sue's face scrunched up. "Hell, no! What made you think I was talking about Jake? I was talking about the jerk-off over there." She sloshed a little of her drink when she tried to point. "Dan Horn. Yuck. Remember how he tried to get everyone to call him *horny*? He may have been, but he certainly couldn't keep it up for long, if you know what I mean." She took another sip then said, "Uh-oh."

"What now?" Why wouldn't the woman take a hint and leave her alone?

"Looks like your sister's abandoned you."

"What?"

"And Jake is in hot pursuit," Sue said with a smile over the rim of her glass. "Nice to see someone finally got his attention."

Time to regroup. Megan popped a Peppermint Pattie and pushed the elevator button again. She'd make a quick pit stop in her room to cool off and de-stress. After years of counseling, she knew the importance of relaxing to relieve stress. Heaven knew, she had a boatload of stress going on. She'd splash her face, reapply her makeup, brush her teeth. All the Peppermint Patties she'd been scarfing down were probably busy making cavities, along with more junk in her trunk. And if all that activity wasn't enough to calm her raging hormones, she'd practice some relaxation techniques before returning to the reunion.

Damn card key. Her hand shook so badly, she had to take hold of her wrist with her other hand to swipe it again. Relief washed through her when the green light flashed on.

Stepping into her room, she took a deep breath of filtered air, leaning against the closed door with her eyes closed.

Jake was gorgeous. Even more so than she remembered. Taller, maybe. More mature, certainly. While her eyes were blah blue, his made her want to dive in and swim around. Was that what they called bedroom eyes?

She knew without a doubt she wouldn't kick him out of her bed. Provided he remembered her name, of course.

That thought should have cooled her ardor. Instead, she found herself attempting to picture him naked while she stripped down to her strapless bra-slip and washed her face.

The air-conditioned hotel air should have cooled her off. Instead, she became increasingly aware of the air current caressing her bare skin. The idea of putting her dress back on held no appeal.

Maybe she should just lie down on the bed and relax for a few minutes, allow the air to soothe her sensitized skin.

She'd just kicked off her shoes and stretched out on the raw silk spread when a soft knock sounded. Probably Suz, wondering why she chickened out with Jake. She sighed. Not answering would not deter Suzanne.

Maybe her sister could give her some advice. Since Megan dumped her cheating fiancé, Bryce, two years ago, she'd basically been celibate. To say Suz had been around the block a few more times was an understatement, but Megan had to admit her sister had knowledge.

Dragging herself to a standing position, she padded to the door and opened it.

Jake Stanton stood on the other side in living, breathing spectacular color, holding a bottle of champagne in one hand, and what looked like a box of Godiva chocolates in the other.

"I bring peace offerings," he said with a grin. "I don't know why I pretended to not know your name, *Megan.* It was a stupid, immature thing to do."

Stepping behind the door to belatedly protect her modesty, she glared at him. "Maybe it was because you truly didn't know which sister you were kissing?"

He slowly shook his head, dark hair glinting in the can light of the entry as he stepped over the threshold. "Oh, no. Trust me. I knew exactly who I was kissing." He placed his bounty on the dresser and turned to pull her into his arms while he shoved the door shut. "The one person I lusted after all through high school. The one I couldn't get out of my mind all through college and medical school. The one who has haunted my dreams for more years than I want to remember."

Wiggling against him, feeling pliant and needy, she smiled up at him, looping her arms around his neck. "That would be me? The person you never bothered to call all through school, let alone ask out, and never attempted to contact after graduation?"

He winced, then brushed a kiss on the tip of her nose. "Guilty. What can I do to make it up to you?"

A few thousand suggestions came to mind, along with a realization.

She was going to get laid.

5

"What are we going to do about that? It really wasn't a very nice thing to do, you know." Her smile broadened when he cupped her buttocks through the silken barrier of her slip and pulled her higher against his hardness.

"Maybe I could be your slave for the weekend. A sex slave?"

She pretended to contemplate that idea for a while, then shook her head. "I'm not really into the whole slavery thing."

He drew the tip of his forefinger along the exposed swell of her breast, sending points of pleasure zipping to her core and making her nipples tingle. "What are you into?"

Besides you? "Mutual pleasure." Dragging her hand down his firm chest, she paused briefly to unbuckle his belt, and slide down the zipper before delving in to cup his cotton-knit covered erection, weighing his heat. "Strip, please," she said in a breathy whisper against his lips.

"Ladies first." He hooked his thumbs on either side of her slip cups and tugged.

"Ah! Wait." She reached into each cup and ripped the double stick tape from her breasts. "Sorry. I didn't want my top to fall down during the reunion."

"Anything else you need to remove?" he asked with a chuckle.

"No, I think I'll let you do it." Rising on tiptoe, she nibbled on his lower lip until he took the hint and kissed her.

The edge of the mattress touched the backs of her knees before the bed dipped with their combined weight as he lowered her.

"Ow!" The edge of his open fly poked her. She grasped the sides of his pants. "Take these off before you hurt someone. Like me."

As soon as he'd tossed his trousers and shirt aside, he pulled the stretchy fabric of her slip down until he'd bared her breasts.

"Poor baby," he said, kissing each of the red marks left by the tape on the tops of her breasts.

Her breath caught at the wondrous feel of his lips on her, the heat of his breath against her puckered nipples. Impatient, she arched her back.

He took what she offered, sucking the nipple deeply into his mouth and drawing rhythmically while he drew the slip the rest of the way off, tossing it aside.

Leaning back on his elbow, he looked at the woman stretched out next to him. A goddess. The monumental effort it took to resist her for the last twelve years made the moment that much sweeter.

"Thank you," he said on a breath against her fragrant skin.

"For what?"

"For staying single." He drew the tip of his index finger around her nipple, smiling when it puckered prettily. "I don't know what I'd have done if you hadn't." He cupped each plump breast in his palms and placed cherishing kisses around and on top of each one before meeting her gaze. "There were times when I'd be almost wild with wanting you. You were my guilty obsession. Between classes and later, between rounds, I'd think about you. Fantasize about what I'd do with you if I ever saw you again."

"You're seeing me now." She'd done some pretty heavy fantasizing over the years, too. She glanced down at his fit body and realized nothing she'd imagined did justice to the real thing.

"Not as much as I'd like to see." He hooked his thumbs in each side of her lace thong and slid it down over her hips.

She arched off the mattress to allow him to remove her underwear.

He dragged his fingers reverently over her exposed pubic area. "Is that a Brazilian wax?"

"Does it look like one?" She popped another candy into her mouth and chewed, wondering how many women's privates he'd been up close and personal with before tonight. She did a mental head slap. Duh. The guy was a gynecologist.

His gaze jerked to her hostile one. "Um, actually, I wouldn't know. I've never seen one. I read about them a couple of times in the magazines in the hospital reception areas." A small smile curved his well-kissed lips. "I always wondered if you did it, and if I would ever find out."

"Oh." She twisted to reach for her purse and another treat, popping it into her mouth and chewing vigorously. She wanted to sleep with Jake. Plain and simple. She'd thought of little else for more years than she'd care to remember. Now here he was, in her hotel room, wearing nothing but boxers and a smile.

While she wore less.

But did she have the guts to act out her myriad fantasies? Her hand closed around another Peppermint Pattie, expertly shoving the wrapper off with her thumb and the back of her index finger, then popped it into her mouth to buy time.

A frown creased Jake's perfect face. "Are you hungry? We can call room service." He leaned back, resting his weight on his hands, causing his biceps to flex in a very distracting way. "Meg?"

"Hmm?" She absently shoved another candy into her mouth. Why was he talking about food at a time like this? Realization caused the Peppermint Pattie to lodge in her throat.

Of course he thought she was hungry. Good grief, she'd been shoving candy into her face since he'd walked into the room. Peppermint burned her nose from the inside, making her nose and eyes water.

Jake sprang to her side, thumping her on the back. "Are you okay? Can you breathe?"

Humiliated, she nodded and attempted to shove him away in a manner that didn't give him the idea she wanted him to leave.

Easier said than done.

His magnificent blue eyes widened a nanosecond before his equally magnificent body toppled over the foot of the bed and landed with a painful sounding thump.

The last of her candy went down. She drew a gasping breath and crawled to the edge of the mattress to peer down at her hopefully-soon-to-be lover. "Are you all right?" she finally managed to wheeze through the peppermint heat.

He sat up, the six-pack of his abs displayed for her viewing pleasure, and linked his arms around his knees. "Not really. Actually, I'm embarrassed." He stood, dusting himself off and reached for the robe lying on the chair. "Here. Put this on or else I might embarrass myself again."

She caught the robe and clutched it to her chest. "I don't think I understand." Was he embarrassed about being with her? Long buried inadequacies reared up. Jake didn't really want her. He wasn't interested in her as anything but a quick and easy diversion. It was high school all over again. Worse. This time she was older. She was worth more than that. She should have known better.

She was naked.

6

Jake hopped around in his effort to put on his pants while he looked at Megan. "What's not to understand? I acted like a jerk, following you up here. You told me no, but did I listen? Hell, no. I kept pushing. I'm sorry, Megan. I guess part of it is because I've wanted you for so long." He zipped his pants and picked up his socks. "And part of it is just the way I am. When I want something, I go for it, regardless of the odds. It's the way I've always been. I don't regret it, most of the time. It was that trait that got me through college and medical school." His gaze softened along with his voice. "But I need to learn to temper my enthusiasm a tad. I didn't mean to scare you."

Scare her? She crawled to the end of the bed, allowing the robe to fall around her knees. Her butt might scream wide load, but her breasts always got male attention. Tonight, she reveled in that fact, and all but shoved them in his face. "I wasn't scared, Jake."

He paused, mid-sock. "No?"

Shocked by her own boldness, she edged closer to the end of the mattress, skimming her hands up her torso, then cupping

her breasts as she slowly shook her head. "No, I wasn't scared."
She gave her breasts a little squeeze and bit back a smile when
his gaze zeroed in on her puckered nipples. "I was turned on,"
she said in a low and, she hoped, sexy voice.

He swallowed. "Well, I was going to suggest we go down to
dinner, but . . . turned on, huh?" He dropped his sock and
shucked his pants.

Meg nodded while she stared in fascination at the bobbing
purple head of his erection, clenching her thighs together to
keep from squirming, and licked her lips.

Jake swept her into his arms and impaled her before she
could take her next breath.

He crawled up on the bed, nudging her back toward the
headboard with each powerful thrust.

Around his thickness, her arousal dripped, making their
union slippery. She clamped her legs around his lean waist and
locked her ankles together. She'd waited too long to let him slip
away in the heat of the moment.

His hips bucked, shoving his penis impossibly deeper, taking her breath away.

Breathing was overrated.

A gush between her legs got Suzanne's attention. Clamping
her thighs together, she edged toward the end of the dessert
table, praying she could remain upright until she regained her
chair, three tables back.

Moisture tricked down her inner thigh. *Damn it, Meg, couldn't
you have played hard to get?* It was slick where her thighs
rubbed together, making her wish she hadn't chosen a miniskirt.
Especially not such a revealing one.

She looked up, her nipples tingling. Ron's hot gaze did nothing to help her discomfort.

The man to her left got up and Ron wasted no time in claim-
ing his chair. "Is there a problem, Suz?" His breath was hot against

her flushed face when he leaned close, his voice barely a whisper. "You look a little, ah, frustrated." He leaned closer still and ran the tip of his tongue around the outer rim of her ear. "I can help you with that."

Her gaze locked with his, and she could do nothing but push air in and out of her lungs while, beneath the linen tablecloth, he walked his fingers up, up, up her leg until he touched the telltale moisture.

She bit down on her lower lip to keep from gasping, not wanting the others to know what was going on under the table. His finger rimmed the edge of her sodden thong, causing her to jerk, then look around guiltily.

Their fellow diners talked and laughed, oblivious to the sensual assault taking place.

Ron tsked, scooting his chair until he was as close as possible. "Must be uncomfortable." His breath ruffled the wisps of hair next to her ear. "Let me help," he whispered. Not waiting for her reply, he tugged until he managed to pull her panties past her hips, down to her knees.

"Oops," he said as he knocked his knife off the table, then ducked to retrieve it.

She felt him tug her panties the rest of the way off. While he straightened with the knife, he tucked the thong into the pocket of his jacket and grinned. "Better?"

Her sister's climax washed through her. She struggled to regulate her breathing, eyes closed, until it passed. She opened her eyes to find Ron staring at her with enough heat to set the tablecloth on fire. No doubt he gave himself credit for her orgasm.

Of course he did. He had no idea of the type of bond she and Megan had with each other. A part of her was sad that she'd never shared real intimacies with Ron, just the intimacy of her body.

His finger slid into her wetness. Even after all the intervening years and her many lovers, it felt delicious. Exciting beyond belief.

Right.

It took real effort to keep her hips from bucking, to refrain from grinding down on his talented fingers. But, despite the force of will, the dam broke as another orgasm washed through her. Given the stimuli, it was a toss-up as to whom it belonged. But it was strong, forceful, gut wrenching.

Orgasmic heaven.

Luckily, she managed to pant quietly to herself and not scream her fulfillment. Or Megan's fulfillment. Or both.

Ron's hot breath fanned her face.

She opened her eyes to his heated blue gaze.

His nostrils flared. Sweat beaded on his upper lip, giving her the insane urge to lean closer and lick it off.

He stood abruptly, half-dragging her to her feet with his firm grasp on her upper arm. "Great seeing everybody. We'll see y'all later."

"Ron," she hissed, pulling back as he tugged her through the crowded dining room. "Maybe I'm not ready to leave yet. Let go. Ron, I said—"

They rounded the corner. He opened a narrow door, just off the hallway, and pushed her inside.

She blinked in an effort to adjust to the sudden darkness. The smell of cleaning solvents burned her nose. "Ron! I said—"

"I know what you said, Suz." He shoved her skirt up around her waist. The sound of his zipper echoed in the little room. His fingers parted her, petted her moistness. "But your pussy says something else."

Her first impulse was to clamp her legs together, but why fight it? Wasn't this what she'd hoped would happen when they saw each other again? She pushed the nagging thought of being used aside and relaxed, enjoying the way Ron's fingers played her. Even after all these years, he knew exactly how to touch her.

A delicious languor washed through her. Widening her stance, she slid her arms around his neck, teasing him through his shirt with the hardened tips of her breasts. "Oh?" she whispered. "And what does it say?"

"It says," he breathed against her neck, giving little nipping kisses that always drove her wild, "fuck me, baby."

He lifted her, his big hands gripping her butt cheeks, flexed his hips, and buried himself deep within her.

Tingling heat filled her, sending pleasure shocks to every nerve ending. Wiggling, she pushed him deeper while she popped the closure on her bustier, arching her back for him to take her nipples in his hot mouth.

"Oh-h-h," she said on a moan, and did a little shiver. "Yeah . . ."

Megan gave a gasping wheeze and jerked to a sitting position, toppling Jake onto the mattress beside her. She squeezed her eyes shut, mumbling under her breath, "No, no, no! Not now. Please, not now."

"Not now what? Did I do something wrong?" Jake pulled the covers over them and attempted to pull her stiff posture into his arms. "I thought women liked to cuddle afterward. Meg?"

Even though it was the last thing she wanted to do, she pushed him away and edged toward the side of the bed. "I should have known better." Luck and love were two things that had never gone together for her. Why should now be any different? She stumbled to remain upright while she searched for her underwear, dragging the sheet from the bed to cover her nudity. "I can't believe I left. What was I thinking?"

"Gee, thanks." He crawled to the edge of the mattress to retrieve his pants and boxers, temporarily derailing her train of thought with the display of his firm backside.

"What? What are you talking about?"

He pulled up his boxers and stepped into his pants. "Doesn't matter. I didn't mean to bother you or interfere with your plans." He jerked up his zipper and reached for his discarded shirt, shoving his arm into it, slinging it around to straighten out the inside-out sleeve.

She bit back a smile. "Need some help?"

"What do you care?"

"Don't be like that, I—ah!" Her back arched, her hips spasmodically bucking. In the effort it took to keep her eyes from rolling back in her head, she saw the look of shock on Jake's face. If she could only draw in enough oxygen to speak, she'd tell him she was okay. But, then again, how would she explain she was experiencing yet another orgasm when he stood on the other side of the room?

Jake watched in fascinated horror as the woman he'd fantasized about for the last ten years had some kind of seizure. His medical training told him to do something. His personal side just stared and marveled.

Strange. If they'd still been having sex, he'd swear she was having an earth-shattering climax . . .

7

"Ron!" Suzanne swatted half-heartedly at his hands when he tried to shove her skirt back up. "Behave. We're in a janitor's closet."

"But I've missed you, babe," he mumbled against her neck while he ran his hands back under her skirt, and rubbed his recovering erection against her butt. He dragged one hand up to cup and squeeze her still exposed breast.

Renewed moisture surged. She wiggled against him.

A squeak of surprise sprang to her lips when he lifted her, his hands digging into her waist.

"Relax," he said from behind her. "Here. Hold onto these so you don't fall off."

Her breasts pressed against cold metal. He'd laid her over something round. Some kind of drum of something. He placed her hands around what she realized were two mops hanging from hooks on the wall in front of her.

She squirmed in excitement. What was he going to do?

She felt him spread her legs, felt his hot breath fanning her wetness. Was he blowing on her?

The next instant, his tongue speared her. Had he not been holding her legs firmly apart, she'd have toppled from her perch.

Arching her back caused the edge of the can to dig into her. It probably would have hurt were it not for the incredible sensations streaking through her, thanks to Ron's talented tongue.

Her orgasm didn't surprise her, but Ron's abrupt penetration did. His action caused another immediate orgasm to rip through her.

Megan's hips bucked, her flesh wept in fulfillment, her breath came in short painful gasps.

Jake watched in obvious horror.

She had to do something. Fast. She'd waited too long for him. She wasn't about to ruin it. She hoped.

Making an executive decision, she dropped her clothes and ordered her legs to take her to stand close enough to touch him.

With jerky movements, she tugged at his clothes until he got the idea she wanted him naked.

As soon as his erection sprang free, she shoved him back on the mattress and fell on top of him.

After two fumbles, she managed to get things aligned and he slid home.

She sighed and smiled down at him. This was the way they were supposed to be.

Every nerve ending began to tingle, warning her of another impending orgasm. Dang it, she was not going to let her sister ruin this for her.

She began rocking, rubbing, searching for the most sensual friction she could stand without bursting into flames. It was time her sister knew what it felt like.

Dueling orgasms.

What a concept.

* * *

Panting, Megan rolled from Jake's sweat-soaked chest to lay spread-eagle on the mattress, while she waited for her heart to resume its normal rhythm.

He turned on his side, dragging the tip of his finger along her ribs to the lower curve of her breast. "Wow. That was . . . mind-blowing. Awesome." He propped his head on his hand and smiled down at her. "But I think maybe I should be jealous."

She forced one eye open. "Jealous? Of what?"

He concentrated on pinching the tip of her nipple until it stood at attention before he answered. "I wonder where you learned some of those moves. But I don't think I really want to know." He leaned to flick the hardened tip with his tongue. "I'm just going to be grateful, and enjoy." He took the morsel into his mouth, sucking deeply.

Wiggling a little closer and arching her back for him to take more, she swallowed a yawn. He would be shocked if he knew what really caused her *moves*. And she'd tell him. Eventually. Maybe. Someday.

8

"I'm glad we decided to come back down to dinner," Megan said to Jake as they entered the ballroom.

Hand on the small of her back, he smiled down at her. "Don't get me wrong, I'd vote for spending the weekend in bed with you, given the option, and ordering room service to keep up our strength. But I know you and your sister probably have a lot of catching up to do with old friends, and it wouldn't be fair of me to keep you from it." He leaned to brush her lips with his. "I just hope you'll allow me to hang around and enjoy your company."

She smiled back at him, slipping her hand into his much warmer one. If this was some delicious dream, she didn't want to wake up. "I wouldn't have it any other way." She responded to his little squeeze with one of her own. "I'm so glad we ran into each other."

"There are two vacant chairs. To the right. You grab them while I get us something to drink. Any preference?"

"A house white wine would be fine." She refrained from letting out a little whoop of joy when he patted her bottom on his way to the bar, but she knew she had to be beaming. Going to the reunion was one of her best ideas to date. Even if she and Jake went nowhere, she'd have the memories of the weekend to hold close for the rest of her life.

"Is this seat taken?"

Meg looked up to see Kathy whatever-her-name-was, Homecoming Queen from their senior year. She looked much the same as Meg remembered her: blonde, cool, disdainfully distant. She smiled up at the aloof blonde, wishing she'd chosen a table far away. "Sorry, yes, it is."

The woman narrowed her overly made-up green eyes. "I know you. You're one of the twins, aren't you?"

"That depends on which twins you're talking about, I suppose."

Kathy shrugged and flipped her hair over her shoulder. Obviously she hadn't read the article about long hair on women approaching thirty. "Does it really matter?" she asked in a bored voice, while scanning the room, then walked away.

"Where the hell have you been?" Her sister hissed in her ear as she plopped down next to her. She shifted on the seat and straightened the bodice of her bustier, which looked less than tidy. "No, don't tell me. Since I know what you've been doing, I can make an educated guess."

"You've been doing the same thing, Suz." She leaned closer and whispered, "Cut it out!"

Her sister batted her eyelashes and flashed a saccharine smile. "I don't have to. I wasn't doing anything you weren't doing. I deserve to have some fun, too."

"You have fun all the time," Megan snapped. "It's my turn." She glanced at the bar to make sure Jake was still across the room. "Do you have any idea what a difficult position I was in?"

"Do tell. Is it in the Kama Sutra?" Suzanne's eyes sparkled with her barely controlled laughter.

"Very funny. You know what I mean." She leaned forward. "Please, Suz. I haven't gotten lucky in so long. I need this."

Suz slumped back in the chair and grabbed a handful of chips from the basket. "You act like I'm doing this on purpose."

"Well, I saw you earlier when you were talking to Ron. I sincerely doubt you tripped and fell on his penis. So, yeah, you are doing it on purpose." She picked up a chip and broke it in three pieces. "Pass the salsa, please."

"Wow. You are upset. You never eat chips. What's the matter, run out of Peppermint Patties?" As if to taunt her, Suz piled guacamole on one chip and salsa on another, then popped them into her mouth, chewing with gusto.

"Forget it." Meg took a dripping piece of chip and popped it into her mouth. The flavor burst on her tongue had her all but moaning from pleasure. Suz was right. She never ate chips, or any starch. She watched Suz take another handful. It just wasn't fair. Suzanne ate anything and everything she wanted, never exercised, and yet was the same size and weight as Megan, who rarely ate carbs of any kind, except for her one vice, Peppermint Patties. She also ran five miles a day, worked out, and regularly attended yoga classes. Where was she when the metabolism gene was passed out?

She swallowed the last of the one chip she'd allotted herself. "Anyway, you're going to have to move. Jake is going to sit there. Here he comes with our drinks."

Suz glanced over her shoulder then back. "And he is looking particularly pleased to see you. Judging by the way you two rocked my world earlier, I can understand why. Way to go, baby sister." She stood. "That's okay. I plan to eat a fast dinner and then have Ronnie-baby for dessert." She licked her lips. "I told myself if I ever saw him again, I'd give him a blow job to put a smile on his face for the rest of his life."

"Well, it's nice to know you set your sights so high." Megan smiled at Jake as he approached and patted the vacated chair. "Not to mention your faith in your abilities," she added before Jake was in earshot.

"It's called confidence." She winked. "And lots and lots of practice." She patted Meg's head on her way to meet a serious looking Ron, who sat at the end of the table by the exit.

With her newfound sibling rivalry, it looked as though Jake would also be getting a blow job later. Meg's smile faltered when she saw a brunette crawl out from under the table on the other side from where her sister stood talking to Ron. The woman stood and straightened her dress, then discreetly wiped her mouth and walked away. The edge of the starched tablecloth was hiked up on the empty chair where she'd escaped. Meg narrowed her eyes while she watched Ron reach beneath the table and rearrange himself, then zip up.

Obviously Ron Daniels had not changed.

How in the world was she going to tell Suzanne?

9

"Meg? Earth to Megan." Jake waved his hand in front of her face, wondering what held her rapt attention.

Following her line of vision, he bit back a curse. He should have known. Ron Daniels was a player in high school, and had obviously not changed.

Had Megan succumbed to Ron's dubious charms? And, if so, did he seriously want to continue whatever relationship they'd started at the reunion? Ron could have introduced her to a whole host of nasty germs.

Their time together flashed through his mind. Damn. For the first time in his life, he'd had unprotected sex. He was a doctor. He knew better.

Megan turned an absentminded smile up at him, derailing his train of thought. Deep within, a piece of ice he'd encased around his heart melted a little more. Throughout college and med school, he'd had to stay focused on his studies and future career. But he'd met his goals. Within the next month or so, his new clinic would be up and running. He had some time to play.

To see if his insane lust for the woman before him could or would develop into something more.

"Is that for me?" Megan tugged at one of the wine glasses he held in a death grip.

"Hmm? Oh, yeah. Sorry. We didn't miss dinner, did we?"

She swallowed a sip of wine and shook her head. "No, I don't think so. There are no dirty plates around." She glanced at the gold watch on her wrist. "According to the itinerary on the web site, we still have about half an hour before they start serving." She smiled when he rested his arm on the back of the chair, rubbing her bare shoulder with the pad of his thumb. "Is there anything you want to do while we wait?"

"I can think of lots of things I'd like to do, but none of them would take less than thirty minutes," he said next to her ear, nuzzling his nose in the fragrant golden blonde hair. No doubt about it, he could definitely get used to touching her. "Meg? Did I say something wrong?"

"Hmm?" She turned and looked at him. "Oh, no. I'm sorry. I guess I'm not being a very attentive date." She slumped back in her chair, snuggling under his arm. "I'm worried about my sister."

"Why?" He watched the woman across the room. He'd bet a dollar she was fondling Daniels under the table, judging from the expressions on their faces. "She's obviously not thinking about you right now."

Meg sighed, the sound so sad it made him wish he could take back his last comment.

"I know. That's the problem. All our lives, I was the only one who ever worried about anything." She shrugged. "I guess it's a habit I need to break."

He kissed her smooth forehead. "I think it's a very sweet habit."

"She doesn't like me very much, you know. She never has."

"Are you kidding? She's your sister. Your twin sister. Isn't there some kind of genetic code, hardwiring you together for life?"

Her laugh sounded forced. "Jake, if you only knew." She took a deep breath. "Let's change the subject. Oh, look. Isn't that Mike McNaught? You remember him, don't you? Class president?" She waved and smiled as Mike headed their way.

"Stanton," he said, extending his hand to Jake. "I heard you were going to be here. How've you been?"

"Fine," Jake responded, then turned and looked pointedly at Megan. "You remember Megan Hartley, don't you?"

"Sure I do." Mike shook her hand, his smile looking less than warm. Then he turned back to Jake. "So," he said in a low voice, "when did you hook up with the twins? Have you done both of them?"

Unfortunately, his voice wasn't quite low enough.

Embarrassment heated Megan's cheeks. It would have been a good time for the floor to open up and swallow her.

"Best piece I ever had," Mike said in a conspiratorial whisper.

"Excuse me?" Discretion may be the better part of valor, but . . . Meg knew she should probably walk away, but the man was purloining her and her sister's reputation to the man she might be falling in love with. It wouldn't do. It wouldn't do at all.

Plus, it was a big fat lie.

Both men turned to look at her. Her opinion of Jake dropped a notch. Granted, he didn't really know her, but somehow she felt he should be saying something in her defense.

True, Suz had sown her share of wild oats, but not until after Ron had dropped her in college. Meg knew for a fact that neither she nor her sister had even gone out with Mike.

"Take it back," she told Mike in a low and, she hoped, threatening voice. "Take it back, you lying scumbag." She stood, drawing up to her entire five-foot-nothing frame. "You know it's a lie. I never went out with you, and neither did my sister."

The creep shrugged, oblivious to the steak knife she clutched in her fist. "Hell, I don't know for sure if we ever did the deed, sweet thing. You two look so much alike, maybe I just did it twice with your sister." He nudged Jake and gave a broad wink. "Killer blow job," he said sotto voce.

Before she knew what she was thinking, she found herself standing with the knife poised at his fleshy throat, her other hand clutching his tie. She jerked on the silk, digging the blade into his Adam's apple just enough for him to feel it. "Take it back! Tell him you're lying."

Through the roar of blood in her ears, she heard Suz's voice, but couldn't understand the words.

Mike's corpulent eyes widened. A bead of sweat trickled along his receding hairline. "Okay, okay. Put the knife down." He looked at Jake. "Tell your girlfriend to back off, Stanton."

"I don't think so." Jake stepped back and crossed his arms. "You'd better tell her what she wants to hear. And it better be the truth."

Mike's gaze shot from one to the other and back again. "Maybe I made a mistake. Yeah, it was a mistake. I never had sex with you. Or your sister. You're right. We never even dated."

She released her hold on his tie and he stepped back. "You're fucking crazy." Mike glared at her, then turned to Jake. "They both are, Stanton. You need to get out while you can." With that, he turned on his heel and strode away.

"Yeah, well, fuck you and the horse you rode in on!" Suz yelled as he stalked away. She squeezed Meg's shoulder, then walked back to Ron.

"Are you okay?" Jake gently removed the knife from her hand and placed it on the table, then led her back to her seat. "Can I get you anything?"

She chuckled. "I don't suppose you have any Peppermint Patties on you?"

He grinned. "Sorry." He held up a finger. "Wait. Maybe I can come up with something. I'll be right back."

He returned a few minutes later, handing her a frosted martini glass filled with something that looked like chocolate milk and smelled distinctly minty. "Try it," he urged at her hesitation. "It's a mocha peppermint martini."

"Oh, wow," she said after her first sip. "It's like drinking liquid Peppermint Patties. Yum!"

"Easy," he said, gently taking the glass from her. "It's loaded with alcohol." He leaned closer and said in a low voice, "I want you completely sober for what I have planned for after dinner."

Since she had no problem with that plan, she allowed him to set the glass aside.

"Are you okay?" Suzanne squatted next to Meg's chair, a concerned look on her face. "I've never seen you lose it like that."

Touched, Meg blinked back tears. Maybe her sister didn't hate her after all. She sniffed. "I'm fine," she whispered back. "Mike was just being, well, Mike. Once a creep, always a creep, I guess." She touched her sister's hand where it rested on the back of her chair, encouraged when she didn't recoil. "It means so much that you asked, though. It's sweet. I—"

Suzanne's face hardened, her lips drawing into a thin line as she stood, breaking contact. "Don't read anything into it, Megan. I'd be concerned about anyone who was upset enough to hold a knife to someone's throat." She glanced at Jake, then back at Meg. "Remember the plan." With that, she turned and walked back to her table.

"What's wrong?" Jake asked, close to her ear. "You and your sister always got along so well."

That's what you think. She took a deep breath and exhaled slowly. "Suz and I get along just like we always did." She flashed a smile she was far from feeling. "Some things never change. You know how siblings can be sometimes, though, I'm sure."

"Actually, no. I'm an only child of only children." His smile was sad looking. "I have no frame of reference."

And you have no idea how lucky you are. She picked up her glass and clicked it against his. "What shall we drink to?"

"Renewing old friendships? The future?"

"Sounds like a plan." Whatever.

Clink.

10

Megan raised her head from Jake's shoulder to gaze dreamily across the dance floor. Where was Suz? She needed to talk to her.

Despite her vow to her sister, Meg had no desire to be with anyone other than Jake for the duration of the reunion. Longer than that, if possible. Suzanne could do whatever she pleased—not that she hadn't always. Jake had never been anything but kind to Meg. She had no reason to use him and walk away, even if she were the type.

In the dimly lit ballroom, it was difficult to see, but the couple dancing like they were attached at the hip appeared to be Suz and that scumbag Ron. Memories of her sister's devastation made Meg want to shake some sense into her. That, coupled with seeing the woman crawl out from under Ron's table earlier, made her especially anxious to talk to Suzanne.

Meg shivered with revulsion while she watched Suz and Ron practically copulate to the music. Talk about dirty dancing.

Jake gathered her closer. "Cold?" His warm breath fluttered the hair by her ear.

Cold was so far from the way she felt when she was with him, it was laughable. "A little," she lied, slipping her arms beneath his jacket and resting her head against his heart.

"I've missed you," Ron said, grinding his erection against Suzanne. "If we stay here much longer, I may come in my pants."

The thought of getting him that excited appealed to the part of her wanting revenge. But Ron looked earnest, eager to please, not the cocky kid she'd known so long ago, who'd say anything to get into her pants.

Maybe he'd changed. Maybe he really did still have a thing for her, had never gotten over her, as he'd claimed. Maybe she'd have to change her love-him-and-leave-him plan for the weekend . . .

She glanced across the floor at Megan. Poor gullible Meg. She had no idea, no concept of doing something for simple sexual gratification. Everything had to have an emotional connection. She may as well take out an ad saying *I like being emotionally kicked.*

She mentally shrugged. Megan was a big girl. Eventually she'd learn. She wasn't her sister's keeper. Never had been, in spite of the efforts of their parents.

"Let's go up to your room," Ron said with a growl.

Why didn't he invite her to his room? Old insecurity reared its ugly head.

She shimmied against his hardness and did a slow grin. "What's wrong with your room? Maybe it's closer."

"I'm not staying at the hotel." At her raised brow, he shrugged. "I only live about five miles away." He jerked her against him, letting her feel his desire. "Besides, I figured if you were here, you'd let me bunk with you." He kissed her neck, making her weak in the knees. "C'mon. It'll be like old times. Remember how you used to sneak me into your room?" He chuckled. "Just the thought of a dorm still gives me a hard-on."

Slipping her hand between them, she outlined him with the tip of her finger. "Back then, everything gave you a hard-on." She gave the tip a little squeeze. "Doesn't look like anything has changed."

"Only you have that effect on me, baby. Only you." He bucked her hips with his and said, "Let's go. We've been apart too long. I need to be inside you."

Meg reluctantly backed away from Jake's reassuring heat, resisting when he attempted tugging her back into his arms. "I need to talk to my sister. I'll be right back."

"Too late." Jake looked over her head. "She and Daniels left a few minutes ago."

"Oh, no! I have to find her. She needs to know—"

"About Rhonda going down on Ron while he was sitting next to Suzanne?"

"You saw that? How—"

"Meg, everyone saw it. That's what all the laughing and talking was about when I went to get your drink."

"They were laughing at Suz?" Horror and anger filled her at the same time. Her sister may not be a sterling example of morality, but she'd punch out anyone's lights who dared to ridicule Suzanne.

"No! They were laughing because Ron hasn't changed a bit." He shrugged. "Most of us have grown up by now. Besides, everyone knows about Rhonda Spader."

"What? What do they know?"

"Well, maybe 'know' is too strong a word. Let's just say we all suspect and have heard, well, certain things."

"Like?"

"She's a pro." At her blank look, he said, "It's how she makes a living. And from what I've heard, she does very well."

"She's a *hooker?*"

"Shh! Keep your voice down!" He led her off the dance floor. "Besides, like I said, it's pretty much speculation."

She felt physically ill. The mocha peppermint martini weighed heavily on her stomach, churning against the braised chicken breast and asparagus tips she'd had for dinner. Her sister was with a guy who'd just had fellatio performed by a hooker.

Suzanne had to be told.

Her sister's earlier cruel words taunted her. Suz didn't want or need anything, including help, from her.

"I'm hungry." She looked around the empty table. "Did they already take away all the food?"

"Yeah, while we were dancing. We just ate. How could you be hungry?"

"I just am. I always get hungry when I'm stressed. The fact that my sister left with that creep is very stressful for me. Is the bar closed? I could definitely use another peppermint martini thing."

"That's not a good idea. If you're hungry, we'll get you something to eat." He stood. "On my way into town, I saw an all-night diner down the block. How about a midnight snack?"

"Let me make a restroom stop and you've got a date."

Meg had just closed the bathroom stall door when she heard some women enter, giggling.

"Did you see the twins?"

"How could you miss them? The one—I can never keep them straight—anyway, the one looked okay, but can you believe what the other one was wearing?"

The women laughed again, and then one said, "Maybe it's what she wears on the job." Her comment earned more peals of laughter.

"No! That would be Rhonda Spader! I heard she's a high-priced call girl these days, although you wouldn't know it to see her crawling out from under Ron Daniels's table tonight!"

"Shh! There's someone in here."

"Oh, don't worry. Rhonda is busy hanging all over the band, and the twins are gone. I saw them leave with Ron."

"Both of them?"

"Who knows? Maybe he likes a three-way."

"Yeah, maybe they'll make a Ron sandwich!"

More giggles erupted while Megan's cheeks burned with humiliation. She swiped at the tears in her eyes, wishing the women would stop talking trash and get out, so she could leave and find her sister.

Finally the ladies' room quieted. To be on the safe side, Meg flushed the toilet again, then opened the stall door. The sink and sitting areas were deserted.

She washed her hands and reapplied her lip gloss with a shaky hand.

Jake stood on the far side of the hall by the elevator, talking to a woman. As Meg walked closer, she saw it was Carolyn Wong. Carolyn had been head cheerleader their senior year. Seeing her standing there, looking like an older cheerleader, made Meg agonizingly aware of the extra weight she'd put on since high school.

Jake looked her way and smiled as she approached. How could he possibly find her attractive after seeing Carolyn?

"Carolyn," he said, grasping Meg's arm and pulling her to his side. "You remember Meg Hartley, don't you?"

Carolyn stared for so long, it was all Meg could do to keep from screaming, *I was on the cheer squad with you for three years. How could you not remember me?*

Slowly, Carolyn nodded, a vague smile on her thin, overly glossed lips. "Right. You're one of the twins, aren't you? I'm sorry, I could never tell you apart. Which one are you?"

"You don't have to tell them apart," Jake spoke up for her,

his voice hard. "I just told you, her name is Megan Hartley. You know *which one she is.*"

Megan had never wanted to kiss someone so much in her life.

"Thank you," she whispered as Jake hustled her toward the lobby.

"No problem. Did you talk to your sister?"

She shook her head. "No. I tried her cell and her room. No answer. She must still be out. Let's go ahead and get something to eat. Maybe she'll be back in her room by then."

The diner was empty. Nodding to the cook, they took a seat in a booth in the far corner.

A few minutes later, a plump redheaded middle-aged woman in a starched yellow and white uniform shuffled over, a coffee carafe in one hand, two mugs in the other.

She thumped the mugs onto the faded red laminate table top and expertly filled them, then asked, "Coffee?"

Meg bit back a smile.

Jake smiled at the waitress and nodded. "Yes, please. With lots of cream."

She brought a bowl filled with enough individual creamers to last them all evening, took their orders, and left.

After they'd prepared their coffee, Jake took a sip and looked at her over the rim of his mug. "Don't let them get to you."

"Who?" She blew on her coffee and took a tentative sip.

"Our esteemed fellow classmates. I saw the look on your face when you came out of the restroom. I also saw the women leaving before you. And your expression only got worse when you were talking to Carolyn." He held up his hand. "I don't blame you. But people like Carolyn, and the women in the rest-room, and Mike, they're not worth getting upset over. Most of them are just jealous. At least the women." He shrugged and took another sip. "Always have been, probably always will be."

She set her mug aside while the waitress placed steaming

plates of biscuits and gravy in the center of the table, along with their omelets. Just the heavenly aroma alone would probably add five pounds to her frame.

"You think people are jealous of me?" she asked when the waitress had gone back to the kitchen.

He nodded while he chewed, then swallowed. "Meg, have you never looked in the mirror? You're beautiful." He reached across the table to take her hand. "Why don't you believe me?"

She stared for a second, then put down her fork, appetite gone. "Because I'm nothing special."

"I don't understand. How can you say that, much less believe it?" He made room on his platter for two biscuits and smothered them with gravy. "And don't deny it now. I can tell by your face you believe it."

"Jake, look at me. I'm average, at best. Besides which, I look exactly like my sister." Emotion clogged her throat. It was the reason Suzanne hated her. "Even my face isn't my own."

"Bullshit! I've known both you and your sister for years, and could always tell you apart."

"How can you sit there and say that? Don't you remember when I asked you to the Sadie Hawkins Day Dance? You thought I was Suzanne!"

He chewed and swallowed, then took a sip of coffee before saying in a low voice, "No, I didn't." He wiped his mouth on his napkin. "I knew exactly who was talking to me. And I did the same stupid thing when I first saw you at the reunion: I pretended not to know which twin you were."

Folding and refolding her napkin, she thought about that. "Why?"

"Because you scared the crap out of me back then." He grinned. "And it's only slightly better now."

"Again . . . why?" For someone who was so smart, it just didn't make sense for him to be afraid of her.

"Because I knew, even back then, you were special."

11

Carefully setting her cup back on the table to prevent sloshing hot coffee all over herself, Megan stared at him.

"That doesn't make any sense. If you thought I was so special, why didn't you ever call or ask me out?"

"Because I also knew I wanted to get an education and go to medical school. Med school requires every ounce of your time and concentration. I couldn't afford the distraction."

Warmth washed through her. "I was a distraction?"

"Damn straight." Under the table, his knee rubbed hers, much the same as his thumb rubbed on the back of her hand. "You still are. Maybe more."

"Yet you're here with me now." She whispered, "We even slept together!" She drew circles on the back of their joined hands with the tip of her index finger. "Aren't you afraid I'll distract you?"

"Megan, honey, I'm counting on it."

Emotion clogged her throat. Tears burned the backs of her eyelids. "Are you sure?" she managed to choke out. How was she going to be able to walk away from him at the end of the reunion? If he truly had carried a torch for her for the last ten years and was still interested, leaving could ruin her one chance at happiness.

Assuming, that is, he was telling the truth.

Suz was always telling her she was gullible. It was a safe bet Suzanne wouldn't jump to conclusions about Jake. In fact, her sister was probably having her wicked way with Ron somewhere right now, riding him while she planned her revenge.

But Megan didn't want revenge on Jake. All she'd ever wanted was his attention. And his love.

Still, it wouldn't hurt to be a little cautious.

"Meg?"

"Hmm?" Why was Jake looking at her like that?

"You don't need to cut your napkin with a knife."

"What?" She looked down and realized she was sawing at her napkin instead of the omelet. "Oh. Guess I wasn't paying attention."

"Do you want to try to get in touch with your sister again?"

Did she? Suz's harsh words came back to her.

"No. Suz is a big girl, perfectly capable of taking care of herself." She forced a smile. "And so am I."

"I never doubted it." He threw some bills on the table. "If you're finished, maybe we could go somewhere else. There's a great little jazz club a few blocks over. Or we could have a drink at the hotel. Their bar is still open." His shoulders slumped, and he looked sheepishly through his lashes. "I'm just not ready for the night to end. But if you're tired, just tell me to get lost."

Wiping her mouth, she stood and smiled at him. "I'm not ready for it to end, either." Summoning all her courage, she said, "Why don't we go back to my room? We can order a drink from room service."

The way Jake's face brightened warmed her to the tips of her toes.

Score one for the shy twin.

* * *

"Stop!" Suzanne drew a shuddering breath and ordered her wet noodle muscles to obey her command to scoot away from the temptation of Ron's magnificent, sweat-slicked nudity. "Let's rest a little." She glanced at the shiny head of his remarkably still erect penis. "We don't want to wear it out."

He climbed up on the mattress, advancing on all fours, his swollen member reflecting light with each move he made.

"Ron," she warned, crab walking as fast as her weakened state would allow, until she felt the headboard at her back. "I know that look."

Lightning fast, he grabbed her ankle, jerking it out from under her. He stretched his arm, causing her legs to spread wide while he inched closer. On one elbow, he reached to flick her swollen labia, sliding the tip of his finger up and down her wetness. "And I know that pussy," he said in a low, urgent voice. "I've missed it and dreamed about it for years."

Her lubrication made his fingers slick while they slid up and down, in and out. Despite her best intentions, the muscles in her thighs vibrated with renewed desire. She watched his tan hand against the much paler skin of her thighs, watched his finger go slowly in and out of her primed sex, disappearing between the close-cropped hairs of her pubic area.

"Don't push me away again, baby," he said in a choked voice.

The sucking sound of his fingers on her moisture echoed in the quiet room.

"I crave you." Hot breath fanned the area he touched when he spoke. "Craved the sight of you, the sight of this. The smell. The taste." His mouth closed over her, his tongue spearing her, then licking her engorged flesh.

Closer, now on his knees, he pushed his free hand under her hips, raising her from the mattress. While he arranged her, he continuously licked and sucked.

He found her nub, first with his tongue, then his teeth. Just as he sucked it deeply into his mouth, he wiggled his fingers deep within her.

Her orgasm shot through her, vibrating her muscles, wringing what little breath she had left from her lungs.

Ron wasted no time in pulling her legs up onto his shoulders and, with her hips still elevated, shoved into her hard, knocking her head against the headboard.

"Your cunt is mine. Mine. Mine." He punctuated each word with a deeper thrust. "Don't. Forget. It."

12

"I see you have one of the remodeled rooms," Jake said, flipping the security bolt.

Smiling, Megan ran her hand along the smooth, cold black granite surface of the wet bar. "Yes, isn't it gorgeous? Did you see the bathroom?"

He stuck his head through the open doorway to the left of the entry, and gave a low whistle. "Pretty classy." His voice echoed from the granite tiled walls. "Hey, that tub looks like it's big enough for two." He looked back out at her. "Want to check it out?"

There was no way she would admit she'd never taken a bath or even a shower with a man. Had never had the inclination. Until now.

Tamping down her inhibitions—after all, not only was he a doctor, he'd already seen her naked—she dimmed the lights and attempted her best seductive walk toward him.

It would have worked, too, were it not for the powerful orgasm that snuck up on her, causing her muscles to melt, refusing to take another step. She tried with all her might not to cry out, clamping her legs together to stem the gush of arousal. She almost righted herself and would have made another step had it not been for the edge of her briefcase peeking out from under the chair. Her heel snagged it and before she could say a word or catch herself or even think, she did a face plant in the Berber carpet, knocking out what little breath remained from her lungs.

Tiny bristles abraded the end of her nose and her cheekbones. They pricked her nipples, hard and erect, through the scant covering of the silk bodice of her cocktail dress.

Before she could attempt to recover, Jake was beside her, his warm hands lifting her.

"What happened? Are you okay?"

"I'm fine, I'm just a klutz. I—ah!" Another climax slammed into her, making her drop back down to squirm on the carpet in an effort to alleviate the gnawing ache between her legs.

"Megan, what's going on? Do you have a medical problem?"

Gripping his legs, she pulled up until she was plastered against his hardness. Her hands shook but she managed to wrestle his belt from the buckle and unzip his pants. The ache between her legs intensified. Wild, she clawed until she freed his erection, then shoved him onto his back on the mattress, his trousers and underwear around his knees.

"Meg? We have all night. Ooph!"

As soon as she ripped off her panties, she hiked up her dress and hopped on him, her knees pushing on his abs as she impaled herself.

The sigh barely left her mouth before the deep itch began, clawing at her, causing her to rock, hard and fast, riding him. Bad enough Suz had almost ruined Meg's romantic evening with Jake with her stupid shared orgasms. Meg would be danged if she'd allow it to continue.

A glance down at Jake confirmed he was otherwise occupied. Good. Maybe sex would take his mind off her weird connection with her sister.

Her nipples drew into tight points. The ache between her legs intensified. She picked up the pace.

Don't you dare have an orgasm without me, big sister!

When Meg could breathe without huffing and puffing, she slid from Jake's heaving chest.

He immediately curled his arm around her, dragging her close to his side.

"I know," he said, panting. "I look ri-ridiculous, but I think we may have destroyed some brain cells. I can't lift my arms or legs." His hot breath fanned her face as he leaned to kiss her temple. "And you know what? I don't even care if I did kill off some cells." He gave her a one-armed hug. "It was worth it."

She nodded, placing little kisses wherever she could reach along his chest. "I'm sure I'm ruining my dress, but I know what you mean. I don't have the strength to take it off."

His chuckle rumbled against her ear. "You had plenty of strength when you threw me on the bed and had your way with me, not that I'm complaining."

"Mm-hmm. I am woman, hear me roar."

"Hungry?"

"That depends." She rallied herself enough to raise to her elbow to see his face. "Do I have to order it?"

"Oh, yeah. I'm much too weak to lift the phone."

She flopped back down, staring at the ceiling. "Then no, I'm not hungry. It's too much effort."

"Do you want to try to reach your sister again?"

She stiffened against him. "Do you think I should?"

He shrugged and pulled away a little, rolling to his side, his head resting on his hand. "I think you're worried and trying to not show it. If it's okay with you, I'd like to spend the night

with you. Hell, I'd like to spend the whole weekend with you."
He reached for her hand and squeezed. "But I don't want to
share the bed with whatever problem you have with your sister.
I'm selfish. I want your undivided attention." He leaned to kiss
her forehead, breathing in her unique scent. "And if that means
I have to wait while you check on Suz, I don't have a problem
with that."

Meg seemed to contemplate what he'd said, then shook her
head. "No. I tried a few times and got no answer. When she's
not busy, she'll see I called her cell." She shrugged. "If she
needs to contact me, she'll call back."

"What's it like, being a twin? What was it like growing up?"
She was so quiet, he thought for a minute she wouldn't answer.

"Being a twin is . . . a lot like being in a dog show. You get
groomed and trotted out to be put on display. When you're little, everyone thinks you're so adorable. Mom insisted we always dress alike." She made a face. "Suz hated it."

"What about you? Did you hate it?" He brushed a strand of
hair from her face.

"Yes." She sighed. "And no. I loved that there was another
person who shared everything about me. But at times, I hated it
for the same reason." A sad chuckle escaped her. He noticed
she wiped her eyes. "Suz hated it twenty-four-seven. She always said I stole her face."

"You could have made the same claim."

"Not really. She's the oldest by about three minutes."
Rising, she pulled her dress over her head and tossed it toward
the chair, then grabbed the robe from the other side of the bed
and wrapped it around her nudity.

"You don't have to cover up on my account." Surprisingly,
he meant it. The human body may have lost its mystique years
ago for him, but he found he couldn't get enough of seeing
Megan—with or without clothes. That probably meant some-

thing, but he was too wiped out to think about it at the moment.

"No, I'm doing it for me. Maybe if I'm covered, I won't attack you again."

"I'm not complaining." He pulled up his boxers, feeling at a distinct disadvantage by his flagrant nudity. "Funny, I always thought you and Suz were inseparable."

"Most of the time we were, but it wasn't by choice. You have no idea how annoying it is to be seen as half a person. And poor Suzanne! Most of the time, I could overlook it, but it bugged her." She looked down, fiddling with the belt on her robe. "Sometimes, I thought she hated me." She snorted. "Heck, sometimes I think she still does." Her eyes sparkled with tears when she looked at him, causing a clenching around his heart. "I didn't ask to be her twin. It wasn't my fault I looked exactly like her!"

"Shh." He pulled her into his arms, and back to the bed to snuggle. "Of course you didn't." He tilted her chin to look into her eyes. "And, for what it's worth, you don't look exactly like her." He shook his head at her look of disbelief. "I could tell you apart from the first time I met you."

"Yeah, right. You're just saying that to make me feel better."

"You're wrong about that. I can prove it."

"How?"

"Well, for one thing, she's left-handed. Which makes her also left-footed. Even from across the room, all I have to do is notice which foot she leads with to know it's her." He pulled her close, inordinately pleased she didn't resist. "But that's an easy one. I also noticed more subtle differences. You have a little mark at your hairline, behind your left ear."

She clamped her hand over her ear, eyes wide. "You noticed that?"

Nodding, he continued, "Yep. And tonight I noticed it looks like a tattoo."

She dropped her hand and turned for him to see the little

blue B next to her hairline, behind her ear. "It is a tattoo. Suz has an A. Get it? Baby A and Baby B. The hospital did that to all identical twins born there." She huffed a little laugh. "No wonder we never had the urge to get another one."

He placed a tender kiss on the tattoo. "I think it's sexy."

"Thanks," she said in a watery voice, then sniffed. "So, was there anything else you noticed?"

"Well, Suzanne is a little taller."

"Nope, we're exactly the same height. She's just in better shape, which is so unfair, since she eats junk food and doesn't exercise, while I watch every bite I put in my mouth and run every day."

He waggled his eyebrows. "Your shape looks great to me." *I love you.* That was the biggest difference. Of course, he knew she'd probably run screaming from the room if he declared his love after less than one day. "I run, too. Maybe we can start running together."

"I'd like that." She snuggled closer. "What else have you noticed?"

"Lots of little things. You're, for lack of a better word, nicer than your sister. You smile and laugh more. You're not as cynical." He shrugged, getting sidetracked by the gaping front of her robe and the firm flesh exposed for his viewing pleasure. "And you're prettier." He trailed kisses down her neck. "And sexier." He parted the robe, feeling his strength return, along with something else.

"And," he said, pulling the robe from her delectable body and covering her with his aroused one, "if I don't make love to you right now, I will surely die of a broken heart."

"Well," she said, sliding her arms around his neck and playing with his hair, "I wouldn't want to be responsible for that." She swatted his bare butt and grinned at him. "Let's have a little less talk and a lot more action, hot stuff."

13

Suzanne sat straight up in bed, wheezing for breath. Sweat sheened her skin. The air conditioning clicked on, raising goose bumps on her nude body. Her sister must be having a hell of a night with Jake Stanton. The arousal burned between her legs, making her look around.

Apparently Ron had left sometime while she slept. She flopped back on the pillows and tried not to feel abandoned or hurt by the fact he hadn't said good-bye. He'd be back.

And, when he did come back, would she be able to walk away as planned?

She'd always teased Meg about her emotions, and yet here she was, getting all warm and squishy at the thought of seeing Ron again, wondering if maybe this time they might make it work.

Sunlight filtered through the crack between the drapery panels.

Megan stretched and smiled, relishing in the slight soreness of her muscles, remembering exactly how the soreness had happened.

The bathroom door opened, bathing the room in filtered light. Jake walked to the edge of the bed, dressed in khaki pants and a starched white shirt.

When he leaned to kiss her smiling lips, a tingle danced along her nerve endings. No doubt about it, she could definitely get used to good morning kisses from him. Or afternoon kisses. Or evening, or midnight kisses . . .

"When you look at me that way, you make it very difficult for me not to shuck my clothes and crawl back into bed with you, you know."

"I wouldn't mind."

"Neither would I, except I already made plans for the day."

Her shoulders slumped. Of course he did. He had no way of knowing they would get together. Glum, she stood, dragging the sheet with her. "I understand. I should probably find Suzanne and talk to her, anyway."

"No, I don't think you do understand."

Stopped at the end of the bed by his words, she turned, determined not to jump to conclusions.

"I made an appointment months ago to do a walk-through of the new clinic." His warm hands gripped her shoulders. "Why don't you get ready and come with me? We can have breakfast along the way, and then find your sister when we get back." At her hesitation, he hurried on. "Unless it's urgent you talk to Suz. Because, if it is, I can always go alone or change the appointment and go after we find her." He slid his hands down her arms to grip her hands. "Your call. I don't want to interfere with your plans."

You are my plan. "Um, okay. I'll try to call Suz, then take a quick shower. How much time do I have?" She frowned when she noticed he'd removed his shirt. "What are you doing?"

His smile caused a melting deep inside. "I figured it would take less time if I helped you shower."

"Ah," she said, nodding. "I somehow doubt that, but you're welcome to try."

While the water warmed, she stole glances at Jake. How could he be so confident, so matter-of-fact about his nudity, while she stood there, with her robe wrapped to her neck, wondering if he'd notice if she showered in it.

Not giving her a choice of showering in her robe, he drew it from her and guided her into the big tub, then followed her in, drawing the shower curtain to cocoon them in the intimate steam.

She stood, rooted to the spot, wondering what to do next, where to put her hands, how she would reach the soap. And was there such a thing as a shampoo faux pas? What, if anything, was the etiquette for communal showers, anyway? She glanced down nervously, then, seeing him at half mast, wondered if it would be a conjugal shower and how, exactly, they would do it.

A shower had never been so stressful.

"Meg," Jake said, close to her ear. "Stop. You look like you're worried. Whatever it is, it will be okay." Lathered hands cupped her breasts, thoroughly massaging them, making her knees weak.

By the time he'd soaped her from head to toe, she was close to melting into a puddle of need.

"Okay," he said, also breathing hard. "Turn around so we can get the rest of this rinsed off."

Obligingly, she turned. Bubbles sluiced over her shoulders, rounded her breasts, trickled down over her abdomen. Her heartbeat echoed in her ears.

The tingling began in her toes. Before she recognized it for what it signaled, it was too late. Her knees grew weak, her heart rate doubled. Before she could take another breath, her sister's climax hit her right between the eyes.

She jerked, her foot connecting with the recently rinsed bubbles on the bottom of the tub. Sensation washed over her, rolling her eyes back in her head, as she felt herself slide bonelessly into the tub between Jake's legs.

"It's not funny," Jake told her, glaring across the examination room.

"Doctor Stanton, please, hold still," the resident on duty at St. Luke's ER told him. "I don't want to mess this up. There." He placed three Steri-Strips over the new stitches on Jake's eyebrow. "I don't think I really need to send the aftercare sheet home with you, do I?" He stripped off the latex gloves, tucking them inside each other, then tossed them in the trash. "How exactly did you fall again?"

"It's none—"

"He slipped getting into his car and hit his head," Meg supplied, cutting off what surely would have been a crabby reply, at best. The truth, that he fell over her in the bathtub, would be too humiliating for either of them.

The resident, who looked all of about eighteen years old, although she knew that wasn't possible, shook Jake's hand and left.

Jake wasted no time in stripping off the hospital gown and tugging on his shirt. "I hate hospitals. Let's get out of here."

"Excuse me? Did you say you hated hospitals? Jake, you're a doctor. Worse, a lot of your practice, delivering babies, takes place in hospitals. If you hate hospitals, you're in the wrong career." He couldn't possibly mean it. Could he?

After they'd exited the room, he looked both ways, then ushered her toward the exit sign. "I'll tell you a little secret. The first time I had to do rounds, I fainted."

"You're kidding." Swallowing her giggle, she bit back a smile.

"I wish." He guided her across the parking lot toward his car. "No problem all through med school, then blammo."

"That must have been embarrassing." She allowed him to help her into the cab of his battered red Chevy pickup truck.

"You have no idea."

After he'd climbed in behind the wheel, she touched the edge of his stitches with her fingertip. "Does it hurt?"

"Nah. It's still pretty numb." Instead of exiting the parking lot, he drove to a secluded corner and put the truck in park, then looked across the duct-taped seat at her. "You need to level with me. Do you have a medical condition? I'm a doctor. Maybe I can help, or direct you to someone who can."

"No!" She jerked away from his touch. "I do *not* have a medical problem! Do you have a hearing problem? Because I told you before, I'm *fine*." After fumbling with the broken handle, she finally shoved open the door and jumped out.

"Megan!" He leaned to glare at her through her open door, the dome light casting a shadow on his cheek from the swelling above his eye. "Get back in the truck."

"No, thanks. I can walk back to the hotel." Hitching her purse over her shoulder, she set off across the grass median, hoping she was going in the right direction.

"Not going that way, you can't."

Shoot.

She pivoted and strode in the opposite direction.

"Not that way, either." His voice sounded like he was laughing at her, but she didn't want to look at him and confirm it. "Get in. I'll drive you."

She wheeled on him, hand on hip. "I can walk. It's not that far."

"Meg, honey, you don't even know which direction to go. How do you expect to find it?" He patted the sagging seat. "C'mon. Let's not argue. We're both tired, and I'm beginning to get a headache."

Guilt tugged at her. If she and her sister didn't have that weird connection, she wouldn't have slipped in the tub and knocked him down. If she hadn't, he wouldn't have had to get stitches.

Guilt sucked.

With a sigh, she climbed into the truck and fastened her seatbelt, then crossed her arms and looked straight ahead.

"You know," he began, pulling onto Fannin Street, "you should be glad I didn't tell them how I really got the cut."

After looking at him for a moment, she took the bait. "Oh? And what would you have told them?"

"It was a sex injury."

14

The sound of breaking glass filled the room. Suzanne cracked open one bleary eye to look around for her cell phone. Whatever her sister was calling about had better be important at— she rolled to look at the digital clock—six o'clock in the damn morning.

After a few fumbles, she flipped open the flat pink phone. "Hmm?" She pushed her leg sideways, her toes feeling to see if she was still alone.

That was a stupid thing to do. Ron was still as hot for her as always. If he'd been in bed with her, he'd have been in her. She yawned. Being with him again was great, but did the guy pop No-Doz? Even the Energizer bunny couldn't perform all night the way Ron had.

"Suz?" Meg's voice echoed in her ear. "Are you there?"

"Where else would I be? I answered the phone."

"Did I wake you up?"

"Of course you woke me up! It's the butt-crack of dawn. Who gets up at this ungodly hour?"

"Oh, good, I'm glad you're awake. Meet us at the breakfast bar in half an hour."

She frowned. "Us? Hello?" She tossed the phone on the nightstand and threw back the covers. "Whatever it is, baby sister, it had better be worth it."

"If you want to talk to her without me, I can sit somewhere else." Jake surveyed the crowd in line for the breakfast bar.

Glancing up at him, with his white strips tracking across his eyebrow, along with the discoloration, she tamped down her guilt. After she talked to Suz, she would take him back to her room and tell him everything.

God, he was gorgeous. The way the lights reflected off his wavy dark hair. The broadness of his shoulders showed off to perfection in the pale yellow starched shirt. The way the dark redness surrounding his eye brought out the depth of the blue color. Oops. That was probably not a good thing.

"But I don't want you to sit with anyone else." Pathetic, but true. "You'll not only be here for moral support, you can verify the things I've heard about Ron. Maybe if we both tell her, she'll listen."

"I don't know, Meg." He ran the tip of his index finger along her cheek, setting off goose bumps down her body. "I don't think there's anything anyone could say about you, right now, that would change my mind."

Good to know, since she would be testing that theory later.

"Okay, I'm here. What is it?" Suzanne skidded to a stop, perched precariously on a pair of hot pink stiletto heels. Her pink and orange paisley print dress looked more like it should be a top. Or part of a set of babydoll pajamas.

"You forgot your pants," Jake said, looking disinterested as well as uncomfortable.

Meg warmed, happy to know her sister did not appeal to him. It was a twin thing.

"Ha. Ha." Suz turned to her. "You really find that attractive?"

"Hey, don't get personal. What your sister and I have is special."

"Really?" Meg knew her question sounded breathy and full of wonder, but . . . well, it was.

"Oh, gag me. You two are sickeningly sweet, you know that? Next, you'll probably be cooing at each other and kissing, and ruining everyone's breakfast."

"Suz, cut it out," Meg said under her breath. "We have to talk to you." She glanced around as they filled their plates. "There's a table over by the window." She inclined her head. "Jake, would you please go save it for us?"

"Damn, Meg, you already have him trained?" Suz tsked and shook her head as she watched Jake walk toward the table with his tray. "I underestimated you."

"Stop joking around." She nudged her sister toward Jake and the table.

"Okay," Suz said, as soon as the waiter took their trays. "What's so important that I had to get up and come here before I'd even totally woken up?"

Meg unfolded her linen napkin and placed it on her lap. "I wanted to talk to you about Ron Daniels."

Suzanne set her mug back on the table, coffee sloshing to mar the perfection of the starched tablecloth. "Don't start."

"Suz, he's using you! He hasn't changed. We—"

"What, Megan? You wanted to protect me from myself? I'm a big girl. I may not make as much money as you do with your booming real estate sales, or live in as nice a place, but I do okay. I've made it just fine up to now, without your advice. What makes you think I'd want it now?"

Meg clenched her fist in her lap and took a deep breath. "Suz, this isn't about you or me or us. It's about Ron and what he did, and what he might possibly do." She leaned forward, pleading. "Listen to me, please. He's a rat fink. Just as much, if not more so, than before."

Suz threw her napkin on the table and shot to her feet, then grabbed the table to steady herself. "Shut up. I don't want to hear it. You're just jealous. You were always jealous of me, and you always will be. It's pathetic, really."

"Everyone saw Rhonda Spader giving him a blow job under the table last night." Jake's quiet voice cut into her tirade. "Everyone except you. You were sitting right next to him." His voice lowered. "Meg is only trying to warn you, protect you."

Tears swam in Suzanne's eyes. "Bullshit." Turning, she strode away without a backward glance.

"Well." Meg put her napkin on the table, appetite gone. "That went well."

Suzanne stood tapping her foot, waiting for the glass elevator to arrive and praying no one she knew was in it. She was not in the mood to be sociable.

The elevator was blessedly empty. She punched the fourteenth floor. Before the doors slid completely shut, a hand stopped them.

Sue wedged her plump body through the opening and smiled at Suzanne. "Boy, that was lucky. I had to wait a long time this morning." She shrugged. "Guess everyone wanted to go down to breakfast before the food was all gone."

Tight-lipped, Suz nodded.

"You heard, didn't you?" Sue shifted from one flip-flopped foot to the other. "About Ron and Rhonda?"

Sue always did love to be the bearer of bad news.

On some level, she knew Jake and Meg had been telling the truth. Well, the truth as they knew it, anyway. "What about them?"

"You didn't know?" She moved closer to Suzanne, and whispered, "She went down on him last night, when you were sitting right there! I wanted to tell you, but everyone said you were probably cool with it, considering you two had broken up years ago and all. You didn't sleep with him or anything, did you? I mean, after that, how could you?"

"Yeah, right, how could I?" Her coffee gurgled in her empty stomach. "Of course, I knew. Same old Ron, huh?" She shook her head, ordering the tears to stay back until she gained the privacy of her room. "A girl would have to be crazy to get involved with him again. I'm not crazy!"

They laughed, then the doors swooshed open and Sue stepped out. "I can't tell you how relieved I am to hear that. Maybe we can get together later, before the barbeque?"

"I'm, ah, busy. I promised my sister I'd help her with some stuff."

The doors slid shut. Suzanne slumped against the rail and watched the people in the lobby get smaller. Ron had been so loving, so willing to talk. So unlike the old Ron. The old Ron would have let anyone have their way with him, but this Ron was different. He only had eyes for her. But why did everyone think he and Rhonda . . . Well, there was only one sensible answer. Either they were mistaken, or Rhonda had forced herself on him and he was too embarrassed to say anything to stop her. Yes, that had to be it.

15

"This is disgusting!" Carolyn Wong jumped up, knocking dishes that landed at her feet with a resounding crash. "There's a used condom in my salad!" She scanned her fellow classmates, her eyes narrowing on Megan and Jake. "And I know exactly who did it!" She pointed at Meg, who shrank back against Jake's solid warmth. "You! Or your evil sister. Y'all are just trying to pay me back for doing it to you our senior year, and it's sick and—and pathetic!"

Jake looked down at Meg and murmured, "I think a used condom in a salad is sick and pathetic regardless of when it's done, don't you?" When she nodded absently, still watching Carolyn's rant, he leaned closer and whispered, "You didn't do it, did you?"

She shook her head. "And I doubt Suz did, either, since I haven't seen her since she stormed out of breakfast."

Jake lounged back on the picnic table, watching all the people hover around Carolyn. "I take it she feels it's payback?"

Meg turned her face to the sun and nodded. "It was really

horrible. For the last two years of high school, either Suz or myself would find a condom in our food. Really gross."

"No doubt." He glanced at his watch. "Are you up for beating everyone in the sack race? It starts in about fifteen minutes."

"Sure." She slouched lower on the bench. "It will give me time to digest some of the barbeque I scarfed down. I can't remember the last time I ate so much! But I love the food from Bubba's Best Barbeque. I rarely eat it, but I love it."

"Yeah, it was great."

They sat in silence for a few minutes before Jake spoke. "We've talked about me and my plans for my clinic, but we haven't had a chance to talk about you. What do you do for a living, Meg?"

"I'm a realtor. Mostly commercial properties. A few high-end homes occasionally."

"Sounds potentially stressful. Do you enjoy it?"

"I love it. Suz is a realtor, too, but she sells to a different market. In fact, she got into it before me. I think she was as surprised as I was to discover I had any talent for it."

A shrill whistle cut through the lazy silence. Someone yelled that the race was about to begin.

With a groan, Meg allowed Jake to haul her up and lead her away. She had no real interest in participating. She'd just as soon stay and bask in the sun and Jake's company. But if he wanted to do it, she would make the effort.

Her left leg was tied to Jake's much longer right one. "I'm not sure how this is going to work." She eyed the rope binding them together.

"Easy. I'll hold you up and run. All you have to do is move your other leg and relax, and let me move the one tied to mine. Piece of cake."

Famous last words.

The whistle sounded. Twenty or so couples hobbled away from the starting line.

"I think the rope is not right—"

"Don't worry. Hang on!" Jake's arm crushed her to his side and he took off, his long legs eating up the distance between them and the rest of the pack.

"Jake! Wait! I—ugh!" His grip on her tank top faltered. Her lotion-slick, sweaty leg slipped around beneath the rope, swinging her backwards between his legs.

Reacting immediately, he bowed his legs to avoid stepping on her, but her momentum took them both down in a heap. With her head wedged between his legs, it didn't take a rocket scientist to identify the soft pillow of flesh pressed against her mouth.

Two short blasts of the whistle ended the race.

People ran over to check on their condition.

Against her laughing mouth, *little Jake* swelled.

"We're okay," Jake assured the crowd, immediately taking his weight onto his knees.

Little Jake nodded his agreement, setting off more giggles from Meg.

"Meg?" Someone called. "Are you okay, too?"

She worked her arm free to give everyone the thumbs-up sign, noticing Jake remained where he was instead of moving to help her up as conversation drifted away.

She tapped on his leg.

"Are you sure you're okay?" He laughed when she nodded. "That felt interesting. Feel free to do it again."

In reply, she swatted his arm. At least she thought it was his arm. With a face full of crotch, it was hard to tell.

Carefully moving away from her, he leaned down to shove the rope off the rest of the way and then helped her up.

"Sack race is next," he said, dusting the dirt from his shorts.

"Go on without me." She motioned to the row of ice chests.

"I'm going to get something to drink. I'll watch and cheer you on."

"Excuse me," a frail looking, yet immensely pregnant red-head walked up to Meg as she popped the top on a Bud Light. "Is this the Champions High reunion barbeque?"

Meg wiped her mouth on the back of her hand, racking her brain. The woman was a stranger. Her high school class had over eight hundred people, but she at least had a nodding acquaintance with most of them. She was pretty sure she'd never seen the woman before.

Swallowing her first draw of beer, she hastily wiped her hand on her khaki shorts and offered it. "Sure is. I'm Meg Hartley."

The redhead's hand felt fragile and childlike in hers. "Oh, hi. I'm Tracey Daniels."

Meg's stomach clenched.

Obviously mistaking her silence, Tracey hurried on. "I didn't go to school with y'all." She shrugged. "I grew up in Louisiana. I met my husband when I came here to go to beauty school. I worked part-time at his daddy's hardware store. 'Course, now it's his. I don't want to intrude, but the reason I'm here now is that I'm supposed to go to the hospital for some tests." She ran her hand lovingly over her bulging stomach. "He insisted on coming to the barbeque, though, since he'd already paid for it and all. When he didn't come home by noon, I decided to swing by on my way to the hospital and pick him up, then just bring him back after we're done so he doesn't miss much."

"You are a very understanding wife," Meg said around the lump in her throat. "I'll help you find him. What did you say his name was?" Please, Lord, let it be some other Daniels. But, since Ron's dad owned the local hardware store, she knew the chances were slim to none.

"Ron. Ron Daniels. Do you know him?"

Of course I know him. He took my sister's virginity and is probably at this moment pounding her into the mattress. But the woman standing before her didn't need to know that. At least not now.

"Sure, I remember Ron," she said instead, pretending to glance around. "But I don't see him right now." *Or at all today,* but the pitiful woman didn't need to know that, either. "What time do you have to be at the hospital? If you want to go on, I'll tell him to meet you if I see him."

Tracey looked around anxiously. "I don't know . . . I don't want him to get mad that I didn't wait for him."

"I'm sure he wouldn't want you to be late. Why don't you go, and I'll try to find him and send him on." *I'd like to send him to hell.*

Tracey looked around once more, her hand resting on her belly. "Well, it is getting kind of late. Will you tell him I tried to find him? Tell him I'll meet him at outpatient."

Meg nodded. "Sure. Outpatient. No problem." *Unless I find him, in which case you may have to meet him in the ER.*

Meg watched the woman waddle away and climb into a dual-wheeled pickup with a King Cab. Just like Ron to want the biggest and most expensive truck around.

"You missed my humiliating defeat in the sack race," Jake said from behind her. "I've come to the belated conclusion that tall people suck at sack races. Who was that?" Jake lifted a beer from the cooler and rolled it across his forehead.

"Ron Daniels's wife."

Jake lowered the bottle in slow motion to look at her. "Shit."

She nodded. "I need to go back to the hotel. I've got to find Suz."

"Damn straight. Let's grab our stuff and head out."

*   *   *

"Do you want me to come with you?"

Meg stretched on tiptoe to kiss his cheek. "Thanks. But I think I need to do this by myself."

"Okay. I've got some errands I need to do. You have my cell number. Call if you need me." He bent to look in her eyes, wishing he could help her through the ordeal ahead. "But I expect a call, even if you don't."

She nodded and walked toward the elevator.

"Meg?" He couldn't let her go without telling her. When she turned back to look at him, he said, "You know I love you, don't you?"

Her sad smile caused his heart to ache. He held his breath, only relaxing a little when he heard her low voice saying, "I know."

That's it? She knew? Sure, she had a lot on her mind, but he'd just made a declaration. Well, okay, maybe declaration was too strong of a word.

She tapped his shoulder. When he turned, she brushed her lips across his and said, "I love you, too." With that, she turned and made tracks to the elevator.

His lips tingled. Did he have the balls to follow through on the plan he'd formulated last night while Meg slept?

16

"Hey," Suz said an hour later, sliding onto the chair across from him in the café. "Have you seen my sister?"

"Um, yes, why?" He flipped the jeweler's box shut and shoved it back into the black and gold bag.

"What's that?" She grabbed the bag from him and had the box out before he could react. "Omigod." The princess-cut diamond winked in the pot light hanging over the table. Her troubled light blue gaze, so like her sister's but not, met his. "Are you sure?"

Was he? He nodded, sitting a little straighter. "Yep. I want to marry her, if she'll have me." He waited a beat. "Is that okay with you?" Not that it mattered, really.

"It's not my opinion you should worry about." She looked back down at the four-carat engagement ring and laughed. "It looks like an ice cube! You're going to be in debt for years . . . Don't you think it's a little soon to propose?" Chewing her lip, she looked up again. "I mean, you never even dated in high school. No communication at all for the last ten years. Then you hook up at the reunion and two days later, you pop the question?"

Put like that, it did sound somewhat absurd. "I've loved your sister for ten years. No, more like twelve or thirteen. So . . . it's not so sudden, if you think about it."

"Loved her? You never even dated her. Not once." She put the box back in the bag and pushed it toward him. "But what do I know? It's not like I'm an expert on relationships."

Guilt heated his skin while he tucked the bag into the pocket of his cargo shorts. "Have you talked to Meg?"

"No, that's why I came over when I saw you sitting here. I'm leaving early. I already checked out and put my suitcase in her room. The problem is, I must have left my card key on her desk and she's not answering her cell. The cab will be here any minute and I can't get my stuff."

"I have a key." He stood. "I'll go up and let you in. But I really wish you'd wait and talk to your sister." At her narrowed eyes, he shrugged. "It would be nice if you were there to congratulate her." He chuckled. "Or buy me a drink to mend my broken heart if she says no."

Softening her expression, she gave him a quick hug then patted his cheek. "Don't worry. She'll jump at the chance to marry you. Don't let on I told you, but I think she's loved you for a long time, too." She swallowed, a definite sheen in her eyes. "I'm sure you'll be very happy. Meg deserves to be happy, you know. So if you screw this up, I will personally kick your ass."

"Yes, ma'am." He motioned for her to lead the way, hitting the send button on his cell phone.

Meg's voicemail came on just as they stepped into the elevator. He flipped the phone shut, trying not to look concerned.

"No answer?" Suz looked distinctly edgy.

"Nope. She may be taking a nap or out socializing." The elevator doors slid open. He placed his hand on the door, motioning her out. "We'll soon find out."

Suz stopped and looked back at him. "You're okay, Jake Stanton. My sister is lucky."

"Don't spread it around."

17

Meg turned, craning her neck to see the back of the super short miniskirt she found in her sister's suitcase. "It's not as gross as I was afraid it might be," she mumbled. "Maybe I'll update my wardrobe when I get home." Would Jake like her to dress more like her sister?

And, speaking of her sibling, why was her luggage in Meg's room? She sincerely hoped it was because Suz finally saw Ron for the rat fink he was and had packed up.

Ordinarily, the thought of sharing a room with Suz would have been thrilling. Maybe it was selfish, but she'd planned to spend the remaining time with Jake. Alone.

The card key clicked in the door as Meg struggled to remove Suz's bustier.

"I was just trying them on," she hurried to explain to her sister when the door opened and closed. "The suitcase was unzipped, so it's not like I was snooping." Her shoulders slumped. "But now I can't get this thing off. I'm sorry I didn't ask first. Could you help me? Is there a trick to it?"

"Oh, yeah, there's a trick, all right," Ron's voice came from directly behind her. He grabbed her waist, jerking her back against him, and the hard ridge pressed against his jeans. "It comes off real slick and easy," he said with a growl against her ear, "when my cock is buried deep in your pussy."

Breath lodged in her throat for a second, then she began to struggle but he held tight. His hands snaked up to painfully squeeze her breasts through the skimpy half-cups of the bustier.

"Let me go," she managed to choke out. "I'm Megan, not Suz!"

"Let me be the judge of that." With one hand, he shoved down on the unzipped skirt until it puddled around her bare feet.

"Please, Ron, I'm telling the truth! I'm not Suz!" Blinking back tears, she struggled against his iron grip. "Don't do this. Let me go!"

"I know who you are," he assured her, both hands once again pinching her breasts. "I always begged Suz for a three-way with you, but she's not big on sharing. So, naturally, when I saw the card key for your room laying there, I assumed she'd changed her mind." He ground his erection into her, her thong giving little protection. "But that's okay, I'll just do my research on my own."

"What about your wife?" Meg gauged the distance to her cell phone.

Ron went still. Unfortunately, he didn't let go.

"Leave her out of it."

"Did you tell Suz about Tracey? Is that why she brought her stuff to my room?"

"Shut the fuck up!" He jerked her back, causing her to cry out in equal parts fear and pain. "You always thought you were too good for the likes of me. That's why you tried to turn your sister against me."

"You did that all by yourself, Ron."

"Well, now you're going to find out why your sister can't get enough of what I have to give."

The rasp of his zipper echoed in the room. He'd obviously done it often enough to successfully use one hand.

Struggling, she kicked, tears streaming down her face. She knew the floor was deserted, everyone still at the barbeque or down in the bar. No one would hear her scream.

Bile rose in her throat when Ron ran his finger along the back of her thong.

"I love them thong panties. Makes it nice and easy to slip in and out." As if to demonstrate, he slid his finger between her legs.

"Please, Ron, don't," she whimpered.

"Don't what, sweet thing? Don't stop? Spread your legs for me. I want to see if your cunt feels like your sister's."

"I really think you should wait and talk to Meg before you leave," Jake said as they walked down the hall. He took his card key from his shirt pocket and inserted it into Meg's door.

"Please," Meg's trembling voice sounded from the other side.

He pushed open the door and felt his heart seize at the sight of the woman he loved half naked, bent over in front of Ron Daniels's bare and fully erect penis.

Both people looked up as they entered. Ron held Meg's breasts in both hands.

Jake looked at Suz. All color had drained from her face. Her tear-filled gaze moved from her sister to Ron and back.

"Jake! Suz!" Meg looked horrified.

Horrified she'd been caught, no doubt.

Jake didn't resist when Suz put out her arm, pulling him into the hall with her as she backed out of the room.

"Have fun." She slammed the door and stalked toward the elevator.

"Suz!" Meg screamed from behind the closed door. "Jake! Come back! Come . . . back!"

Suz paused, her hand hovering over the down arrow. Meg hadn't sounded like a woman in the throes of passion. In fact, now that she thought about it, the feeling in the pit of her stomach wasn't all hers. And it certainly wasn't arousal. "We need to go back." She worried her lower lip with her teeth.

"What for? An orgy?" He reached past her and stabbed at the button. "I'm not into that, but if you are, go on."

18

Meg twisted within Ron's grasp. "Damn you, Ron Daniels! Not only are you a lowlife scumbag, you're a lying, cheating scumbag. Tracey deserves better than you."

He jerked her back by her hair, bringing fresh tears to her eyes. "I done told you, keep Tracey out of this."

"Suzanne deserves better than you, too."

"Suzy-Q loves me, always has, always will. She'll take whatever I want to give her."

"Not anymore, you idiot. Don't you realize you sealed your fate just now? She'll never forgive you. Never." Her questing fingers closed around her computer case. Taking a deep breath she swung up and around, putting all of her weight behind it. The case and its computer hit Ron's head with a satisfying thud.

Suz shot her hand out and stopped the elevator door from closing. "Something's not right. I'm going back."

"What if you're wrong?" Although the idea sickened him, he had to verbalize it. "What if what we saw is exactly what we thought? Two consenting adults engaging in sexual activity."

"What if I'm right? Ron has a mean streak. I thought he'd changed, but when he left me yesterday, I started thinking. I don't think he's changed, Jake. Meg is in trouble."

"Do you really care?" Meg didn't think so, but he had a feeling Suz hid her true feelings about her sister.

She was quiet for a moment. "Yes. I do care. Even with our sicko connection. She may be a drag at times, and can get prissy, and is opinionated as the day is long, but . . . she's my sister and I don't want anything to happen to her." She stepped out of the elevator, still holding the door open. "We both love her. There's a small chance what we saw was what was happening. I doubt it, but there is a chance. I'm willing to risk it. What about you? Are you going to just walk away without a fight?"

"I don't know. I do know I've never felt the kind of pain I felt when we walked into that room. But I also know there is no way in hell I'd let you go back alone." He stepped out. The elevator door whooshed shut. "Let's go."

Meg sat on the edge of the bed, staring at the limp form of Ron Daniels and wondered if he was dead. She nudged him with her toe, relieved to hear him grunt.

He'd wake up soon. If she could just stop crying and shaking, she would be able to think of a plan of action. If he woke up, he would definitely rape her.

Not an option.

Keeping a wary eye on him, she edged to the other side of the bed. Just as she reached for the phone, the door opened.

Her sister swooped in like an avenging angel. "Meg! Are you hurt?" She spared Ron a cursory glance. "He didn't . . ."

Uncontrollable shaking took over, but she managed to assure Suz. At least she thought she did. All she could do, held tightly in her sister's arms, was lock gazes with Jake while she shook and cried.

She'd seen the look on his face when he and Suzanne had

walked in. She knew the evidence was damning. But she also knew she loved Jake with all her heart and soul, and if he turned his back on her now, she might never recover.

But she'd rather live her life alone than with someone who thought she could make love with him and have sex with another guy behind his back. She would survive.

Jake dropped to his knees and checked Ron's vitals. "He's okay, just knocked out. Did you call security?"

She shook her head, still shaking.

He flipped open his phone and did the honors.

A few minutes later, he left with the security guards, and a still unconscious Ron, to fill out the paperwork.

Suz brushed aside the strands of hair sticking to Meg's forehead. "Can I get you anything?"

"No. Thanks." *The only thing I want just walked out the door.* "Thank you for coming back," she whispered, tears welling again. She drew a shaky breath. "What made you do it?"

Suz laughed and wiped her eye. "I think I knew I was wrong as soon as I closed the door. You were always the sensible one. No way would you do the nasty with someone like Ron. You have better taste. Besides," she added in a soft voice, "I wasn't turned on. It was a dead giveaway, once I thought about it. And I know you love Jake. You'd never cheat."

Meg struggled to sit up as soon as her sister tucked her in. "Speaking of cheating . . . that's why I needed to talk to you. It's why I came back to the room. I had to find you."

Suz sat in the armchair and crossed her legs. "Here I am. What was so important?"

"Ron is married," Meg blurted out. "Her name is Tracey and she's *very* pregnant." She held her hand in front of her abdomen to demonstrate.

"How long have you known? Geez, Meg, that's not the kind of information you putz around about telling someone." Suz got up and paced back and forth. "How could you let me keep—wait. You've been pestering me to talk about something for quite a while. I know you. You wouldn't have let me keep sleeping with him, knowing he had a wife." Her eyes narrowed. "You knew something else, didn't you? Spill it."

"Rhonda Spader blew him under the table Friday night during the mixer." She wrung her hands. "I wanted to tell you right away, but you didn't want to hear it."

Suz huffed a laugh. "I already heard it, baby sister." She nodded. "Yeah, I heard, but I didn't want to believe it. So . . . when did you find out he's married?"

"Today. At the picnic. That's why I had Jake bring me back early. I didn't want you to keep seeing Ron. Not without knowing the truth."

"You think I'd keep sleeping with him if I knew he had a wife? Gee, thanks."

"No, I didn't think that! That's why I knew I had to talk to you, to tell you."

"That still doesn't explain how Ron was in your room with his pants down."

"I don't know! He had a card key. I assumed he got hold of yours. I was trying on one of your outfits—don't be mad—I know it was wrong. I just couldn't seem to help myself."

Suz sat down on the bed next to her and put her arm around her. "I'm not mad. It's okay. Now. Tell me what happened."

Meg took a deep breath. "I heard the door open and assumed it was you since I knew Jake was waiting for my call. I was having a problem getting the bustier off—"

"Which, by the way, looks way better on you," Suz interrupted.

"Really? Thanks!" At Suz's rolling hand signal, she continued. "Oh. Anyway, when I turned, it was too late. Ron was already in the room. Primed and ready for action, if you know what I mean."

Suzanne shuddered. "Unfortunately, I do know what you mean."

"Not much else to tell." Meg selected a personal bottle of wine from the honors bar, opened it, and poured a little into the bottom of two glasses, handing Suz one. "The rest, as they say, is history. I fought him off, but was losing by the time you and Jake walked in." She briefly closed her eyes and shook her head. "That must have looked so bad, I'm sure."

"It definitely wasn't a Hallmark moment, to say the least," Suz said with a laugh.

"Do you think Jake will ever get over it?"

"There's nothing to get over," Jake's beloved voice said from the doorway. "But I do want to know about the orgasmic connection you two have. Believe it or not, I've heard of it, but I've never actually met anyone who had it."

"Well." Suz set her glass down on the wet bar. "I just remembered I need to go check on, um, something. I'll see you later."

"Suz?" Her sister turned at the door. "Thank you."

"Don't get all sappy on me." She grinned. "I just did what sisters do."

After Jake and Meg had polished off the rest of the wine in the bar, and made love twice, he pulled her close on the bed, arranging the covers while kissing her forehead.

"So what are the chances of getting your sister to loan you that outfit? Ow! What was that for?"

"Jake Stanton, I love you but you're being an insensitive jerk. Ron almost raped me in that outfit! Why on earth would I ever want to see it again, much less wear the thing?"

"Right." He rubbed his bicep. "You pack a mean punch. Anyone ever tell you that?" He held her close and kissed the top of her head. "Why don't we blow off the rest of the re-

union? All that's left is the good-bye brunch tomorrow morning."

She snuggled closer. "What do you have in mind?"

"Rest. After all you've been through, I am prescribing rest."

"Sounds like a plan. Will that be bed rest, by chance? And
will you be keeping an eye on me?"

"Bed rest would be good, but any rest will do."

She stilled and sat up, putting some distance between them.
"Are you trying to tell me something, Jake?"

He kissed the tip of her nose and got out of bed, stepping
into his boxers. "Yes. I love you and I want you to get a good
night's sleep. You won't do that if I stay." He pulled up his
pants and zipped them, then shrugged into his T-shirt. "The
sedative I gave you will be kicking in soon." He leaned down
and kissed her numb lips. "I love you, Megan Hartley. Sleep.
Good night."

She wanted to call him back or at least tell him good night,
but her mouth failed to form the words, then her eyelids refused to stay open.

The banging on her door awoke her early the next morning.
"Just a minute." She crawled to the end of the bed and grabbed
her robe. "Don't get your hopes up," she muttered, "Jake has a
key."

"This was just delivered for you," the bellman said, handing
her a brightly wrapped square box.

"Wait. Let me get some money—"

"Not necessary," he replied, backing out and closing the
door.

The bright yellow, orange, and green striped foil paper glowed
in the early morning sunshine streaming through the open drap-
eries. She tugged at the silver and gold striped bow, then saw a
card and ripped it open.

Dear Megan, I missed you. Enclosed are my plans for us for the next month while I wait for the clinic to open. I'll see you soon. Love, Jake. P.S. There is a special surprise at the bottom of the box. J.

Finally shoving the ribbon aside, she pushed back the lid to find condoms in every color, flavor, and texture imaginable.

Laughing, she dumped out the box. A small jeweler's box tumbled across the mattress and hit the floor with a thunk.

Before she could get out of bed to retrieve it, the door opened and Jake walked in, looking lean and luscious in khaki shorts and a pale yellow polo shirt. His sturdy feet ate up the distance in a pair of brown leather flip-flops.

"Is that a bad sign?" he asked, stooping to pick up the little box. "That you threw the box off the bed?" He brushed a kiss on her lips. "Hi. How did you sleep?"

"Hi, yourself. Lonely. I've already become addicted to having you next to me."

"Oh, yeah?" He sat next to her and pulled her into his arms for a proper good morning kiss. "Open the box, Meg."

She knew what she hoped it would be, but told herself not to be stupid. It was too soon for a proposal. The box was definitely too small to be anything but a ring. Maybe a friendship or a right hand ring. Or possibly earrings.

"Meg, it won't bite. Put me out of my misery and open the thing." When she just stared wide-eyed at him, he huffed out a breath and took the box from her limp hands. "Forget it. I can't wait." He threw the top aside and pulled out a black velvet box. Opening it, he exclaimed, "Oh, wow, looky here."

"What?" She edged closer.

Tossing the box aside, he turned to her. "Megan Hartley, will you sleep with me forever?"

"Um . . . okay."

"I forgot something." He slid off the bed to his knees and took her hands in his. "Will you also marry me?"

The cool feel of a ring slid onto the fourth finger of her left hand. Smiling through her tears, she could only nod.

After they'd kissed, she looked at her hand and gasped. "It looks like an ice cube!"

Jake laughed and hugged her. "That's exactly what your sister said."

Grinning, she flipped open her cell. "Hi, Suz. How would you like to be my maid of honor?"

DOUBLE THE FUN

1

Suzanne Hartley pulled up to the rental beach house her friend Royce's husband, Jack, owned on Pleasure Beach. Royce and Jack were on their honeymoon and the beach house was awaiting new renters at the beginning of the month. She buzzed down the window, allowing the Gulf breeze to ruffle her hair, tugging strands from the loose ponytail, and took a bracing breath.

She needed this break. A break from all the craziness associated with her twin sister's wedding preparations back in Corpus Christi. A break to work on her tan, rest, and regroup. A break to mend her broken heart.

Oh, sure, technically, her heart wasn't really broken. She knew that. Ron had been and would always be a loser scumbag. But ten years ago, and then again more recently, for a brief moment in time, he'd been her loser scumbag. Of course, his martial status and impending fatherhood had put a crimp in any future plans she may have had with him.

The sound of breaking glass filled her rental Tahoe. Her sister calling. Again.

With a sigh, she flipped open her phone. "Hi, Meg."

"Are you there yet?" Her sister spoke over what sounded like power tools.

"What? Yes, I'm here, but I can barely hear you. What's that racket?" She held her hand to block the noise of the waves from her free ear.

"Oh, Jake decided we needed to say our vows on the beach under a gazebo. He hired some contractors to build one. I'm calling to ask if you picked up your bridesmaid dress. I just was at the salon for my final fitting, and I didn't see it."

So much for her hoping Meg would grow out of her control issues. "Yes. I picked it up on my way out of town. I have it in the car." She pulled her suitcase out and shut the tailgate, eyeing the stairs leading up to the deck.

"Why did you do that? What if it gets ruined? There won't be time to get a new one, and have it fitted, and—"

"Meg! Meg, listen to me. The dress will be fine. Everything will be fine. I need you to do me a favor, though."

"Of course. Anything. What is it?"

"I need you to find Jake. Ask him to write you a prescription for a chill pill because you are driving me *fucking nuts!*"

As usual, her sister's reaction pierced her heart. You'd think after all these years she would have learned that hurting her sister would ultimately hurt her. The sicko connection was obviously still strong.

"I just want everything to be perfect," her sister said in a small voice, making her feel like she'd kicked a smurf.

She sighed and headed for the stairs, dragging her suitcase behind her. "I know. I'm sorry. I didn't mean to hurt your feelings. But, honestly, Meg, your obsessive *bridezilla* attitude is wearing on everybody. Everything is done. The wedding will go off without a hitch. Now, please, let me have a little peace and quiet. That way, I will be calm and collected, and the maid of honor I need to be. Can you do that for me, please?"

She finally climbed to the deck and looked out across the white sand to the breathtaking view of the Gulf of Mexico. Boy, did she need this.

"Suz? Suz? Did you hear me?"

"No, the reception must be bad," she lied. "What did you say?"

"I asked if you were coming to the condo or the church first on the day of the wedding?"

She lifted the welcome mat and found the key Royce left for her. "I thought we agreed to meet at the church and get dressed there. Remember? You were afraid you might get your dress dirty in the limo."

"Oh. Right. Well, have a great vacation. Just don't forget to show up for my wedding!"

"Don't worry, I won't." Unfortunately. "Well, I need to get my suitcase in the house and unpack. I'll see you Saturday." She flipped her phone closed before her sister could say another word. And Meg always had another word to say.

Flipping open the phone again, she powered down. If someone wanted to contact her, they could leave a voicemail and she would get back to them when she turned on her phone again.

Stepping into the dimness of the house, she waited for her eyes to adjust from the bright sunshine.

"Wow," she said when she could see again. "Royce has been busy." The massive great room, open to the second floor, had recently been redecorated in a Tuscan style not totally dissimilar to Royce and Jack's new home.

Overstuffed brown leather couch, loveseat, and two recliners grouped around a massive square coffee table holding a large wooden bowl of decorative spheres. On the far side of the table sat three wrought iron candleholders of varying heights, each with squat candles that gave off an herbal aroma. The fieldstone fireplace soared to the point of the ceiling high above her head.

She kicked off her sandals and wiggled her toes in the plush area rug, and looked around. Dark granite adorned the countertops of the large kitchen, as well as the island. She flipped a switch, illuminating the kitchen, its gleaming stainless appliances glowing in the pot lights and recessed can lights. It was unfortunate her culinary skills were so limited.

She laughed. Limited was an understatement. If she couldn't nuke it, it didn't get cooked. Too bad she didn't have more time here, she thought, trailing her hand along the cool, smooth granite. Maybe she could learn to cook. She looked at the large hot tub on the deck. Maybe not. Cooking wasn't nearly as much fun as the ocean and hot tubs.

Trudging up the stairs to the master suite—Royce had told her there was only one bedroom, which boggled the mind, given the size of the place—she paused at the double door. "Wow."

The outer wall, made entirely of glass, curved, giving a panoramic view. She looked around for the remote Royce had told her about and found it on the dark espresso color dresser. A press of a button started a whirring noise. Slowly, the glass opened, disappearing into the wall, and the sound of the ocean filled the room, giving the impression of standing in a gigantic seashell.

"I could definitely get used to a place like this," she said, tossing her suitcase on the round bed and padding to the accessible balcony.

Below her, what looked to be a prime male specimen ran along the beach.

Maybe Royce and Jack would have an opening soon so she could rent the place for longer than forty-eight hours. She might even take up jogging.

Guilt tugged at her. She really should get back to her sister in time for the rehearsal dinner. But Meg had told her to take some time for herself. They all knew what they needed to do, and after all, it would be a small wedding. But her sister wasn't as selfish as Suzanne.

"One day. I'll just stay one day to rest, work on my tan, relax, then head back."

2

Braedon Wright turned over on the scratchy chaise on the deck of his twin brother's beach house, and winced at the relentless sunshine. Where was a cloud when you needed one? No doubt, Pleasure Beach was just too damn cheerful. From the blue sky, to the pristine sandy beach, to the uber cheerful employees at the restaurant down the beach, to the baby soft yellow his brother's decorator had painted the beach house.

He was not in the mood for cheerful.

The cool beer bottle dripped its condensation onto his belly while he took a sip, listening to the endless sound of wave after wave crashing onto the shore. What was the attraction of living on the beach? Peace and quiet? Between the waves and the sea gulls, it held neither of those qualities for him.

Although he had enjoyed running on the beach for the last two weeks, he was ready to go back to Corpus Christi and get on with his life. His brother, Ryan, was right about one thing: It was past time to grow up.

Thoughts of Ryan brought thoughts of his brother's upcoming nuptials. Braedon took another swig of beer in an attempt to calm the uneasiness that thought provoked.

"Time to face fact, Braedon, old man," he told himself in a low voice. "In about forty-eight hours, Penny will be your sister-in-law. Isn't that just ironic as hell?"

A few months ago, Penny, his future sister-in-law, had been his fiancée, living and sleeping with *him*. Sure, the engagement hadn't really been his idea, but rather a way of hiding behind the needy Penny to keep away from her loan shark father. Now, thanks to Ryan, all that was behind him.

Still, he suspected it might feel a bit weird to stand at the altar and watch his brother make vows to a woman Braedon knew in the biblical sense.

He gave a bark of laughter, and tossed the now empty bottle into the recycle bin on the deck. If he steered clear of all the women he'd slept with, he'd have to become a hermit.

Kind of a sobering thought.

Ryan had given Braedon his life back, and for that he would be forever in his debt. If it meant standing up at his wedding as best man, so be it.

Penny's granddad may be senile, but he had a point when he used to say it was never too late to start over. Braedon was going to start over. Or, at least, give it one hell of a try.

Suzanne stretched and smiled, her toes rubbing on the silk sheets, as she listened to the sound of the surf. Today would be the only day she had to enjoy Pleasure Beach, and she didn't want to miss a thing.

After a quick shower, she donned her new bikini and slathered on sunscreen while the coffeemaker gurgled. She'd work on her tan for a while, then go for a run when the hunky runner ran by. Who knew? Maybe he would turn out to be Mr. Right. One thing was for sure: If she didn't try, she'd never know. So what if she'd never ran in her life. Megan ran every day. Since they'd initially been one person, that would mean she should have the running gene, too. She hoped. There was only one way to find out.

She smiled, liking her new motto for her life. No more tried and true. She was woman, hear her roar. Suzanne Hartley, adventure woman.

After two cups of coffee, she was ready to face the sunshine. Arranging her towel and the chair for optimum even exposure, she stretched out, willing relaxation to take her to a place she'd never been: tranquility.

Evidently, relaxation was on a coffee break. Huffing a breath, she turned to her stomach, wishing she had a hot cabana boy to apply sunscreen to her back. Or maybe her front, which would make it more interesting.

Sweat trickled along her hairline, then dripped on the towel next to her nose. Damn, the sun was hot.

She turned over again, idly wondering how long the waffle bumps from the towel would stay on her thighs like some weird form of cellulite. Shielding her eyes with her hand, she scanned the deserted beach. Didn't anyone go to the beach in May?

Then she saw him.

He looked to be running at a fast pace, even from a distance. She sat up straighter, sucking in her stomach. Oblivious, he blasted past her to become a speck in the distance within seconds.

Exhaling, she slumped down in her chair.

Her nipples began tingling, a warning of things to come. Throughout their lives, she and her sister had shared not only identical looks, but a sicko connection for feelings. All feelings, not just pain. Pain she could handle. Sadness she could handle. It was the escalation of sharing, in adulthood, that got to her. In all fairness, it probably wasn't a thrill for her sister, either. Experiencing each other's sexual activity and resulting orgasms was, by far, the worst. Not to mention downright draining. And embarrassing as hell, especially if it happened in a crowd.

Oh, yeah, here it comes again. She clamped her legs together in an effort to staunch the moisture. Of course, it didn't help. It never did.

She supposed it was payback. For years, she'd been blissfully unaware of sending her sister into orgasm after orgasm. Meg had paid her back from time to time, but nothing like the activity of late. Since Megan had hooked up with Jake, things had never been the same.

Sure, Meg deserved to find love and have that special relationship. Suz knew that, on some level, and would never think of denying her sibling. Well, okay, maybe never was too strong of a word. For sure, there were times, of late, when her sister's sexual bliss had served as an agonizing reminder of her lack of a significant other. Or even an intense sexual relationship. Right now, she wasn't too picky. She'd settle for either one.

Beneath her bikini bottom, her femininity swelled and wept in preparation for the act and its inevitable resolution.

Her back arched, her hips bucking. She held onto the armrests of the chaise in a white-knuckled grip, her chest heaving, praying her sister's fiancée would act out of character and do a quick wham, bam, thank-you ma'am.

Fat chance.

Instead, she rolled from side to side, her body aching for fulfillment. When it finally came, it took her breath away. Her eyes rolled back in her head at the sheer ecstasy of the wave of completion washing over her.

Drained, she lay there panting, waiting for her heart rate to return to something less than stroke level. This one had been a biggie. The muscles in her legs and arms felt wrung out.

There he was again. A speck in the distance, growing larger with each step, bringing him closer to her.

Struggling to get out of the chaise, she ordered her wobbly

muscles to hold her in an upright position. Keeping a watchful eye on her quarry, she stretched and bent like she'd seen her sister do hundreds of time in preparation for a run. Gauging the distance, she set off to intersect his path along the water.

"Ooh! Ow! Hot, hot, hot!" She did a little skipping hop across the lava-like sand, breathing a sigh of relief when her bare feet touched the wet and much cooler sand closer to the water.

Jogging in place, she watched him close the distance. Oh, yeah, baby, the jogger was one hot piece of work. She set off, *accidentally* falling into step next to him.

"Hi," she said with a smile while she tried not to wheeze. "Great day for a run, isn't it?"

He flashed a blinding white smile which would have melted a less determined woman into a puddle of need. "Hi. I don't remember seeing you around. Do you live here, or just visiting?"

"Um . . ." Huff, huff, huff. "I, ah . . ." Huff, huff, huff.

Then, unbelievably, things got worse, if that were possible.

Her sister's climax roared down on Suz without warning, buckling her knees. She fell to the wet sand, wheezing and sobbing, partly from exertion, partly from her sister's rotten timing. Mostly because she really was attracted to the man looking down at her with such concern.

"Are you okay?" Braedon tamped down his self-directed anger. He'd been happily jogging next to the goddess in the hot pink bikini, wondering if he was about to get lucky, when she collapsed. If he hadn't been such a self-centered asshole, he might have seen she was in distress and been able to slow the pace, or even help her. So much for turning over a new leaf.

Hope dawned.

The old Braedon would have taken her to his place to allegedly help her, and ended up between her shapely legs. Determined to learn from past mistakes, the new Braedon would take a different, more noble, course of action.

He touched his running shorts where his cell should have been and came up empty. Damn. He'd put it on the charger last night.

"Stay there. I'll call nine-one-one. Hang on. I'll be right back!" With that, he turned and sprinted toward his brother's house, feeling good about his actions for the first time in years.

3

Two days later, Braedon breathed a sigh of relief as he left Ryan and Penny's reception to find some solace in the hotel bar. He'd had about all the happiness he could stand for one day.

He was happy for Ryan, he really was. Well, sort of. The fact that his former fiancée was now married to his brother would take some adjustment.

As he made his way down the floral carpeted hallway to the lobby, he again thought of the bikini clad goddess he'd left on Pleasure Beach. Oddly, instead of viewing her disappearance as a missed booty call, he realized he hoped she was okay. The paramedics had arrived within minutes of his emergency call to find a deserted beach. With no sign of his mysterious stroke or seizure victim, they'd left, leaving him to wander the beach for the next two hours, to no avail. It was like she'd been a figment of his imagination.

Even his imagination wasn't that good.

He paused inside the bar entrance to allow his eyes to adjust, then made his way to the polished bar and took a seat on the leather clad stool.

He was on his third—or fourth—Manhattan when a vision appeared in the doorway.

Okay, maybe vision was too strong. But she was definitely a sight. Wearing what had to be the world's ugliest bridesmaid dress—it had to be a bridesmaid dress since it went way beyond street-clothes-ugly—in a color his mom called *puce,* her blond hair in a partial updo, with pieces of roses and leaves hanging from the dangling strands. One sleeve had an oversized ruffle larger than the woman's head. The other appeared to have been ripped off. A jagged tear went from one armpit halfway across one plump breast, partially exposed by the rent in the fabric. As he watched in horrified fascination, she hobbled toward the bar.

Halfway there, she stopped and lifted her long skirt, and the reason for her hobbling became obvious. She wore one spiked high heel and one . . . not. Leaning against a vacant table, she took off her shoes, kicked them under the table, and continued her trek to the bar.

With a grunt, she pulled herself onto the stool next to him. "Tequila shot," she said to the bartender when he walked up.

After the bartender set her drink, a salt shaker, and a bowl of sliced limes on the bar, her eyes widened as she frantically patted her torso. "Shit."

"Problem?" Braedon motioned to the bartender to give him another drink.

In answer, she downed her drink, then motioned for another.

"Are you staying with us?" the bartender, whose name tag said Raj, asked. "I can start a tab for you . . ."

Her shoulders slumped. Well, the bare one did. It was difficult to tell about the other. "No, I'm just here for my sister's stupid wedding. I—"

"Room 403," Braedon interrupted. "Put her drinks on my tab."

The bartender nodded and walked away after setting her up again.

He watched her lick the salt off the back of her hand, and throw back the shot, then suck on the lime wedge.

"Don't you think you should slow down on those things?" He knew what he was talking about since his own lips were pleasantly numb. "Have you had anything to eat? You really don't want to drink on an empty stomach."

She glared at him with the eye not covered by a hunk of hair, then attempted to blow the offending piece of hair away from her face. The attempt failed, but it didn't prevent her from continuing to try. Giving up, she shoved the hair aside, only to have it flop back into place. Or out of place, depending on your point of view.

"Too late," she said in a slightly husky, slightly slurred voice.

Oh, man, he could see how things could get ugly quick. "Why don't you let me buy you something to eat? I had a hamburger here last night and it was pretty good."

"Maybe I'm a vegi-vegetarian." She threw back another drink.

"Are you?"

"Am I what?"

"A vegetarian."

"What makes you think I'm a vegetarian?" She started to slide toward the side. He grabbed her and pushed her back on the barstool.

"I have no idea. I think you're drunk."

"Nah," she said, waving one hand in his general direction while motioning to the bartender to bring another shot with the other. "You're not drunk, you know, if you can lie on the floor without holding on." She winked and picked up her drink.

Why he persisted in trying to help was a mystery, but he felt compelled. "Why don't you let me buy you something to eat?" he asked again.

"Okay, why?"

And why did he have the urge to bang his head repeatedly on the bar? Instead, he said, "I didn't get much to eat and it's past lunchtime. Let's both have a hamburger." He waved to the bartender to place their order.

Suzanne watched the man next to her, part of her wishing he'd just leave her alone, and part of her admiring how cute he looked in what appeared to be a very expensive tuxedo. Although she could do without the cloying scent of the rose in his lapel. Wait, maybe it was the crappy roses tangled in her hair she smelled.

It was wrong to allow him to pay for her drinks and food. She had plenty of money. She just didn't know exactly where any of it was at that precise moment.

It was also wrong to let him assume she was drunk. But it was easier than talking or, worse, explaining. Watching her beaming twin sister walk down the aisle that morning was one of the most difficult things she'd ever endured. Nothing like watching the closest person to yourself getting married to depress a girl.

As soon as possible, after the interminable picture-taking, the obligatory toasts, the bland food, and sickeningly sweet cake, she'd made her exit. She should have gotten in her car and driven to the little cottage down the beach her sister had rented for the bridal party. But something had driven her to the bar. Something besides the urge to drink herself into oblivion. Maybe she wasn't ready to be alone again.

Only this time, she was truly alone. Except for those first moments of life, her sister had always been right there with her. Although they'd disliked being lumped together as *the twins,* she more than Megan, now the idea of being separated was . . . odd.

To her horror, tears welled, then spilled down her cheeks.

The guy looked distinctly uncomfortable, but she had to give him credit for not running screaming from the bar. Instead he put his arm around her, awkwardly patting her bare shoulder, murmuring, "It's okay. Please don't cry."

She'd get used to her sister not being around, cramping her style. Hell, she'd probably revel in it, once the newness wore off. But, for right now, she'd rather not be alone.

And the babe consoling her, buying her drinks and making sure she had some food, was a slam-dunk winner over the alternative.

She squinted her eyes. Oh, no, it couldn't be. What are the chances she'd bump into the runner from Pleasure Beach all the way in Corpus Christi? Even though it had only been a few days, he obviously didn't recognize her. Which was a good thing, since she really, really thought he was totally hot, and felt almost desperate to get to know him.

"So," he said, fiddling with the torn sleeve of the bridesmaid-dress-from-hell. "It looks as though we have something in common." He motioned to his impeccable tuxedo. "Looks like we were both in weddings today. My brother got married." He looked expectantly at her.

"Sister," she said, then slammed back another shot. She tried to ignore the way he stared at the mess her dress had morphed into, but finally sighed and said, "I had a sort of accident." She shook her head. "Damn bridesmaids. They're vicious! I didn't even want the stupid bouquet. I only stood there because it was expected of me. One second I was standing, looking up at my sister on the little balcony as she got ready to throw the bouquet. The next, I was tackled by a bunch of jackals, being rolled from one end of the dance floor to the other while they fought over it." She shuddered. "Don't laugh. It was terrifying. I could have been killed."

As it was, she had just a slow death by mortification by having to tolerate the hideous dress her normally sane sister had chosen.

"You win," he said, wiping tears of mirth from his eyes.

"The wedding I was in was a distant second. All I had to do was watch my brother marry my ex-fiancée."

She winced. "Ow. That sucked, I bet."

"Let's just say it wasn't on my top ten list of things to do." He motioned to the wonderful smelling burger basket the bartender had set before her sometime during her sob story. "Eat before it gets cold."

Braedon watched the woman beside him as she ate. She looked vaguely familiar. Damn, he hoped he hadn't done anything to her to make her want to do bodily harm to him. She seemed harmless enough. Then again, he'd dated some real whack jobs over the years who had seemed harmless at the time.

It was a pretty safe bet he'd never taken her out. He'd have remembered her appetite. When she finally came up for air, he felt it was safe to offer his hand. "I'm sorry, I didn't introduce myself earlier. I'm Braedon Wright."

She wiped her hand on an extra napkin, and shook his hand. "Hi. Suzanne Hartley." She looked at her empty plate and shrugged. "Sorry for all the theatrics. Guess I was just hungry."

He thought her tears had nothing to do with food, but it was none of his business. "No doubt. How about dessert? They have a great dessert menu. I can personally recommend the Snickers turtle cheesecake." Even if she was full, he'd order some since it was his newfound favorite. Maybe he could coax her into taking a bite, just to try it.

"Yum! Sounds delicious. Absolutely. Bring it on!"

Okay, then. With an appetite like that, he couldn't help speculating what other kind of voracious appetite she might have.

4

"Thanks for lunch." Suz extended her hand to Braedon as she hopped down from her barstool. "And the drinks. It was nice meeting you." She took a reluctant step back. "I should probably be going now." *Tell me to stop, ask me out, kiss me, anything. Just don't let me walk away.*

He jumped to his feet, clutching her hand. "Wait. Do you have to leave right now?"

She glanced down at her dress, then back up at him with a deadpan look. "What do you think? Do you really think I want to hang out in this monstrosity?"

He chuckled. "Yeah, it is pretty bad. I didn't say anything earlier because I didn't want to hurt your feelings."

"Oh, so now you do?" She smiled to let him know she was teasing.

"Hey." He put both hands out, palm up, and shrugged. "I figure I bought your drinks and lunch, I can be honest now."

"Gee, thanks." She raised on tiptoe and kissed his cheek. "Thanks. Really. For the drinks, the food, and the company. I had a great time." Turning, she started walking from the bar.

"Wait," he said, falling in step beside her. "I heard you say you're not staying at the hotel. Where are you staying? Or do you live around here? I thought maybe we could go out to dinner or something. Later." He grinned. "After you change."

What the hell? "Sure. I'd like that." Surprisingly, she would. Braedon seemed like a nice guy. The fact that he was hot was an added bonus. She hadn't dated a guy who was both hot and nice in, like . . . never. Maybe her penchant for picking losers was finally ending. "No, I don't live here. I have a place in Houston. My sister rented a beach cottage not far from here for me." She paused. "How about you? Since you're staying here, I guess you don't live around here either."

"Actually, I do. I have a condo not far from here, as a matter of fact. Unfortunately, my ex-fiancée, rather, my new *sister-in-law* and my brother are staying there until they leave for their honeymoon."

"That was really sweet of you, all things considered, to let them use your place."

"Actually, Penny—that's her name—put down half of the down payment, so she owns half of it. Plus, her grandparents live in the unit next door." He shrugged. "I guess, after they get back from their honeymoon, we'll have to straighten it all out. Ryan lives in Houston, so it's not like she's going to want the condo anyway. Still, I'll probably sell it."

She nodded. "Bad memories?"

Grinning, he plucked part of an orange rose from her hair and tossed it in the hall trash as they walked past. "More like no memories. Just a giant, money-sucking lesson."

"Well," she said, pausing at the beach access door, "if you ever decide to relocate to Houston, I can help. I'm a realtor there."

"I just may do that." He held the door for her. "I'll walk you home."

"That's really not necessary." Instant images of her clothing strewn all around the little cottage flitted through her mind. "It's not far. I'll be fine."

"Well, maybe I won't be fine. I'll worry about you." He stepped onto the sand and tucked her hand in the crook of his arm. "Humor me."

"I love the beach." As they walked along the sand, Suzanne inhaled deeply and smiled up at him. "If I didn't have to work, I'd seriously consider relocating."

"There's real estate at the beach, too, you know."

"I know. I guess I just didn't think about that. Plus, right now I have to stand in for my sister while she's on her honeymoon. She's a realtor, too."

"You two work together?" That would be his idea of hell, if he had to work with Ryan.

"Lord, no! I'd have to kill her. We get along better now than ever before, but I still couldn't work with her." She motioned to the next bungalow-style cottage. "This is where I'm staying."

Smiling up at him, bathed in the glow of the late afternoon sun, she made even the butt-ugly dress look sexy. He should just leave her and come back later to take her to dinner. Maybe in a minute.

"What time should I pick you up for dinner?" He slid his arm around her, pulling her close, breathing in the scent of roses.

"I'm too full to even think about eating anything right now." She grinned up at him. "You don't have to take me to dinner."

"Sure I do. I asked. You accepted. It's a date." He narrowed his eyes, leaning closer. "Unless you're trying to get rid of me?"

"Nope. Just trying to give you an easy out." She toyed with his tie, slightly rubbing against his increasingly excited body.

"You could invite me in. That way, when you decide you're hungry, I'll already be there to take you out." Arms around her, he swayed to and fro. It was absurd. He'd never felt the urge to hang around any woman ever, before meeting Suzanne. What was it about her that seemed so familiar?

"I can't. Trust me. The place is a total pit. It's embarrassing."

"How much of a pit can it be? How long have you been here? Maybe two, three days at the most? No more than a week. You're one small woman. I doubt you could really mess up a place in that amount of time." He nudged her toward the door. "I'll even help you clean up."

Admittedly, that would be a first. Penny used to always complain about his lack of domesticity.

But Suzanne was not Penny. His cock knew the difference from first sight. Why was he continuing to make comparisons? Maybe it was safer. Something about the short woman standing next to him scared the hell out of him. Yet, even so, he found he didn't want to leave her. Scary, if he thought about it for too long.

"Okay." She tugged him toward the door. "But don't say I didn't warn you."

Yowza. For one small woman, she did a great impression of making it look like a tornado had whipped through the place.

"I told you it was a mess." She snatched up what looked like several pieces of sexy lingerie, and he had to wonder what activities had gone on before she'd left for the wedding. And, hot on that thought, did he want to be one in a potentially long line? Wasn't that what his dates had always been? A sobering thought, for sure.

"Did you do this all by yourself, or did you have company?" He picked up a lacy bra and twirled it around on his index finger, telling himself it didn't really matter. They were simply passing time together.

"Give me that!" Cheeks pink, she stuffed the bra into a duffel on the couch. "I didn't get around to doing laundry before I left, so I washed after I got here. I don't put my underwear in the dryer, so I laid them around to dry. And I slept in yesterday, then couldn't decide what to wear to the rehearsal dinner." She waved her hand at the strewn clothing adorning the chair and sofa. "The only mirror is on the back of the door. Let me tell you, that makes doing hair and makeup an adventure."

He reached out and flipped her less-than-tidy hairdo. "I see that," he said with a grin.

"Very funny." Yanking at the dead flowers in her hair as she talked, she continued picking up clothes with her other hand. "I know there's furniture under here somewhere. I—oh!"

Kissing her at that moment was probably not his brightest idea, but it was the only one he had at the time.

As soon as his mouth covered hers, she melted against him with a sexy little squeak.

It was all the encouragement he needed.

5

Oh, wow. Braedon really knew how to kiss. Her muscles were weak. If he weren't holding her up, she'd surely melt into a boneless puddle of goo. His fingertips traced the plunging neckline of her dress. Well, what was left of the neckline of her dress. Regardless, it felt decadent, wonderful. Everywhere he touched her, he left a little trail of sparks. Heat flushed her cheeks, moisture—oh, no! Her sister and Jake must have left their reception and decided to start the honeymoon early.

Her breathing became labored. Beneath her bridesmaid dress, her nipples tightened to hard peaks, scraping painfully against the half cup of her lace bra. Moisture surged. Her knees went weak, making it increasingly difficult to remain upright.

Abort! Abort! Her mind screamed subliminal messages to her sister in a frantic, useless plea. If she went into another orgasmic swoon, Braedon would put two and two together, and realize she was the woman on the beach. How embarrassing.

It could not be happening at a worse time. True, Meg never had the best of timing, for anything, but since she's been with

Jake, it's like she's rediscovered sex. Meg Hartley, Energizer sex bunny.

Braedon's obvious erection bumped against her. *Hello.* Maybe inviting him in wouldn't be a total disaster, after all. He was obviously revved up and ready to go. Thanks to her sister, she was primed and ready for action, too.

It could work.

Braedon knew he should back away before he embarrassed them both. And he would. In a minute. It felt so good to hold her, kiss her, taste her.

Inside his tuxedo trousers, her hand closed around him, rubbing up and down, squeezing, torturing.

What was happening to him? The woman had put her hand down his pants. The old Braedon would have had her stripped in a nanosecond. But, instead, her actions gave him pause. Make no mistake, it felt wonderful, but . . .

She tugged at his trousers until they fell around his feet. His boxers followed.

He could salvage the moment. He could back away with his dignity intact—assuming he didn't fall over his pants. And he would have, if she hadn't chosen that moment to drop the ugly bridesmaid dress and stand before him in nothing but her underwear. The orange lace thong and matching itsy-bitsy bra left very little to the imagination.

When it came to women, he always did have a great imagination.

Still, even he had his scruples. She'd had a lot to drink. They both had. Even though it felt as though he'd known her all of his life, in reality it had only been a few hours.

"Are you sure this is what you want?" He couldn't believe he said that. But, suddenly, her answer was important.

She nodded, running her hands appreciatively over his buttocks and hips, shoving his shirt aside, the buttons pinging in several directions. Panting, she said, "You have a fantastic body."

He swallowed. He must be in a lot better shape than he thought, since she was already panting. "Thanks. I'm a runner. My body is a temple." What the hell was he babbling about? His body was a temple? Where had that come from?

She popped the front closure on her bra, her exposed breasts smooth and supple looking in the indirect light coming from the other room, and nodded. "Absolutely. My body is a temple. Five days a week." She hopped into his arms, wrapping her legs around his waist, her now naked, moist center pressing intimately against him. "The other two days, it's an amusement park." She jiggled her breasts against his chest and whispered in his ear, "Want to go on an E-ticket ride?"

He'd have to be a fool to turn down what she was offering.

His mama didn't raise a fool.

She cried out when he entered her, still standing with his pants around his ankles, and climaxed, squeezing his cock before he was even totally in.

He flexed his hips, going deeper, and prepared to set the rhythm.

His natural rhythm of sex was immediately shot to hell by her second screaming orgasm within as many minutes.

Damn. He must be better than he thought.

Her inner muscles began clamping again. Furiously, he pumped, forgetting technique in his effort to go for his personal land-speed record. Her nails dug into his shoulders. Her breath came in guttural groans, her hips flexing faster and faster.

Her back arched, her internal muscles clamping and unclamping, milking him. He tried thinking of baseball. Football. Laundry. Anything to take his mind of the intense reaction of his body to hers.

Her hips bucked, causing her pelvic bone to rock hard into his at the same time her back arched again. The force of her movement, combined with the beginning of his own climax, caused him to stumble backwards.

His feet tangled in his pants, refusing to cooperate with his efforts to not fall. On his way back, his hip hit the edge of the sofa, ricocheting him in the other direction, where he took out the floor lamp.

The crash barely registered, due to the blood roaring in his ears.

Falling backward, he tried to roll to keep from landing on her with his entire weight. His head hit the hardwood floor with a painful thump as he finished coming.

Amazingly, Suzanne wasn't finished with him yet.

Drawing her knees up, she rode him hard and fast, clamping her legs against him with enough pressure to crack a rib, while she finished sucking him dry. With an exhausted cry, she collapsed on his sweat-slicked chest, her heart pounding against his rib cage, while his heart felt like it was trying to break through from the other side.

They lay there for several minutes, while their breathing and heart rates slowed.

Pain originated between his shoulder blades and radiated outward. Exhausted, he ignored it as long as he could before rolling, holding her clamped to his chest, and reaching behind to see what he was laying on.

"I assume this is yours?" He held a red high heeled sandal in front of her face. "I think it stabbed me."

She laughed and snuggled closer. "Don't be so dramatic."

"Who's being dramatic? Didn't you ever see *Single White Female?* The guy from *Wings* bought the farm by being stabbed between the eyes with one of these things." He tossed the shoe aside. "Gave me nightmares for months. Not to mention a whole new attitude toward women's footwear as weapons."

She raised her head to prop her chin on her hands and look him in the eye. "Do you want me to kiss it and make it better?"

Damn, she was cute. Not to mention sexy. And hot. And did

he mention sexy? Still buried deep within her, his cock stirred in agreement.

And she was also in all probability still drunk. He'd made it a lifelong rule to not do drunk women. They inevitably turned out to be more trouble than they were worth.

With a sigh, he disengaged their bodies and set her aside to stand with as much dignity as he could muster, while he pulled up his drawers.

Grabbing her dress, she covered herself and watched him finish dressing. "Are you really hurt?"

"No. Well, yes, if you're talking about my dignity." He snickered. "We're lucky we didn't do more damage than we did. I'll pay for the lamp, if you find out how much it is."

"Don't worry about it. I'm sure they're charging my new brother-in-law a bundle as it is. A lamp will hardly matter." She stood, wrapping the voluminous skirt closer around her nudity. "Are you mad?"

"What? Why would I be mad?" He gave up looking for the rest of his shirt buttons. "I'm the one who acted like a caveman, throwing you around while I tried to screw your brains out. Are you mad at me?"

"Did I act like I was mad?" She shoved some clothes aside and sat down on the couch, pulling her feet up under the skirt. A shy smile curved her kiss-swollen lips. "It was fun."

Reality dawned. It was fun. He honestly couldn't remember ever actually having fun and sex at the same time. Hell, or even with the same person.

He liked it.

He liked her.

6

Suzanne tossed aside another blouse and dug around in her suitcase, glancing nervously at her watch. Braedon would be back in less than half an hour, and she still couldn't find anything to wear.

Thoughts of their wild sex that afternoon elicited a flush of arousal. She couldn't remember laughing with any of her other sexual partners. It was nice. Different, but nice. And she wanted it again. All of it. An orgasm that was entirely her own would be nice, too.

After Braedon left, she'd experienced three more empathetic orgasms during her shower. She was lucky she could still walk. All had been quiet for the last two hours, so she could only assume her sister and her groom were asleep. Now, if they'd just stay that way for the rest of the night.

Fanning herself while she thought of all the yummy things she'd like to do with Braedon, she wondered if it would be too obvious to meet him at the door naked. They could always order a pizza. Hmm. Pizza. She could come up with some creative things to do with pizza. And none of it added calories.

The sound of shattering glass filled the room twice before she located her cell phone. "Meg, you're supposed to be on your honeymoon. Why are you calling me?"

"I was worried about you. Are you okay?"

"Of course I'm okay." She held up a red dress and wondered if she remembered to pack her red bra. "Why wouldn't I be?"

"Well, you kind of got knocked around during the bouquet toss. Then you disappeared." She lowered her voice to a whisper. "And I had some very unusual orgasms. You know, what you used to call headbangers? Did you meet someone, or did Jake do all that?"

"Of course it was all Jake, you lucky girl! Now get off the phone and go wear out your new groom." *And stop calling me.* She flipped her phone shut.

Braedon knocked on the door of the guest cottage and shifted from foot to foot. He'd like nothing more than an instant replay of the mind-blowing sex he'd experienced with Suzanne that afternoon. But he didn't want to scare her away.

"Hi," she said, opening the door for him in nothing but a red thong and matching push-up bra. At least he assumed it was a push-up bra since her breasts looked like they were trying to make an escape.

"Are we eating in? I gotta tell you, that's a little too casual for where I had in mind." He bent to kiss her as he walked past, then waited until she'd closed the door to pull her into his arms. "'Course, I could always be talked into staying right here."

"Down, boy," she said when he rubbed the proof of her effect against her. "I just haven't gotten dressed yet. Where are we going?"

"There's a steak house down Ocean Drive a ways that's pretty good. Then I thought we might go to the carnival that's in town. Do you like carnival rides? How about cotton candy?"

"All of it sounds great. Just give me a few minutes to throw on some clothes."

The steaks were good, the company better.

She looked up from her dessert coffee to meet Braedon's heated gaze. "What?" She ran her tongue over her lips to check for cappuccino foam. "Do I have something on my face?"

Slowly he shook his head. "No, I'm just admiring the view." He frowned and picked up his cup. "But I wish I didn't know what color your underwear is." He took a sip and set his cup on the table again. "All I can think about is stripping off your sin-with-me red dress. The bra and panties would be the next to go."

She met his gaze and tried not to squirm on the leather chair. "You promised to take me to the carnival. I want my cotton candy."

Throwing some bills on the table, he stood and pulled her up. "That I did. Let's get going before they're sold out."

"Carnivals have a unique smell," Suz said, skipping along next to Braedon, her hand in his. "Did you ever notice that?" She inhaled and smiled up at him. "It's like a combination of cotton candy, candy apples, and barbeque. Don't you just love it?"

"If you love it, I love it," he told her, steering her toward the ticket booth.

"Omigod!" Suz had a stranglehold on his neck, her head burrowed against his neck. "I forgot I'm afraid of heights! Get me down!" The Ferris wheel car they were in began to rock. "Oh, no! Make it stop!"

He held her tight, not minding a bit. "Are you really afraid of heights?"

She peeked up to meet his gaze, her eyes sparkling. "Not

really. I thought I'd just give you a chance to play macho protector."

In retaliation, he set the car to rocking, eliciting shrieks from Suzanne that sounded suspiciously like screams.

"Okay, okay! Maybe I'm just a little bit afraid. That doesn't mean you can scare me, though." She pretended to pout. At least, he thought she was pretending.

"How about if I make it up to you with some cotton candy?" He helped her down when the ride came to a stop at their car and the operator threw aside the safety bar.

"Cotton candy is good." She thanked the ride operator's wife for holding the duck Braedon had won for her at the ring toss booth.

"It won't hurt my feelings if you throw the goofy duck away," he said, pulling her toward the cotton candy maker's cart.

Relief washed through her, since she'd never been the type of person who liked stuffed animals, even as a child. "Maybe I'll give it to the next little girl I see."

Half an hour and two cotton candy cones later, she still had the stupid duck.

"What is this world coming to when parents suspect the motives of someone who wants to give their little girls a stuffed animal?" She sat glumly on the bench next to Braedon while he finished off his ice cream. "Did you see that last lady? My gosh, you'd think I'd asked her daughter to do porn or something, the way she acted. I think maybe I'm offended."

"I saw a toy donation barrel by the entrance. Let's just drop it in there on our way out." He wiped his hands on the napkin, then threw it in the trash.

"You don't want to go on any more rides?"

"I can't find the only ride I'd be interested in."

"There's a map on the bulletin board over there." She tugged him along behind her. "What's the name of the ride? Maybe we can figure out where it is."

His whispered reply made her gasp. "Braedon Wright! That's perverted."

He laughed, hugging her to his side as they walked toward the exit. "I know where we can find a ride like that."

She dropped the duck into the donation bin and gave him a disinterested look. "Oh, really? Gee, what a surprise."

"You need to carry a stool in your truck," she said when he lifted her into the passenger side.

"This is much more fun," he told her, running his hand up under her skirt.

She swatted his hand. "Cut that out! Someone might see us."

"So I can do it if no one is watching?" He closed his door and started the powerful engine.

"Maybe, if you're lucky." Leaning over the console, she pushed his zipper down, freeing his erection. Her fingers traced the veins, circled the head.

"Careful, missy, you're playing with fire."

"I doubt it. Not with this huge console separating us." She sighed. "I bet you never got lucky in this thing."

"You got that right. I've only had it a little over a week." He signaled and pulled onto Ocean Drive.

"What did you have before? Was it any more... accessible?"

He snorted. "Worse. It was a sports car. European. Fast, sleek, expensive as hell." He sighed. "Man, that thing purred and got to a hundred in the blink of an eye."

"Sounds like you liked it."

"I loved it. But I didn't love the price tag. It was a stupid thing to buy." He signaled again and turned into a gated drive. "I sold it and paid off some debts I'd racked up, then used the rest to buy this." He punched a series of numbers into a steel box and the gates parted.

"Do you live here?" It didn't look like any condo complex she'd ever seen.

"Nah. It belongs to my ex's dad."

"Um, should we be here? Isn't it trespassing? Besides, you may not be welcome since you're no longer engaged to his daughter."

"Don't worry. I'm sure they're all still at the reception. The whole family's big partiers. And since he's paying, it could go on all night." He followed the drive past a huge home and two smaller buildings that could be garages, finally coming to a stop by a dock, his headlights reflecting on the water. He turned to her, one hand draped over the steering wheel. "Ever done it on water?"

"With or without a boat?"

7

"Are you sure we're not trespassing?" she asked, stepping down into the rowboat, clutching his arm when the little boat rocked wildly.

"Shh. No, we're not trespassing. I told you, he said I was welcome to use it anytime I wanted. I think he was relieved I wasn't going to be his son-in-law."

"If we're not trespassing, why do I have to shush? And why are you whispering?"

"We don't want to alert his guard dogs."

"Guard dogs!" The boat rocked violently, almost throwing them out.

"Will you be quiet?" he whisper/yelled. "Are you afraid of dogs like you were afraid of heights?"

She edged closer to him, straining her eyes for movement along the shore. "No, I really am afraid of dogs. Especially guard dog types. What kind of dogs are they?"

"You probably don't want to know."

Shivering, she scanned the yard.

"Here, come sit closer to me. I'll keep you warm."

"Oh, ha! If you think you're going to get lucky in this little thing, think again, mister. We'll drown."

"While the aspect of you finishing what you started in my truck is appealing, a boat this size isn't exactly my fantasy, either, darlin'." He pointed into the bay. "We're going out there. See that big boat yonder? That's where we're headed."

Several minutes of quiet rowing brought them to the boat anchored in the bay.

"Wait a sec while I go aboard and turn off the alarm." Standing, he grasped the edge of the larger boat and hopped up, tying the line from the rowboat to a metal peg before disappearing.

"All clear," he announced a few minutes later, smiling down at her in the moonlight. "Need some help up?"

She started to stand, only to flop back onto the metal seat, clutching the sides of the rocking boat. "I think I'll stay right here."

Laughing, he climbed down, causing the rowboat to pitch and roll from side to side.

Screaming, she held on for dear life. "Cut it out! You're going to capsize us!"

"Stop fighting me. Now put your foot on the seat and climb up. I'll lift you the rest of the way."

After three false starts, her bare feet were firmly on the high gloss varnished deck of the boat. "I lost my sandals."

"You took them off in the truck."

Good to know, since they were her sister's shoes.

"Is this a small yacht?" Running her hand along the sleek smoothness of the rail, she made her way toward a stairway.

"Nah, it's more like a really big fishing boat. Charley loves to deep water fish." He motioned to the stairs. "After you. It sleeps six."

She looked around the compact quarters. "Six what? Small children?"

"The table and benches make beds, and the master bedroom is through that door."

Walking below deck in a boat was a little tricky. "This feels weird. Like my head isn't attached to my body. And my knees don't feel like they're working right." Placing a hand on each wall of the narrow walkway, she staggered to the door. "Oh, wow! It's like a tiny little bedroom."

"It *is* a bedroom," he said, close to her ear, setting off goose bumps. "Are you sure you're okay?"

"That depends, I guess," she said, flopping back on the plush gold and green silk comforter. "What do you have in mind?"

Several scenarios came to mind, but he'd vowed, after Penny, to stop vying for the title of Playboy of the Western Hemisphere. Their activities that afternoon had been a minor setback. If his brother could find a meaningful relationship, damn it, so could he.

And, if he planned to take the nobler route, the first course of action would be to get them out of the bedroom, away from temptation.

While he stood trying to come up with a safe alternative to what he really wanted to do, she scooted to the edge of the bed. Before he could do much more than look down at her, she had him unzipped.

Contrary to popular belief, Suzanne wasn't as free and easy as she let everyone believe. Sure, she'd had her share of relationships, both long- and short-term. She knew Meg thought she had enjoyed a lot of one-night stands of late, thanks to their shared orgasmic connection, but the reality had been much tamer. Not to mention safer.

But tonight, no batteries were required.

Standing before her was a drop-dead gorgeous, red-blooded male. Closing her hand around him, she bit back a smile. And he was ready, willing, and oh-so-able to satisfy her.

His velvet tip pulsed against the pad of her thumb, his shaft swelling impossibly harder in her hand.

Fish or cut bait seemed an appropriate analogy to shore up her courage now. *What are you waiting for?* It was not as though she'd never gone down on a guy before. Well, okay, not as many times as she'd have people believe, but still . . .

The fact that Braedon seemed different, the alarming possibility she may have finally found Mr. Right—she bit back a smile at the thought he was Mr. Wright and possibly Mr. Right—brought a hesitance, a shyness she hadn't experienced in a long time.

Shy? Her mind snickered. *You're holding the guy's family jewels, your mouth watering from anticipation, and you're shy?*

Scooting closer to the foot of the mattress, she spread her legs, trapping his, and gave a gentle tug.

Braedon took the small step to bring his legs against the edge of the mattress.

"I've been waiting all night to do this," she said, more to herself than Braedon.

Her tongue moistened her lips, then swiped at the tip of his penis. She placed a gentle kiss on the head, then took him into her mouth, not stopping until he touched the back of her throat.

They both groaned.

Setting her rhythm to the rhythm of the undulation of the boat, she began sucking, her tongue drawing lazy circles around his shaft.

She squirmed at the sensations zipping through her. Soon. He'd be in her soon. Anticipation would only add to the experience.

His hips bucked.

Unfortunately, so did the boat.

Her jaw jerked, but she didn't think she bit him. Well, not hard, anyway.

She was sure Braedon's roar could be heard for miles. Or, on boats, was it knots?

"Braedon!" She reached for him with one hand, the other gripping the comforter as the boat continued to rock. "I'm so sorry! Did I hurt you?"

"Well, you sure as hell didn't help me!" He tucked everything back into his pants and zipped up.

She noticed he stayed more than an arm's length away from her. Not that she blamed him, but, really, it had been an accident. He didn't seem to relax when she told him as much.

"We should have stayed up on deck." He raked a hand through his short blond hair. "Look, you probably don't believe me, but I didn't bring you here for this."

"You didn't?" Hearing it should have been a relief. After all, she'd worried about the impression she'd made by jumping his bones earlier. Why did it feel more like disappointment?

8

Braedon looked down at the sexy bombshell on the bed, and cursed his brother. It was all Ryan's fault for putting the stupid idea in his head that he could have a meaningful relationship with a woman.

The old Braedon Wright would have been buried deep in her lush heat by now. But, no. Now, thanks to some asinine competition he's had with his brother from birth, instead of looking to score, he was looking for . . . something more. Something deeper. Something real.

And it scared the shit out of him.

But, damn it, if Ryan could find it, why couldn't he?

"It's not that I'm not attracted to you." That sounded lame, even to him. "I mean, hell, look at you. I'd have to be dead to not be attracted to you." Or stupid. Or insane. At the moment, he wasn't sure he wasn't both. "I had fun today. And tonight."

"You could have more fun," she said, leaning back on her hands, breasts thrust against the snug top of her knit dress.

Even though a part of him leapt at the idea, his mind said no. Now if he could just get his mouth to say the same, he might have a shot at getting to know someone before jumping her bones.

Sure, technically, he'd already jumped her bones. But that didn't mean he was doomed to repeat performances. Or mistakes.

Guilt tugged at him. Having sex with her in the messy little beach house had definitely not felt like a mistake. Maybe that was the reason he wanted to take a step back, take things slower.

Maybe she was *the one*.

And if his other thought hadn't scared the shit out of him, this one sure as hell did.

Suzanne stood and brushed past him on her way out. "Forget I said that," she mumbled.

"Wait." He grabbed her arm, turning her to face him in the dimness of the cabin. "It's not that I'm not interested. After this afternoon, you know I'm attracted to you." He rubbed the smooth skin of her outer arm, not ready to sever the physical connection. "In fact, I can't remember when I've been more attracted to anyone."

Suzanne looked up into his earnest blue eyes while she tried to ignore the rub of his skin on her arm. Following the direction of his gaze, she did a mental groan when she saw the hard peaks of her nipples protruding. She'd always felt they were the female equivalent of a hard-on. Maybe Braedon wouldn't notice . . .

In slow motion, he reached out to glide his fingertips over the sensitized bumps.

Her breath caught, her nipples getting impossibly harder. Darn. He noticed.

"Maybe we could talk down here." His voice was husky, quiet in the intimacy of the cabin, his fingertips rubbing, rubbing, rubbing, robbing her of coherent thought and, quite possibly, the ability to stand.

"What—" she croaked, then licked her lips and tried again. "What did you have in mind?"

"How do you like being a realtor?" He tugged one strap off her shoulder. Then dragged his open mouth along the exposed skin.

"Um . . . I like it. Most of the time, anyway." She tilted her head to one side, giving him greater access. "I wish I could make a little more money, sometimes," she finished on a whisper.

"I thought there was big money in real estate." He tugged the other strap down, baring her to the waist, her breasts perched on the shelf of her half bra cups like she was serving them up for a snack. "So pretty," he whispered, bending to take a nipple into his mouth, bathing it with his hot tongue, then sucking it deeper.

Suddenly the allure of wearing naughty lingerie for more than the way they looked made sense. Functional. Who knew?

Moisture dampened her new thong. Her knees grew weak. Make that weaker.

When he'd said he wanted to talk, relief had washed through her. Now he obviously wanted to do more than talk, which was better.

Still sucking, he lifted her, his hands sliding beneath her skirt to cup her buttocks, grinding his hardness against her front.

Now what? Should she lock her legs around his hips to let him know she was interested in more than conversation, casual or otherwise?

Frustration built, along with her passion. Her sister would be surprised at her confusion. Hell, she was surprised. Although she wasn't really the free spirit Meg assumed her to be, she'd been around the block a few times.

Her last trip around the block, at her ten-year high school reunion, had really done a number on her confidence. That had to be the reason why, after she and Braedon had had sex in her rental beach house and he'd made his escape, she'd felt so dirty. Used. Yet anxiously anticipating their next encounter. How sick was that? If not sick, definitely confused.

Did she want a repeat of those emotions?

Braedon's finger insinuated itself under the elastic of her panties, rubbing her slick folds, ratcheting up her excitement another notch. He slid his finger in and wiggled it, his thumb now working her aching nub.

Her climax washed over her with such speed and ferocity, she wondered if it was all hers, or if her sister and her new husband were in on the action.

Braedon had just inserted his finger, pleased at how obviously ready she was, when her inner muscles began clamping on him, her juices drenching his hand.

Beneath his zipper, his cock jerked, impatient to be free to join the party.

Suzanne's dress bunched around her waist. He looked down, watching as he pleasured her.

It wasn't nearly enough.

Fumbling, he finally unzipped and freed his eager cock. Releasing her nipple, he shoved aside her scrap of underwear and flexed his hips once, driving deep into her welcoming heat.

She came apart in his arms, her back arching, eyes rolled back, nipples standing at attention. Her pussy clamped him, her inner muscles fiercely squeezing, milking him.

The muscles in the backs of his calves tightened. The backs of his thighs and ass followed. He couldn't have staved off the powerful orgasm that rocked him any more than he could have stopped the tide rocking the boat.

With a roar, he toppled them to the bed, clutching her to him while he struggled to remain conscious, to regulate his heartbeat. To take a deep breath.

Small. She felt so small in his arms. He tightened his grasp, attempting to get closer. Emotion clogged his throat. Hell, if he could, he'd crawl under her skin.

What was happening to him? He'd had sex many times in his life. It had never affected him the way it had tonight.

Must be the rocking of the boat. It made everything more intense. Yeah, that had to be it.

She moved, her inner muscles still clamping, caressing him from the inside. Renewing his erection.

Damn. He needed to buy a boat.

9

Suzanne wanted to protest when Braedon began to sit up, but she didn't have the strength. Hoping her body language conveyed the message, she whimpered and did a little wiggle, thrilled to feel him harden deep within, his penis stroking her passion-engorged passage. Exciting her all over again.

But instead of rolling her back and renewing his thrusting, he continued to sit up.

Luckily, he was still deeply embedded. Tugging on his shoulders, she thrust her hips up, rotating in an effort to deepen the connection.

He pulled her up, breast to chest, for a hug, his chuckle vibrating her chest.

"Turn around for me, darlin'." His voice rumbled against her ear. "I'm holding you. You're not going to fall. Trust me."

Amazingly, she did trust him.

While she pondered the latest revelation, he rotated her on his shaft until she faced away from him, his hands possessively cupping each breast.

He tugged, gently pulling her down until she was practically lying on her stomach, his hands beneath, squeezing her breasts

while he rotated his hips in lazy circles, achieving deeper penetration than she'd experienced to date.

Excitement built. She arched her back, pushing her breasts
further into his hands, begging for release, her hips grinding
against his.

It happened again. Her climax roared up, washing over her,
pulling her under, nearly drowning her in its intensity.

Behind her, Braedon increased his tempo. His hands gripped
her in a pleasure/pain grasp. His hips pounded into her, shoving her chest down into the mattress, dragging her sensitized skin
along the coarse texture of the spread. With a roar, he slammed
her back against him, once. Twice. Then his lean hips ground
into her as though he were trying to reach deep inside.

A slow slide took them to the mattress, his weight a solid
warmth along her back.

His heart pounded against her back in a duet with her own.

She wheezed in an attempt to drag air into her oxygen-
starved lungs.

Against her neck, his breath came in harsh pants, the huffs of
air ruffling her hair where it had escaped from her ponytail.

"Fuck," he said in an awed tone.

Right. She needed to remember that was exactly what it was.
Nothing more. So what if he rocked her world. Obviously he'd
had lots of practice. That thought caused a vague ache in her
heart, so she resolutely shoved it aside and attempted a worldly
sounding chuckle. "I thought we just did."

*Say it. Tell me it was more than that for you. That I am more
than that to you.*

Which, of course, was really stupid, since they'd just met.
What was wrong with her? Had her Goody Two-shoes sister
somehow crawled into her head and warped her brain?

Suzanne swirled the remnants of her wine, her goblet held
loosely between her fingers, while she watched Braedon in the
moonlight.

Sitting across from her on the polished deck, one leg bent at the knee, with his bare foot resting on the warm wood, it wouldn't take much to see up the leg of his shorts.

Using the rim of her glass to hide her smile, she took a tiny sip while she attempted to regulate her breathing. Just remembering he went commando under his khaki shorts sent a flush of arousal from her head to the tips of her bare toes.

"We should probably head back," he said in a low, intimate tone, his relaxed, fit body rocking along with the waves.

"I thought you said you had permission to use the boat." She drained her glass, smiling against the rim at the way his gaze caressed her throat . . . and farther down.

He cleared his throat. "I do. But even though old Charley is relieved as hell I won't be in his family, he still might take offense at me bringing another woman on board." He crawled to her, relieving her of her goblet, then tossing it and his overboard.

"What are you doing?" She grabbed for the glasses, but it was too late.

"I don't trust myself to go below deck and wash them."

"I'd have helped."

He shoved the neckline of her dress aside and placed a sucking kiss on each nipple before sliding the bodice back in place. "That's what I'm afraid of, darlin'. If you went down there to help me, we'd end up right back in bed. And the glasses wouldn't get washed. So I just bypassed temptation and the glasses still didn't get washed, but now no one will know."

Frowning, she pursed her lips, then nodded. "For some weird reason, that makes sense. Sort of."

"C'mon." He held out his hand.

"Wait. We're going to have to go down there anyway." She shrugged. "I'm missing my panties. Remember?"

He grinned, running his hands under her skirt. "Oh, yeah, I remember. I've just been enjoying the view."

She swatted at his hands. "You wouldn't let me put them

back on. So we have to go back. While we're down there, we should also look for your underwear."

"Talk to me," she ordered, intensely aware of him, of his body heat directly behind her as she made her way down the ladder on wobbly legs. Maybe if she concentrated on their conversation, she could ignore the bed and what had transpired there long enough to retrieve her underwear and get out.

He bumped her back, his obvious erection making her question her plan. Would an instant replay be so terrible?

Hard on that thought came the possible horror of being caught, literally, with her pants down on a stranger's boat. Yes, it would be terrible and she needed to remember that.

But it was difficult when Braedon was such a hot, sexy presence so close to her, his heat and scent surrounding her.

Her breath caught at the feel of his hand dipping under her skirt, slowly progressing up her thigh. "How long have you been a realtor?" His breath was hot against her ear as he picked up the thread of their earlier conversation.

"A-about s-six years." Her breasts grew heavy, her breath shallow.

"Successful?" He ran the tip of his finger between her legs, making her even moister.

Swallowing around a sudden lump, tamping down her need, she glanced around the tiny room, hoping to take her mind off the sensations zinging through her. "Um, I guess. It depends on what you call successful. Most people would think my sister, Meg, was the more successful one. She sells a lot of high-end units. Also commercial stuff."

She bit her lip when he slid his finger deep within her weeping flesh, pulling her up on her toes. Despite her best intentions, she ground against his hand, swallowing a moan.

"Oh?" He nudged her until she was bent over the mattress, his hands smoothing the short tight skirt of her dress up and over her buttocks, baring her from the waist down. "What about you?"

His finger still deep within her, he spread the rest of his fingers until she widened her stance.

"W-what about me?" Muscles vibrating with excitement, she had to lock her knees to keep them from buckling when she felt his hot breath between her legs. His hand on her back kept her from straightening up.

The tip of his tongue slid round and round her eager flesh before darting out to spear her. A brief kiss followed, then, "You're not as successful as your sister?"

He moved his head between her legs to suck on her nub while his finger continued to move deep within her.

Breath lodged in her lungs for a second before she found her voice. "I guess that depends on how you measure success," she said in a breathy voice, frowning to keep her mind on the conversation, instead of focusing on more physical things.

His hot tongue swiped her. He took a few teasing nips, then said, his breath hot, "How do you measure it?"

She swallowed. "I think I'm a success when I can find good, affordable housing and help someone get approved so they can have a home." His tongue speared her again, causing a blip in her thought process.

"You like that?" He petted her dripping folds and it took her a moment to realize he meant finding homes for people.

"Y-yes. I love it."

Both his hands came around to shove down her bodice and tweak her nipples. Before she could do much more than gasp, he entered her from behind.

"And I love this," he said on a growl, thrusting impossibly deeper, rolling her aching nipples between his thumbs and forefingers in counterpoint.

Her knees threatened to buckle. Her breath came in wheezing gasps with each powerful thrust, as the pressure built.

Oh, yeah, she loved that, too.

10

Braedon rolled on his side, dragging Suzanne along until she was spooned against him. "Are you awake?" he asked, playing with her nipples until they obediently pebbled, and placing little kisses along her hairline at the back of her neck.

In answer, she smiled and reached back to drag her hand along his naked hip, then patted his firm butt.

"We should get going," he said, making no move to leave the bed or take his hands off her breasts.

She nodded, and they lay together for a while longer.

"What about you?" She reached down and brought one of his hands up to kiss it. "What do you do?"

He chuckled, but it didn't sound like he was amused. Breaking contact, he sat up and reached for his clothes. "I guess I'm technically unemployed."

"Okay. What *did* you do?"

"I was an accountant."

"What did you . . . account?"

Smiling, he pulled up and zipped his pants. "Nothing much, which is why I'm unemployed."

Somehow, she got the feeling there was more to the story. "You must have done all right. You bought a condo and a new truck." For lack of anything better to do, she smoothed the bedspread.

"Right. And let's not forget my car. The one I had to sell to pay some bills? There was a wise financial decision."

"That's what doesn't make sense. You are or were an accountant, and yet you managed to get into such financial problems that you had to sell your car."

Silence greeted her.

Braedon turned to make his way above deck. "Drop it," he said over his shoulder.

The urge to call out to halt his progress was strong, but she swallowed it. They'd just met. Even though they'd shared their bodies, it didn't mean they had to share everything. She, of all people, should know and respect that. After all, wasn't that the very thing she always told her sister? Just because she and Megan shared a physical bond and looked alike, didn't mean they had to share everything.

Thoughts of her sister tensed her shoulders. She would not wonder about Meg's honeymoon or how she liked married life. She didn't care. Never had, never would.

But even she had to admit her sister had made a beautiful bride. Then again, maybe all brides were beautiful. Kind of like how all babies and puppies are cute. Maybe there was some law of nature about those things. Of course. That was probably exactly where those thoughts came from. It was only natural.

The warm humid air caressed her skin, wrapping around her like a soft cocoon when she climbed up on deck. After the intense sex, she'd have liked to take a moment to regroup, to bask in the afterglow. However, one look at her date stopped those thoughts in their tracks.

Braedon stood stiffly by the railing, obviously waiting for her so they could get underway.

"Sorry, I didn't realize you were ready to go so soon." She accepted his help down into the row boat.

"No problem." He untied the line, dropped his shirt to the floor of the boat, and shoved off.

"Did you already set the alarm?" No doubt he had. What was her problem, she wondered. It was like she was morphing into her sister.

"Shit!" Grabbing wildly for the line again, he jumped up on deck, tied off, and then disappeared before she could say another word.

Less than a minute later, he hopped back into the boat, causing it to rock crazily.

Suzanne reached for an oar at the same time as Braedon.

"What are you doing?" He tugged, but she did not relinquish her hold.

"I thought I'd help." She tried pulling the oar from his iron grip, then had to grab for the edge of the boat to maintain her balance. "Braedon, stop being a macho jerk. I'm perfectly capable of rowing."

"I got us out here, I'll get us back, princess," he said through clenched teeth.

"Why can't we both paddle?"

"Because I don't want to end up going in circles, that's why. Now let go of the damn oar."

"No."

"Yes!" He jerked on the hard wood, cutting into her palm.

Tightening her grip, she braced her knees on the edge of the boat and jerked right back. "No!"

Their impromptu tug of war ended abruptly when the boat flipped, tossing them into the warm Gulf water.

Water roared into her ear canals. All around her was nothing but inky blackness. Blindly, she kicked out, pulling with her arms toward the top. At least she hoped she was going in the right direction.

She broke the surface first, coughing and clawing at the wet hair clinging to her face.

Braedon immediately followed, slinging his head like a wet dog.

Continuing to tread water, she edged a little farther away, unsure of his mood after their recent dunking. Why did she always have to push? It was her fault they were in their current predicament. Would it have killed her to allow him to row back?

She coughed, stalling for time until she could force her apology past the knot in her throat.

Moonlight gleamed from the smooth skin of Braedon's broad shoulders, his muscles flexing with the movement of his arms.

"Are you okay?" The words grated, dragging on the lining of her throat.

She expected him to rant. She expected him to rave. She even half expected he'd want to do her bodily harm.

She didn't expect him to laugh.

Softly at first, his chuckles soon grew to an outright belly laugh.

"I take it that's a yes," she said, edging closer. Did sharks hang out in the coves at night? What about jelly fish? One sting in childhood was enough for her. "Um, Braedon, we probably shouldn't be hanging out here in the water. At night." She shuddered. "I don't want to end up as some shark's midnight snack."

That made him laugh harder.

"I'm serious!" If she hadn't needed both hands to tread water, she'd have punched him.

"I know, that's what's so funny." A smooth stroke took him closer to the overturned hull of the boat. "Be ready to grab that edge when I pull up."

She was ready, but evidently the boat was not. It conked her on the head as it flipped upright.

Warm water surged into every orifice. Her immediate reflex to pop back up was thwarted by the bottom of the boat.

More than just a surprise gulp of water seized her lungs, tightened her muscles, caused her heart to threaten to escape through her rib cage.

Blindly, she clawed at the cold hardness of the boat, wanting to scream her frustration, knowing if she did, she very likely would drown.

A hard hand gripped her just past her armpit, jerking her up. Water whooshed with the motion. Air, blessed air, surrounded her, filled her starving lungs.

A coughing spasm shook her.

Holding onto the boat, he cradled her against his chest while she shook and gagged and coughed, then wheezed for good measure.

"I thought you'd know enough to stay clear of the hull," he grumbled next to the ear that wasn't still filled with ocean water. "Hey, you all right?"

Clenching her teeth to prevent breakage as they chattered, she nodded and clung to his neck.

"Good." He flopped his sodden shirt onto the seat of the boat. "Let's get back into the boat and get to shore."

They bobbed around for a few seconds, then Braedon's soft curses filled the air.

Following his line of vision, she saw the reason for his frustration: the oars were floating out to sea.

He struggled to de-manacle her from his torso. "Suz, let go. Here, hang onto the boat. Suzanne? Baby, if you don't let me go, I don't have a prayer in hell of getting to the oars in time."

On some level, she knew that was true. But she also knew the waters of the Gulf of Mexico harbored all kinds of sea creatures, most of whom she did not want to meet, up close and personal. Especially not at night.

"Suz," he said in a strangled voice. "You're choking me."

"Oh!" She loosened her hold but didn't dare let go.

Gripping her wrists, he pulled her from him, not releasing her until he was sure she had a firm grasp on the boat. "Wait here. As soon as I grab the oars, I'll be back to help you into the boat."

He struck off with sure smooth strokes and disappeared as he rounded the boat and swam out of sight.

Wait here. Where would she go?

Maybe if she were really careful, she could climb into the boat.

It rocked, looming precariously over her, causing her to shriek. So much for that idea . . .

An eternity later, she froze in horror at the sound of something slapping water, before she realized it was Braedon swimming back.

"Too late," he said, stopping and treading water next to her. "They're gone."

Shoving the rising panic down, she asked as casually as possible, "H-how are we going to get back to shore?"

His hard hands gripped her waist. "Don't worry. I'll get us back. Here. Hold onto the boat while I hoist you up. Reach up with your foot. That's a girl. Good job! Now roll into it."

The hard bottom of the boat bit into her knees. Peeking over the side, she drew comfort from his presence. "Aren't you getting in?"

"Nope." He edged to the end, one hand gripping each side of the stern. Or was that the bow? Or did it matter on a little boat? "I'm going to push us in, it'll be easier than trying to drag it. But you'll have to guide me, since I can't see over the boat."

"Oh. Okay. Um, Braedon?" She assumed his grunt was a reply. "Go a little to the left if you want to go back to the same dock."

"Of course I want to go back to the same dock." It sounded

as though he spoke through gritted teeth. "The neighbors might not appreciate us docking on their property."

She thought maybe his ex-future father-in-law might not be all that thrilled, either, but decided it was probably best not to mention that little tidbit.

Then she remembered the guard dogs.

11

As soon as the boat nudged the dock, Suz jumped out to tie off.

"Thanks." Braedon's shoulders and biceps flexed when he pulled up onto the dock. He sat, head down, arms resting on updrawn knees, his chest heaving.

After admiring the view for a moment, she glanced around at the darkened house, squinting to see in the shadows of the tropical landscaping. "Do you think the guard dogs are still out?"

He gave a bark of laughter devoid of humor, and wiped his palm over his face. "Bastards are always out." He looked up at the house before getting to his feet. "We need to get out of here before they catch our scent."

She scrambled back to the boat.

"What are you doing? We have to leave!"

Her head jerked up at his harshly whispered words, once again scanning the land leading to the dock. "I was just getting your shirt." Scooping it up, she jumped back onto the dock. "Okay. Let's go."

Clutching the shirt against her chest to keep her heartbeat from echoing like a tom-tom from the touch of his hand in hers, she scampered along behind him, ever vigilant for the attack dogs.

Braedon froze, arms slung back to protect her. She ran into his back, squishing her nose against warm skin. "Ow!"

"Shh," he hissed, edging them toward the parking area. "I thought I saw one."

Braedon turned the air blue with his cussing and ran, half dragging her along.

His scream split the night as he fell to the ground. Growls filled the air. The dogs were on him, their growls mixing with the sounds of his terror.

They were vicious. They were single-minded in their attack. They were . . . Chihuahuas?

Of course, the way Braedon was carrying on, you'd have thought they were Rottweilers.

Laughing, she plopped down on the damp grass and tried to regain her composure.

One of the dogs stopped mauling long enough to look up, its big dark eyes luminous in the moonlight, dark spots standing out in its predominantly white coat.

She tapped her leg. "C'mere, sweetheart," she cooed.

The dog left Braedon rolling on the grass and trotted over, its spiky tail wagging, tongue lolling in a doggie smile.

Scratching behind the dog's ear, she made little kissing sounds to gain the attention of the second dog, still intent on gnawing on her date.

It took a few minutes, but eventually the dog joined her.

Braedon, curled in a fetal position, eventually lowered his arms from his face and watched her loving on the dogs.

"Did the big man scare you?" she cooed, alternately rubbing both dogs' ears and scratching their throats.

"Scare them?" Braedon stood a few feet away, shrugging on

his discarded shirt. "They're vicious. They hate me. Always have. Whenever I came to the house, they attacked me." He paused, tucking in his shirt. "Don't look at me like that. It's true. Just because they're small doesn't mean they don't bite." He edged closer.

"Braedon, look at them. How could you possibly be afraid of something so small? You could stomp them into the ground."

He mumbled something and took a quick step back when the smaller dog's ears perked up.

"What? I didn't hear you."

His hand came up to run over his closely cut hair. "I said I'd never stomp anything into the ground, even a dog that was trying to kill me." He backed away. "Don't let them go until I get to the truck, okay?"

"How could anyone be afraid of you sweet things, hmm?" She kissed the dogs' sleek heads, but watched until Braedon reached his truck before releasing her hold on them to follow.

"Okay," she said, once they were back on the road. "You want to tell me what that was all about?"

"Buckle up."

"Stop trying to change the subject." The seat belt clicked in the quiet.

"Drop it."

"But—"

"We had fun today. And tonight. Don't spoil it."

"Did you have a bad experience?"

"No, this is probably the worst date experience so far."

"Gee, thanks."

Grumbling, he pulled to the side of the road and threw the truck into park. Her seat belt gave a hollow click when he unlatched it to drag her over the console, not stopping until she was on his lap. His lips covered hers before she could say another word.

Not that she could think of a word to say, which, for her, was pretty unusual in itself. All of her thoughts, her senses, were centered on the way his mouth tasted, the way his lips felt on hers, his scent filling her nostrils. His zipper digging into her rear end.

Twisting to alleviate the pain, she finally gave up, breaking lip contact. "Are you trying to divert my attention?" she whispered against his mouth.

"I guess not, since it's not working."

"Ow." The steering wheel pressed painfully against her spine. "This truck is really not conducive to romance."

He chuckled, vibrating parts that begged her to at least try for a more conducive position. "So you're saying sex is out?"

She twisted, wincing at the pain shooting through her hip. "I think at least one of us would not enjoy it." Wedging her hip closer to the console, she tried to scoot down lower. "Maybe if you'd move a little toward the door. Yes, like that. See? There's plenty of room for me to sit in the same seat." Of course, she'd have to forgo breathing, but she could do that for a little while. Surprisingly, she enjoyed being close to Braedon. Even when they weren't having sex.

When was the last time that had happened?

"My butt is wedged against the armrest," he complained. "In fact, I can't feel much in that area of my body." He shifted a little and grunted. "This isn't going to work. If we're not going to do anything, you may as well get back on your own side."

"Define not doing anything." His skin was smooth and warm through the opening of his shirt, tantalizing her fingertips as she ran them up and down. His warm scent, part lingering aftershave and part male, surrounded her. Twisting, she inched her leg up until it was over his lap. "There. I gave you some more room."

"Not to mention more possibilities." He kissed her neck, his hand running along her thigh, up under the edge of her hiked-up skirt.

His fingers skimmed the crotch of her thong, making her shift on the seat. Whether it was for greater access, or to find a more comfortable position was a toss-up. The cooler air of the cab bathed her heated skin.

Braedon paused in sucking her earlobe long enough to whisper, "Open a little wider for me, darlin'."

Without pausing to debate the wisdom of following his instructions, she spread her legs as wide as the steering wheel permitted, moaning when his questing fingers found their target.

Her breasts tingled, causing her to rub them as discreetly as possible against his chest.

There were those who would not be surprised at the idea of Suzanne Hartley having sex or even a hot and heavy petting session in the driver's seat of a pickup truck. They'd be surprised if they only knew the truth.

Excitement coursed through her.

Braedon withdrew from her wetness, patting and caressing her along the way. His warm palms cupped her shoulders, smoothing the straps of her dress and bra down her arms until she was bared to the waist, the blast furnace of his hard chest and abs burning her nipples.

His hands bracketed her ribs, lifting her until she was aligned with his mouth. His hot breath bathed her aching nipples a second before he drew a puckered bud into the dampness of his mouth. With each strong draw, his sucking caused a corresponding surge of moisture.

Whimpering with need, she straddled him, wedging her knee against the armrest, better aligning her breast to his greedy mouth. Moaning, her head thrown back, back arched, she reveled in the sensation of his mouth suckling her while he palmed and squeezed her breasts.

His erection rubbed against her engorged sex, the zipper

heightening her excitement. She bucked her hips, meeting him thrust for thrust, rubbing shamelessly against him, seeking closer contact. More contact. Release from the raging desire driving her, pumping her hips, causing her breath to come in fast, short, panting gasps.

He gently bit down on her nipple, subtly stretching and grinding it between his teeth.

She'd heard of being blinded by passion but had never experienced it firsthand. Until now.

Wild with need, primal in her urge to mate, she shoved her skirt to her waist and wiggled. She clawed at his zipper until she'd freed him. So great was her need, she didn't pause to enjoy the tactile pleasure of his turgid weight in her hand, revel in the heated flesh about to give her pleasure. With little frustrated cries, she manipulated herself until she was aligned with him and sank home.

Braedon gave a guttural cry and arched his back, burying himself in her wet, welcome heat.

Her hands gripped his head, all but smothering him in the fragrant flesh. He sucked her deeper, wanting more, wanting all she could give. And it wasn't nearly enough. His hips bucked, buried deep within her wetness, her slick walls sucking at him, milking him of his strength, his staying power, robbing him of his breath.

Suzanne rose higher, her knees resting on his outer thighs, giving him enough leverage to pound into her with more force, driving deeper into her weeping flesh.

Her inner muscles contracted, squeezing him. He picked up the pace. Her breath hitched, signaling her completion as she shrieked.

He knew immediately it was not a shriek of sexual fulfillment, since it coincided with the blaring of his horn.

She shifted, blasting the horn again. "My—" *Honk.* "Heel—" *Honk-honk.* "Is caught—" *Honk.* "In the wheel!"

"Stop." He gripped her hips to prevent more Morse code with his horn. "Move your foot."

"Well, duh! Why didn't I think of that?" She jerked her dress back up to cover her assets. Her eyes widened. "I know!" She leaned closer, her eyes narrowed to evil looking slits. "Maybe because my damn heel is stuck in your steering wheel!"

"Don't yell at me. It's not my fault."

In response, she shot him another evil look, and moved her leg in frantic jerks.

Honk! Honk—honk—honk—honk. Honk.

It was his turn to narrow his eyes when he realized two things: he was still embedded inside her, and her jerky movements were causing an unwelcome reaction.

She must have felt the telltale swelling, because her gaze shot to his, her kiss-swollen mouth forming a surprised O. "Could you be any more of a—a . . . man?" *Honk, honk.* "Hello? I'm stuck here and quite possibly doing serious bodily damage. My ACL could be tearing as we speak. Would you get your mind out of the gutter and give me a little help?" *Honk—honk—honk.*

"The sex was your idea," he pointed out, withdrawing from her warmth as discreetly as possible, and zipping up. He nudged her hip with his hand. "Maybe if you move that way you can get your foot out."

"Are you laughing at me?" Suz was sure she heard a distinctive snicker. Warmth surrounded her ankle, then his hand gently manipulated her foot in an effort to free her abused heel from the steering wheel.

"Nope. I'm laughing at *us.*" Her heel finally slid sideways enough to disengage from its prison. Laughing outright, he scooted her to sit sideways across his lap and gave her a little hug. "Damn. I can't remember when I've had so much fun on a date."

Pleasure washed through her. "Really?"

He kissed the tip of her nose. "Really." He gripped her ribs, lifting her across the console to settle into her seat. "Much as I want to continue what we started, I don't want to do it in my truck." He leveled an intent gaze on her. "Your place or mine?"

Nipples tingling in anticipation, she leaned back against the door, kicked off her shoe, and rested her foot on the console. Of course she knew it was a provocative position. Well, she hoped it was provocative anyway. Heck, she was feeling pretty provocative. Rubbing the tips of her toes along his arm, she smiled at his indrawn breath.

"Whichever is closer."

12

Braedon dropped his truck into gear and spun in the gravel shoulder as he took off. Watching her out of the side of his eye, he grabbed her ankle before she could lower her foot and turn away.

When she didn't protest, he rubbed her ankle bones with the pad of his thumb, marveling at how small they felt in his hand. Delicate.

Quiet echoed in the cab as they sped through the darkness. His left hand gripped the wheel while his right stroked her ankle, then higher.

She shifted, getting as close to the console as possible, her legs splaying wider.

He walked his fingers up the velvety skin of her inner thigh, his nostrils flaring at the smell of arousal filling the cab. Hers? His? Probably both.

Beneath his zipper, his cock stirred, straining against the wet confines of his shorts.

He slipped his finger under the elastic of her panties, his excitement ratchetting up another notch at the slick wetness he found.

Her shallow panting blared in his ear, his every nerve ending so acutely attuned to her, it felt as though his skin would burst into flames at any second.

Blood pounded through his veins, roared in his ears, heated his cheeks.

Where the hell was his exit?

By the time he located the hotel marquee illuminated in the distance, he was shaking with need. It was all he could do to gather enough strength to shove down the turn signal indicator and turn the wheel, while his other hand pleasured Suzanne, buried deep in her wet heat.

The truck tires squealed as he made the turn on practically two wheels, skidding to stop just short of flattening the valet stand.

With one brisk move, Braedon removed his wicked fingers and tugged her dress back down before jumping out of the truck, and all but running to open her door.

If the valet noticed their urgency, he didn't acknowledge it as Braedon hauled her out of the truck and half carried her at a little less than a dead run into the hotel.

She tucked her face tightly against his neck as they hurried through the lobby. She didn't want to contemplate the picture they made, still half wet from their dunk in the Gulf, barefoot, her wet hair streaming down her back.

A shiver ran through her. She hoped it was sexual excitement and anticipation, and not because of a draft from exposing herself as she was carried to the elevator.

Instead of setting her on her feet once they were in the elevator, Braedon tightened his hold, tickling the side of her neck and her ear with tiny flicks of his tongue.

Instead of laughing, though, the actions made her nipples

harden into tight needy peaks beneath her damp clothing. Had he not held her so close, she would have squirmed in a pale attempt to assuage her ache.

Finally the number four lit up. A ding sounded. The shiny brass doors whooshed open. In the blink of an eye, Braedon strode down the burgundy carpeted hallway, not stopping until they were outside a polished door adorned with the brass number 403.

He fumbled with the card key. A metallic click and a green light, and they were in.

Braedon kicked the door the rest of the way shut, then flipped the privacy bolt.

Cool hotel air bathed her fevered skin.

To their left she glimpsed the shiny dark tile of what looked to be an opulent bathroom. Braedon walked so fast, it was kind of a blur.

But she wasn't complaining.

A small red-shaded lamp on a tasteful cherry desk lent the room a soft, warm glow. A cherry armoire, dresser, and nightstands glowed with a well oiled patina in the low light. At the far end of the room was a sitting area with a small comfy looking sofa and matching wingback chair, done in some kind of print, clustered around an entertainment center.

But the star of the room, in her opinion, the piece that held her rapt attention, was the California king-size bed with the deep burgundy silk spread, piled decadently high with assorted decorative throw pillows.

The low light from the lone lamp cast the bed in a hypnotic glow, making everything else in the luxurious room fade into the background.

Her bare toes sunk into the plush navy and burgundy tweed carpet. Before she'd had time to assimilate the fact that he'd put her down, she was naked.

Another blink, and he was equally naked.

He followed her down onto the big bed, his mouth ravenous on her face, her mouth, her breasts.

The cool silk of the spread caressed her back. The top of her head pushed against the throw pillows.

Incapable of doing more than grunt and groan her pleasure, she clasped him tightly to her, scrabbling for a hold on his undulating body.

He grabbed her ankles, lifting until her legs rested on his shoulders, bracketing his head.

Heat radiated from the head of his penis, poised at the opening of her weeping flesh.

He reached down and drew it round and round, smearing her moisture, tormenting her, his other hand holding her hips when she would have bucked to take him into her eager body.

A frantic whimper escaped her. She pulled at his head, his shoulders, in a blind attempt to drag him closer, to scratch the proverbial itch. Breasts heavy and aching, she panted, desperate for release. Desperate for him.

What the heck was he waiting for?

Obviously the guy could not read body language and she wasn't entirely sure she was capable of communicating at the moment. Eyes were supposed to be the window to the soul. Or was it the mirror? Regardless, she fervently hoped he could read her desire when she opened her eyes.

The whole window/soul thing was going on, loud and clear, in Braedon's blue gaze, which was fiercely focused on her.

Her breath caught. Could she handle all that passion, that intensity, focused on her? It could be overwhelming, all consuming.

Something had changed. Shifted. She wasn't sure what it was, or how it might factor into her life. She'd felt it earlier on the boat. The look Braedon gave her confirmed he felt it, too.

If they acted on whatever it was between them—and although the sex was awesome, she knew deep down their connection went way beyond sex, casual or otherwise—they could never go back.

The thought scared her.

Not going there scared her more.

Still he hesitated, despite her nonverbal urging.

Eyes locked, his body probing hers, he said in a voice so low only her soul could hear it, "Are you sure?"

Her whispered answer released the floodgates.

"Yes."

13

Eyes locked with hers, he slid into her and paused, his muscles vibrating with the effort.

Beneath him, she shook, her entire body quivering.

He assumed it was passion induced. He prayed it wasn't fear.

Before he could ask, or begin the single most important act of his life, the silence was shattered by the sound of breaking glass.

Or the mood.

Suzanne's eyes widened, then darted to a place somewhere near the side of the bed before looking back at him.

"It—it's my cell," she said when the sound of it again filled the room. "My sister. Ignore it." She attempted to pull him closer, only to stop and throw her arm over her eyes when the cell phone rang again. "I should probably get that."

He nodded and withdrew, feeling oddly vulnerable in his nudity while he watched her scramble to the edge of the bed and reach down for her phone.

She extracted a small pink cell and flipped it open. "This had better be good," she whispered.

Suzanne looked back at Braedon. He'd scooted to the other side of the bed and covered himself with a pillow.

"What. Is. It?" Meg had always had lousy timing, but this went way beyond.

"Suz? I can barely hear you. Are you all right?"

"Yes, I'm all right," she fired back through clenched teeth.

"I just had the strangest feeling," her sister lowered her voice. "I woke up barely able to breathe, my heart pounding. And totally turned on. But it was more. A lot more than that. It was like my skin was on fire. I know you met someone." Her voice dropped again. "And I also know you had a *really* good time this afternoon, and again tonight." She laughed. "Jake told me to call you and remind you which one of us was on our honeymoon." Pause. "Suz? This scares me. Talk to me."

She glanced over at Braedon, who was flipping through the room service menu, then lowered her voice and turned away. "I'm scared, too, Meg."

"Do you need me? I mean, I know we've never been exactly close. But you're my sister. If you need me, I'll be there."

Suzanne's throat constricted. Horrified at her reaction, she blinked back her sappy tears. Must be hormonal. There was no other explanation. She swallowed. "Thanks," she managed to choke out, then cleared her throat. "But I'm okay. Besides, you're supposed to be on your honeymoon. Don't you have anything better to do than call me?"

"Judging by the way I felt when you woke me out of a sound sleep, I'd say whatever is going on with you is more interesting." Meg laughed then sobered. "This is important, isn't it?"

"Uh-huh." She pulled the edge of the bedspread up to belatedly cover her nudity.

"Monumental, if the vibes I'm getting are anything to go by."

" 'Fraid so."

"Don't be afraid, Suz," Meg whispered, then hung up.

After dropping the phone into her bag, she realized at some point in her conversation, she and her sister had made an emotional connection. Miracles do happen.

Braedon hung up the phone by the bed. "I ordered room service. I'm kind of hungry. Knowing you, it was a safe bet you were, too." He winked and patted the bed, flipping back the covers to reveal he'd slipped on his boxers. "Why don't you come over here and let me keep you warm while we wait?" He held up his hand. "I'll be on my best behavior."

After splashing her face in the bathroom, she wrapped the fluffy white hotel robe around her and padded back out to join him while he waited for their food.

As soon as she snuggled next to him, she felt the tension ease, all awkwardness leave her body. Cuddling with Braedon Wright, regardless of where they were, felt comfortable.

They made a healthy dent in the laden room service cart while they watched *Some Like It Hot* on the classic movie channel.

Suz sighed and leaned back on the pillows they'd stacked on the couch as the credits scrolled across the screen. "I love that movie. I can't count how many times I've seen it, and I love it each time."

"Well, there's a reason it's a classic." Braedon licked buffalo sauce from his fingers, then took a swig from a bottle of water.

"Maybe it's because times were simpler back then."

"Not so simple, if you think about it." At her raised brow, he continued. "Hear me out. I thought about it while we were watching the movie." He held up a finger. "First off, two musicians, one of which is a player. Not only is he irresponsible, gambling, and womanizing, he takes advantage of his best friend. They witness a mass murder and have to get out of town. The only way to do that is with an all-girl band. They dress in drag, but the one friend is having to watchdog the player to make sure he doesn't *rise* to the occasion and blow their cover. Meanwhile, an old millionaire is pursuing him, thinking he is a woman, and he is finding himself weirdly flattered and maybe even attracted." He grinned and nodded. "Sex. Sex is never simple. Take Marilyn Monroe's character, Sugar Cane. She's been around. And, like I said, sex is never simple. Even back then. And I'm not even going to get into the whole cross-dressing, gender-bending thing."

"Speaking of sex. I never noticed how revealing her costumes were! How did that ever get by the censors back then?"

He laughed and tugged at her, towing her toward the bed. "I noticed, believe me, even as a kid."

"Why does that not surprise me?" She slid her arms around his neck when he pulled her into his embrace. "Were you a naughty little boy?" Smiling, she rubbed her hips back and forth against his.

Tell her. She's different. Important. Tell her. She deserves to know the truth, everything about you. Don't make the same mistake you made with Penny. Suzanne likes you. You. Not half of a matched set. She connects with you. Only you. Tell her.

"Nothing compared to what I'm going to be if you don't behave," he said, instead, nuzzling her neck.

The woman made him hot, he told his screaming conscience. He'd tell her everything soon. Later.

"Have you ever done it in a hot tub?" He slipped his hand beneath the robe to stroke her pebbled nipple. "Each room on this floor has a private balcony with a hot tub."

Her first thought was to decline. But something in his eyes stopped her. For some reason, she realized he assumed she would turn him down.

Something strange was happening to her, and she knew it was connected with Braedon.

And she was pretty sure it had very little to do with the mind-blowing sex they'd been indulging in. It went much deeper.

Meanwhile, why not enjoy everything being with him offered?

Sliding her hands down, she circled his waist, then slid his boxers down his legs. The instant heat in his gaze made her smile as she dropped her robe. "Let's go."

Wrapping towels around their nudity seemed like a prudent thing to do, on the off chance their balcony had a view of more than the skyline.

Once they'd settled into the churning water, Suz sighed, leaning her head back and looking up at the stars.

"This feels great." She looked over at Braedon and smiled. "Good idea."

Tell her.

Instead, he communicated the only way he knew she'd understand, the way she'd obviously come to expect.

14

Suzanne leaned against the slick side of the hot tub, gripping the edge to keep from slipping beneath the churning water while Braedon pumped into her.

Idly, she watched her breasts bobbing on the surface of the water, jiggling with each powerful thrust of his hips. She glanced down, watching the ripped muscles of his abs contract with his movements, squinted in an effort to see beneath the illuminated churning water on the off chance she might be able to watch his body merge with hers. The thought sent little fizzes of sexual excitement zipping to her extremities.

Having sex with him in the hot tub on the balcony of the hotel should have been thrilling. Exciting. At the very least titillating, and sexy as all get out.

It was pleasant enough. Enjoyable. If she really concentrated on the things he was doing to her body, she might even work up a plausible orgasm.

Assuming she could disengage her mind.

Why did it feel as though he was just going through the motions? Where was the intense connection they had earlier? Maybe it was one-sided, but she hadn't thought so at the time.

Braedon watched the distracted look on Suzanne's face and ground into her, willing her to join him more than physically. Funny, there was a time when physical intimacy was all he thought he wanted or needed from his partners. When had that changed?

It changed when he met Suzanne. For the first time in his life, he wanted to share more than his body.

Tell her.

He reached between them and massaged her clit with one hand while tweaking a puckered nipple with his other.

Their gazes met.

Her passage softened, internal muscles stroked him.

Tell her.

Eyes locked, they increased their pace.

He moved his hands to her shoulders, willing her to join him, to crawl under his skin just as he wanted to crawl under hers, as he picked up the pace.

Her smooth legs circled his hips, gripping him as she met each hard thrust.

Sexual combatants, neither willing to sublimate, they battled in the bubbling water, their thrusts growing in intensity, occasionally blurring the line between pleasure and pain.

Suzanne's breath came in harsh panting gasps. Her pubic bone ached with exertion. Still, she kept pounding against the man who held her with such a fierce look of determination.

Watching the shadow play beneath the water, her breath caught at the sight of his body joining hers, retreating and slamming home again. The sight pushed her over the precipice she'd been tottering on, tumbling her into a cloud of sexual fulfillment, weakening her knees.

She may have lost consciousness for a second.

When they could breathe without gasping for air, Braedon helped her out of the tub, dried her off, then carried her back to bed.

Lethargic, she hung from his arm as he lowered her to the cool, soft sheets, too exhausted to even lift her hand to cover her nudity.

The distinctive smell of almonds surrounded her. His big hands smoothed over her from shoulders to ankles and back again, warming everywhere they touched.

Lifting heavy eyelids, she managed to mumble, "Warm."

Concentrating on thoroughly massaging her breasts, he said, "Like it? The bottle said it was self-heating massage oil. Relax." He pushed down on her shoulders when she tried to sit up. "Let me do this for you."

Had her muscles not felt like overcooked spaghetti, had her mind not been drifting toward nirvana, the feel of his skin on hers might have lead to another lovemaking session.

She knew it was no longer just sex.

When he crawled into bed, pulling her tightly against him, she thought she wouldn't mind if he slid into her relaxed body. What was surprising was how thrilled she was when he tenderly kissed her shoulder and fell asleep.

In the dark, she listened to his deep breathing, loving the feel of his strong body pressed intimately against her back.

She was in so much trouble.

She couldn't possibly be in love with someone she'd known for less than twenty-four hours.

Could she?

15

Impending sunrise bathed the room through the open drapes.

Gasping from her sister's orgasm, bathed in sweat, Suzanne jackknifed next to a sleeping Braedon.

Tell him. He had to suspect. *Admit you're the girl from Pleasure Beach. Tell him. Tell him you're a twin, and explain the sicko twin connection. Make him understand.*

But . . . what if he didn't? What if, like other men in her past, he saw her as some kind of freak?

Easing from the bed, she reached for her clothes. Maybe time alone, to sort her thoughts, would help.

Braedon grumbled something and reached for her in his sleep, bringing a smile to her worried face.

She finished dressing and slipped the spare card key he'd given her the night before into her pocket before stepping out into the hall, clicking the door shut.

Maybe things would be clearer after she'd showered and had time alone to examine the many thoughts and feelings vying for attention, jumbling her mind.

* * *

Braedon opened his eyes when the door clicked shut, fully awake. No surprise to find the spot next to him vacant.

He sat up and stretched, glancing around for the note she hadn't left. Not that he'd expected one.

Something had shifted the night before. Something powerful.

For the first time in his life, he'd fallen in love.

Now what?

After a quick shower and some cold leftover room service, he flipped open his phone. He snapped it shut. He didn't know her number.

The cell vibrated his palm. His brother. He flipped it open, forcing a smile and joviality into his voice.

"Hey, stud! What are you doing calling me? Need some pointers?" He winced. Damn. Not the thing to say when your brother just married your ex. "I mean, um . . ."

Ryan's good-natured laugh echoed in his ear. "In your dreams, little brother. My bride is worried about your sorry ass—something about the way you looked at the reception—and insisted I call to check in. You okay?"

"I don't know. I'll let you know later." He snapped the phone shut and headed for the door. He had to see Suz and tell her he loved her.

Tell her everything.

Suzanne looked up at the cloudless sky while she stretched. She needed to clear her head, to come up with just the right words to say to Braedon to make him understand.

Understand what, her mind scoffed, *the connection you and Meg have defies understanding.*

She winced at the idea that only another twin could begin to understand it. She'd die celibate and alone before she'd dip into that gene pool.

Running wasn't her thing, but Meg swore it cleansed the

mind and body. Since her mind was choking on toxic thoughts, running in circles like a drunken squirrel, maybe a run would help.

Beginning with a slow half walk/half jog, she made her way to the water, enjoying the feel of the cool, smooth, wet sand beneath her bare feet. Hopping in the remnants of waves, she made her way down the beach, keeping an eye out for jellyfish corpses.

Braedon banged on the door of the beach house, yelling her name again for good measure. Where the hell was she? Hands blocking the sun, he peered through the window. Judging from the clothing strewn about, she had not checked out yet.

A pink bikini-clad woman hopping along the shore caught his attention. Eyes trained on her, he kicked off his flip-flops and jogged out to meet her.

"Hey," he said when he was close enough for her to hear. "I wondered where you went."

She gave a tight smile but didn't dodge his kiss, which was a good sign. He hoped.

Wait. The ocean lapping the shore. Her in a bikini, running next to him . . .

"We met before the wedding. At Pleasure Beach." He watched her chew her lip while she avoided eye contact. Placing his finger under her chin, he tilted her head until she looked him in the eye. "Where did you go that day? I searched for hours. Why didn't you say anything when we met again in the bar? Or didn't you recognize me, either?"

Her shoulders slumped, but she maintained her gaze. "I recognized you." She shrugged. "I guess I was hoping you wouldn't remember me. It was so embarrassing."

Cold fear washed through him. "Are you sick?"

"What?" He was relieved to see she looked genuinely surprised. "Oh, no. Nothing like that." She watched a seagull land close by. "It's a long story."

"I like stories." He slipped his arms around her, pulling her into a quick hug. "Especially ones with lots of sex."

She chuckled and shook her head. "Braedon, you have no idea . . ."

"C'mon, it can't be that bad. Are you married? Really a man?" he teased. "Tell me. We can work it out." Bright green and white stripes caught his attention. A few feet away stood a portable canvas cabana. Suddenly desperate to make love to her, to feel her sweet body against his, he tugged her toward it.

As soon as he'd claimed her again, made her understand they were meant to be together, he'd tell her about Ryan. Hell, he'd tell her where Jimmy Hoffa was hidden if he could make her believe in his love. In them.

"Brae, what are you doing?" Her voice held a bit of warning, although he noted she wasn't really resisting. "This probably belongs to someone."

Pulling her into the shade, he closed the flap, tied it securely, then pulled her back into his arms. "I'm not stealing it, Suz. Just borrowing it for a little while. I didn't like waking up alone." He bent his knees to meet her gaze. "You were coming back to me, eventually, right?"

Cupping her hand on Braedon's cheek, she smiled, relief washing over her. Everything would be all right. He'd understand, once she explained everything. He had to.

Rising on her toes, she kissed him. "I missed you, too," she said against his lips, barely having time to take a breath before his mouth came down with a hunger she felt clear down to her toes.

A hunger she matched.

The sounds of the surf and sea birds faded, her world narrowing to the four narrow walls of their canvas cocoon.

Clothes fell away.

Talking would wait. For now, they let their bodies do the communicating, expressing in ways beyond words.

Lifting her high, he impaled her while his mouth greedily sucked her breast, each pull eliciting a deep answering tug all the way to her womb.

Her oxygen-starved lungs burned. Gasping, she held onto the smooth skin of his shoulders, her legs wrapped around his waist, and met him thrust for thrust.

Breathing was so overrated.

Sweat slicked, they strained against each other, the air of the little tent thick with the heavy scent of sex and desire. And love.

Their release rushed at them, smashing into them, dragging them under in a tidal wave of sensation.

Braedon sank to his knees in the sand, Suzanne clinging weakly to him, his arms banding her closer still.

Did he whisper "I love you" against her hair?

She had to tell him. She had to tell him now.

She prayed he'd understand.

She wiggled in an effort to gain a little space, but he was having none of it.

Growling, he tightened his hold. "I thought women liked postcoital cuddling," he grumbled.

Stroking his sweat-soaked bristled head, she brushed a kiss on his cheek, then leaned back as much as his arms would allow. "I don't know about *women*, but I do. I love it. Only with you, though."

"But? I know there's a but. I can hear it in your voice, feel it in your body."

This time he let her go when she pulled away. Stalling for time, she pulled on her bikini bottoms, then slipped on the matching halter. "We need to talk."

He groaned. "I hate those four words."

"You don't have to say anything. Just listen. Here." She handed him his trunks. "Put them on. It's hard enough for me to concentrate on what I'm about to tell you." She winked. "You distract me."

"Distraction can be a good thing," he noted, stepping into his trunks. He crossed his arms over his chest. "Okay, so talk."

"Sit down." She tugged on his hand. "It's difficult enough without you towering over me. The reason I didn't mention our first meeting is, well, I was embarrassed—"

"People collapse all the time from overexertion, heat, blood pressure—"

"Will you shut up, and just listen?"

"Yes, ma'am." He took her hands, balancing their clasped fingers on the knees of his crossed legs.

"I didn't collapse because of any of those things. I'm sick, all right, but not with anything medical." She took a deep breath, and met his gaze. "I'm a twin. An identical twin, actually. And we share way more than looks."

"You mean like mirror-image twins? I've heard of those." Duh. He was one. Damn, he knew he should have told her. Now he'd have to sit and listen to her tell him stuff he knew only too well, and then tell her. And pray she wouldn't think he'd played her, like Penny had. Or worse, hate him. "But that doesn't explain your collapse."

"I'm getting to that."

Maybe he could distract her while he came up with a plausible reason why he hadn't told her of his own twin. "What were you doing at Pleasure Beach?"

"I was getting some rest before my sister's wedding. My friend Royce's husband, Jack, owns a rental house there. But this isn't about them or Pleasure Beach." She heaved a sigh. "I'm trying to tell you something. Meg, my sister, and I share a lot more than most twins. We have what is called an empathetic relationship."

"You mean like when she gets hurt, you feel the pain?" He'd heard of that. Thank God he and Ryan didn't have that kind of connection. They'd have killed each other long ago.

"Yeah, there's that, too." Her thumbs worried the backs of

his hands. "But it goes way beyond that. We feel each other's emotions, too. And . . ."

"And?"

"Sexual desire and, um, fulfillment."

"Fulfillment?" Was she saying what he thought she was saying?

She nodded, her cheeks darkening. "When we met for the first time, on the beach, I collapsed because Meg was having an orgasm."

Scenes flashed through his mind. "And the first time we . . . ?"

Nodding miserably, she turned pleading eyes to him.

He dropped her hands.

16

Suz grabbed his arm when he tried to stand. "Please. I know it sounds bizarre. Believe me, I know. I live it! I realize only another twin could possibly understand, but I'm begging you to at least try."

"What makes you think another twin would understand?" *Tell her. Tell her before you dig yourself in deeper.*

Shoulders slumped, she wrapped her arms around herself, absently rubbing her upper arms, and gave a mirthless bark of laughter. "I guess I don't. And I swear I never will," she swore. "Everyone thinks having a twin is so great, oh, so . . . special. It's special, all right. Most of my life, it was a special kind of hell. The only thing worse than being a twin would be dating one." She shuddered. "I'd rather slit my wrists."

"I take it you and your sister aren't close."

She shook her head, her ponytail flicking from side to side.

He could relate to that. Until lately, he and Ryan had been like strangers who just happened to have the same face. But although he'd never given it any thought, he didn't think he had an aversion to dating another twin. "Just curious. Why wouldn't you consider dating a twin? Identical twins are not hereditary, you know. It's not like you'd be condemning your future children to being a twin, even if you married one." *Tell her.*

"Too much baggage. It's enough dealing with my sister. I'd rather live and die alone than hook up with another twin."

Abruptly, he stood and untied the door.

Before she could scramble to her feet, he was gone.

Sinking back down to the hard packed sand, she swiped a tear from her cheek. Telling him was a mistake. She'd known it, could see it in his shocked expression. But once the floodgates opened, she couldn't close them again.

Telling herself it was just as well, that she couldn't keep living a lie, she stood and wearily made her way back to the beach house to pack.

Drapes drawn against the relentlessly cheerful sunshine, Braedon sat in the gloom and popped the top on another beer.

A knock echoed.

He glanced at the sex-rumpled bed. He'd already sent the maid away but maybe the afternoon crew wanted to try again.

He didn't want his bed made. He especially didn't want the sheets changed. He wanted to sleep in them and smell her. Smell their sex. He wanted to wallow in them and grieve.

Whoever was at the door clearly did not intend to leave.

It was slow going, but he eventually made it to the door and threw back the bolts. "I told you to go away," he said, swinging open the door.

Ryan placed his hand on the solid wood and pushed his way in, Penny right behind him. "No can do, little brother."

"Aren't you supposed to be on your honeymoon?"

"Yep. But you're messing everything up, as usual."

"We're worried about you," Penny put in from behind her

new husband, peeking around his arm. "We never meant to hurt you, Brae, we're both so sorry," she added in a soft voice. It was the tone of voice people used in funeral homes.

Rage bubbled up. "Don't be! Hell, Pen, I never loved you. Don't look at me like that. You know it's true. I wasn't the love of your life, either. We used each other, plain and simple." He ran a hand over his head. Maybe he'd let his hair grow out. Trade in his truck for a motorcycle . . . get the hell away.

"Brae?" The concern on Ryan's face sucker punched him. "What's going on?"

All fight gone, he slumped to the edge of the mattress. "Tell me something. Did you ever feel what I felt?"

"I don't understand. What are you talking about?"

"Nothing. That was my answer." He stood. "I'm hungry. All I've had today was a cold chicken wing and—" he paused and looked at the coffee table—"four beers. Want to grab something to eat?"

"Sure," they both said.

"Great. Let me catch a quick shower."

Standing beneath the hot shower, he let the water sluice over his tense muscles. The water running down his face was just that: water. He never cried.

"Damn!" he pounded the marble wall of the shower with his fist. Why did she have to be a twin?

"I don't care what your sense told you, Meg, I'm fine." Suz balanced the phone on her shoulder and haphazardly folded the bridesmaid-dress-from-hell, then shoved it to the bottom of her suitcase. "There's nothing to do here, now that the wedding is over. I thought I'd go home early and get some work done."

"I really appreciate you taking on my clients while I'm gone," her sister was quick to say. "But there's nothing that can't wait a few more days. The beach house is rented for the rest of the week. Why don't you stay and work on your tan or something?"

"There is sun in Houston, and I have a pool."

"You're running away. I can hear it in your voice and I feel a deep down sadness. Since I have no reason to be sad, it has to be you. I know you met someone. What happened?"

"Nothing. Literally. I stupidly thought I loved him. Are you satisfied?" She scrubbed the tears from her face and reached for a tissue. "I told him. Everything."

"Everything?"

"Yes, everything, including our dirty little secret."

"What did he say to you? If I have to, I'll come down there and beat the crap out of him for you. Jake can help."

That earned a watery laugh. "Thanks, but there's no point. He didn't say anything. Just walked away without a backward glance." And she'd thought he was different. "Oh." She picked up her lingerie and stuffed them in her tote bag. "I sort of had an accident. Before you ask, I'm fine, but I broke the floor lamp in the living room. Tell Jake to send me the bill."

"We don't care about a stupid lamp, Suz. Have you seen or talked to him since he left?" Her sister was like a dog with a bone, bless her heart.

"No." She sighed, sinking down on the pile of clothing stacked on the chair. "There's nothing to say, Meg. I said it all, and he said nothing. Which spoke volumes."

"Does he live close to the hotel? I'm thinking maybe you could *accidentally* run into him, and see how it goes."

"Why are you pushing?"

"Because I'm your sister, like it or not, and I care about you. I want you to have what I've found with Jake. I know you've never had the feeling you had with this guy with anyone else. It was special. You owe it to yourself to at least talk to him again. Plus, you owe it to me. I don't want to cry through my honeymoon!"

Meg was right, Suz realized. With their sicko connection, her mood would wreck her sister's honeymoon. That wasn't fair. "Okay. I need to return his spare card key, anyway. As soon as I finish packing, I'll walk to the hotel and try to talk to him again." If nothing else, maybe she could get closure so at least her sister could have a shot at a decent honeymoon.

The hotel lobby was blessedly cool. Wiping the sweat from her forehead, she made her way to the elevator and pressed the button for the fourth floor.

Too soon, the door dinged and whooshed open. Wiping the nervous sweat from her hands on the legs of her shorts, she made her way to his door.

The sound of a shower greeted her. Relief washed through her. She would have a few minutes to gather her wits, plan what she would say.

Her relief was short-lived.

As she entered the room, her gaze darted to the unmade bed, filling her with longing. Why couldn't she have kept her big mouth shut for the rest of the week and enjoyed Braedon's company? Why was it so essential that she reveal all so soon into their relationship?

Movement by the sitting area drew her attention from the bed.

Braedon.

Braedon passionately kissing a woman sitting on his lap.

Pain filled her chest, constricted her breath. Tears blurring her vision, she turned and ran for the door. Above the drumming of her heartbeat in her ears, she heard him and the woman call out to her. Evidently, Braedon was a player.

She told herself it was better to find out now, before she got in any deeper, or humiliated herself further. But it didn't change the pain lancing through her.

Running blindly down the hall, she pounded on the button for the elevator. Luck was finally with her, the doors sliding open.

She jumped in, slapping her hand against the lobby button, praying he wouldn't follow her.

Praying he would.

17

She hit the sand leading to her rental at a little less than a dead run. As she opened the beach access door, she heard Braedon's voice as he stepped out of the elevator and picked up her pace.

Unfortunately, Braedon was a faster runner.

"Suzanne?" He bent, still gripping her arm, gasping for breath. "Wait. I can explain everything."

The woman skidded to a stop next to him, her face flushed, breathing hard. Suzanne only hoped it was from the exertion of running. "Wow," the woman said to Braedon, holding onto his arm, "no doubt about it. We need to get in shape."

We? They were already a we? Rage consumed her. She wanted to snatch every hair from the woman's head and rip her hand away from her man. She had no right to touch him like that.

The roar of blood in her ears prevented her from hearing what their lying mouths were saying.

They turned, and she looked in that direction to see what distracted them.

Braedon came running, barefoot, dressed in nothing but a pair of brief running shorts.

Braedon?

Her gaze darted from one man to the other while the pieces fell into place with deadly precision.

"Suz, don't run. Please, let me explain," the second Braedon said. "I love you. We can make this work," he said in an urgent whisper.

"Love?" She knew her voice shrieked, but was beyond caring. "Love? We've only known each other two days. What would make you think you loved me?" She made a jerky motion encompassing what had to be his twin brother and the woman. "People who *love* each other don't keep stuff like this a secret."

He tried to take her elbow but she twisted from his grasp. "Don't touch me! Don't ever touch me." Blinking back tears, she sniffed. "I trusted you. I gave you my body. I even thought I might be falling in love with you. Oh, don't look so pleased. Whatever I felt, you killed it on the beach." She wiped her eyes and nose on the hem of her T-shirt. "I felt guilty for keeping my secret. Then, when I told you and you just walked away without a word, I worried you were repulsed by the whole twin thing."

Her watery laugh ended on a hiccup. "Not that I'd blame you. I've been pretty repulsed by it for most of my life." She pressed trembling fingers to her lips. "You could have helped by telling me you were a twin. Instead, you let me go on and on, and never said a word."

"You know now. We can make it work. Hell, I'll even go to counseling, if that's what you want. Don't shut me out, Suzanne."

"You did that yourself. Good-bye, Braedon."

Megan rolled away from Jake and stretched. "I'm sorry, honey. It's difficult to concentrate when I know Suz is so miserable."

The phone rang. She made a face when she checked the Caller ID. "Hi, Braedon. No." She shook her head and flopped back on the pillow. "I haven't heard a word." She sighed. "That's not how it works. All I know is she's incredibly sad. And hurting. As soon as we got back, she arranged to transfer her clients over to my office and took off." She chewed her lip and glanced at her husband. "I know her friend Royce has a place out on Pleasure Beach. Suz said something about renting it. Royce's husband is a cardiologist. Jack MacMillan. He should be listed. Sorry I can't be more help. You, too. Bye." She turned to find Jake grinning at her. "What?"

"You know damn well where Suz is."

She smiled and crawled across the mattress to him. "I kind of got used to those double orgasms."

Suz frowned and pushed the button to erase message number twenty-six from Braedon. Somehow, he'd maneuvered her home number out of her secretary. According to Meg, he also knew hers.

"Message number twenty-seven. Six thirty-five A.M., today." Her throat ached at the sound of Braedon's voice. "Suz? Suzanne, if you're there, please pick up. It's been two weeks. I miss you," he said in a low, miserable sounding voice.

Click. "Message erased. Message number twenty-eight. Six forty-two A.M., today." Braedon's voice again caressed her ear. "I'm not accomplishing anything. I'm going to stay at my brother's beach house for a while to think about things. I'll call you when I get back." As sort of an afterthought, he added, "I love you."

Click. "Message deleted. There are no more new messages. To review saved messages, press—" She hung up. She didn't want to review messages. She just wanted to be left alone to get on with her lonely, loveless life.

"No news?" Ryan slid into the booth at Riley's Tavern and signaled the bartender.

Braedon shook his head, not bothering to look up, and took another swig from his longneck bottle.

"Did you call the sister?" He handed the waitress his credit card when she brought his beer. "What did she say?"

"She hasn't heard from Suz either. But she did tell me where I might find her." He grinned and set his bottle on the table. "Pleasure Beach."

Ryan chuckled and took a draw from his beer. "What a coincidence. I just happen to know of a place there with a vacancy." Their eyes met. "But are you sure about this?"

"Ryan, I'm even more sure, if that's possible, than you were about Penny. Without Suzanne, I'm nothing. It's like I never lived before I met her. In a matter of hours, it was like she became my best friend." His brother snickered, and he shot him a look. "Okay, we're more than friends. I realized that what you and Penny have, I could have, too. And I want it. I want it so bad, my teeth ache." He shook his head, twirling the bottle on the cocktail napkin. "I don't want to live without her. I *can't* live without her."

"You need to tell her exactly what you just told me. Convince her she's the one, the only one for you. If you leave now, you won't hit traffic. Go get her."

Braedon stretched in preparation for his run. It was his second morning on Pleasure Beach, and he'd yet to find Suzanne.

He'd walked to the house she was allegedly renting as soon as he arrived, but it looked dark and deserted.

Yesterday, he ran up and down the beach, hoping for a glimpse of her, until his legs threatened to collapse.

And yet, here he was, ready to do it all over again.

A slow jog took him past the beach house. The shutters were closed. No one sat on the deck or in the hot tub.

He decided to run down to the pier and do another turn before giving up for a while.

A shapely tanned woman ran ahead of him, the bright pink of her bikini showing off the expanse of golden brown skin.

His eyes narrowed. That tush looked awfully familiar. So did the swinging golden blond ponytail.

Suzanne.

Energized, he picked up the pace, soon overtaking her.

"Hi," he said, smiling at the look on her face before she could control it. "Come here often?"

"Go away." She sped up but was no match for him.

"I see your running skills have improved," he said when they were side by side once again.

"I've been training."

"Yeah? It shows." He wanted nothing more than to feast his eyes on her gorgeous body, but knew it would not help his cause. "I trained, too. I took a class in CPR." He winked. "Next time you collapse from sexual exhaustion, I'll be ready."

"But I won't be willing." With that parting shot, she picked up her speed.

He stopped, chest heaving, hands on hips, and watched her run out of his life.

No! Damn it, he deserved a happy ending. They both did.

With renewed determination, he gained on her. "Suz. Suz! Stop. Please."

When she picked up speed again, he saw red.

He meant to swing her off her feet. He hadn't counted on his forward momentum taking them both into the sand.

"Get off me!" She struggled, twisting in an effort to buck him off.

"Not until you listen to me. Are you listening?" She nodded, but he continued holding her wrists firmly above her head. His knees held most of his weight off her slender frame, but their position kept her effectively pinned. "I love you. I don't care if you want to believe it or not. It's true. If I have to spend the rest of my life proving it to you, I'd be honored to do it. All I'm asking for is the chance."

"You had the chance."

"I know I should have told you about Ryan right away. And I even understand why you'd feel like I didn't trust you enough to tell you. Especially when you told me everything about your situation. Stop struggling. I don't want to hurt you. I love you. And I think you love me. Right now you're mad and hurt. I get that. You can punch me if it will make you feel better. Whatever you want. But you damned well better not stop loving me."

He leaned to brush his lips over her surprised mouth. "We're both twins. We can't change that, no matter how much we might want to. The point is, we survived, despite being twins, and all that it entails. We love each other. It's time to survive together."

Gripping his sun warmed shoulders, she shoved, toppling him to the sand. Blinking back tears she refused to shed again, she scrambled to her feet. "Stop." Holding her hand up, she took a step back. "You're missing the point, Braedon. Maybe I haven't survived being a twin. I meant what I said in Corpus."

"But we love each other—"

"No!" She turned on him, blinking furiously in an effort to stem the flow of tears. Throat thick, she had to force the words to come out. "If you really loved me, you'd have told me. Even before I told you. But you didn't. And when I poured my heart out, you still kept quiet. Worse, you walked away without a word. Your actions just reinforced everything. Don't you see? I meant what I said about never ever being with another twin." She shrugged. "I don't know. Maybe I'm just too scarred from my own experience."

"But you and your sister—"

"Yeah, we get along all right. Now. But for how long? I can't take the chance. I can't love you, Braedon. I won't love you."

Pain lanced his heart. Fists clenched, he watched her walk

away. Kept watching until she was a dot on the endless span of sand.

She didn't want to love him. She didn't want to make the effort it required to be involved with someone who was a twin.

How could he argue with her when he'd felt pretty much the same throughout most of his life?

"I'm coming down there."

Suz pushed the hands-free button and set the phone on the counter. "Don't be ridiculous, you're supposed to be on your honeymoon." She frowned at the stainless steel toaster that refused to surrender her waffle. "I'm a big girl. I handled it," she finished in a choked voice, swallowing a sob.

"No offense, but I don't think you did. Lying to the guy and walking away isn't *handling it.*" Meg's huff of breath echoed in the kitchen as though she were standing right beside her sister. Suz could just imagine the famous Megan eye roll.

"Who said I was lying?" Oven mitts on, she turned the toaster upside down and shook it.

"Please. Suz, remember who you're talking to here. Don't make me call Aunt Pearl."

Aunt Pearl was their grandfather's sister. A real force to be reckoned with, Pearl had also been a twin. Aunt Pearl was the one who had kept them from killing each other growing up.

"You wouldn't dare."

"Don't push me. Now, are you going to stop being a baby, and go find Braedon and tell him you love him? I'd appreciate it. Then I could get on with my honeymoon without having to worry about you. Not to mention the fact that being sad and crying, thanks to you, puts a definite crimp in my love life." Meg's voice sounded as though she was eating something. Probably a Peppermint Pattie. "Not to mention the fact that I've gone through three bags of Peppermint Patties in less than twenty-four hours. I'll put on so much weight, none of my clothes will fit by the time I get home. You know how much I eat when I'm stressed."

"You're on your honeymoon. I'm sure you can think of ways to work off the excess calories." Suz banged the toaster against the edge of the sink, dislodging a shower of blackened crumbs. No waffle. "Meanwhile, I am starving to death." She dropped the toaster onto the counter. "I'll call you later. There's an omelet bar down the beach calling my name. Bye."

Megan sat staring at the phone still clutched in her hand. "How rude."

"You talking to me?" Jake walked out of the bathroom, looking especially yummy in a fluffy white towel and a smile.

She took a moment to enjoy the view as he sauntered toward her, a predatory gleam in his eye, before holding up her hand. "Wait. Hold that thought. This will only take a minute." Scrolling through her phone book, she found the number and hit send, then winked at her husband. "Hi, Braedon? This is Meg. Let's talk."

Suzanne's stomach clenched at the smell of the steaming golden omelet the waitress just set in front of her. She had to eat. Eating was a necessity. Kind of like breathing.

Breathing reminded her of kissing Braedon, how his scent had filled her nostrils, the smoothness of his tongue. Her nipples tingled at the memory.

Did he miss her as much as she missed him? Impossible. He'd have collapsed in a puddle of misery by now. Men were not strong enough to handle the strength of emotions she'd experienced of late.

An ache radiated from the vicinity of her heart. She absently rubbed the spot. Maybe she wasn't strong enough, either.

Her omelet blurred.

The waitress reappeared to plunk a squat white vase with a lone red rose on the table. At Suzanne's raised brow, she shrugged and walked away.

Braedon? Her heart fluttered, irrational hope filling her. *Don't be stupid. You told him it was over. You told him you didn't love him. You told him you couldn't love him.*

You lied.

The realization hit her, further blurring her vision, deafening her to everything but the sound of her own pounding heart.

Slowly, she became aware of someone standing next to the table. It required several blinks, but finally the man came into focus.

"Hi." Braedon. "Can I buy you a drink? Maybe a tequila shot?"

"Th-they don't serve alcohol until after noon on Sundays." She swallowed and wiped her nose on the edge of her napkin.

Braedon slid into the other side of the booth. For the first time since they'd met, he looked unsure of himself.

"Too bad." He gave a sad looking smile. "I was hoping to get you liquored up and have my way with you."

Scrubbing away the tears, she tried to laugh. It came out watery sounding. "I don't think liquor is a requirement for that, judging by our history."

His warm hands covered her cold ones on top of the lacquered table. "And what about our future? Or do we even have one?"

"After everything I said, would you even still want one?" Her breath refused to leave her lungs, her skin pounding with the jungle beat of her pulse. *Please, Lord, don't let it be too late.* She'd made some big mistakes in her life, but walking away from Braedon took the prize.

He shrugged, sending her hopeful heart plummeting. "I guess that depends." He reached up to wipe a tear from her cheek with the pad of his thumb.

"On what?"

"On whether you really meant what you said."

"I did, at the time." Dreading the look in his beautiful blue eyes, she pulled her hands from his and looked down, concentrating on shredding her napkin.

His finger beneath her chin tilted her head until she was looking directly into his eyes. "What about now?"

What about now? Had she really changed her mind? Truth be told, she'd changed it as she'd walked away from him. She was just too stubborn to admit it, even to herself. She may have even regretted the words as soon as they left her mouth.

Placing her pile of napkin on the table, she finally met his gaze. "Now? Now," she whispered, taking his hand in both of hers, "now I think it was just about the stupidest thing I've ever said."

"But is that how you still feel?" he persisted.

Slowly she shook her head. Never breaking eye contact, she rose and slid into the booth next to him, not stopping until she backed him into the corner and climbed up on his lap. "Now I feel like I may die if you don't kiss me."

When she would have covered his mouth with her own, told him everything with her kiss, he backed his head away, just out of reach. Only his ragged breathing told her he was not unaffected. "Oh, I plan to kiss you," he said, his minty breath so close it made her mouth water. "But not until we're some place where I can do it properly." He grinned. "Or improperly. And for as long as it takes."

The fist around her heart eased, and she smiled for the first time since they'd parted. "Oh? And when would that be?"

"Right after you say you'll marry me."

She wiggled closer, secretly thrilled to feel the hard ridge beneath his zipper. "I haven't heard you ask yet."

"I'm asking."

"Then I'm accepting."

Again, he backed away. "I need to hear the words."

"Maybe I need to hear them, too." Her attempt to scoot away was thwarted by his arms, clamping her firmly against his chest.

"I love you. Will you marry me? Don't just look at me and smile. Answer me, damn it!"

"I love you, too, and yes, I'll marry you. Oh, and Braedon?" She smiled up at him, batting her eyelashes. "The name is Suzanne, not damn it."

With a mock growl he hugged her closer. "Thank God. Now give your future husband a kiss, smart-ass."

EPILOGUE

"Where is she?" Braedon tossed his phone to the bed in the Las Vegas hotel room, and paced to the window before turning to glare at his brother. "We're supposed to get married by the volcano in less than an hour!"

"Take it easy." Ryan attempted an awkward pat on his brother's shoulder. "Penny and Meg are out looking for her." The strains of "I Heard It Through The Grapevine" filled the room. "It's Penny." Ryan reached into his pocket and flipped open his phone. "Did you find her?"

Braedon stood at the window, his head hanging, while his brother's voice droned on. Where was Suzanne? The last week had been magical. Perfect. Had it been one-sided? Had she had a change of heart? Maybe he was stupid for even thinking he could change her mind about the twin thing. Maybe loving her to distraction still wasn't enough.

He might puke.

"Dude." Ryan's voice broke into Braedon's thoughts. "They found her."

* * *

Suzanne licked the salt from her hand, tossed back the tequila shot, and sucked the lime wedge.

Braedon sat at the other end of the bar and watched her down her third drink since he'd arrived. Was she having second thoughts? Did she even plan to tell him she wasn't going to marry him? He deserved better than that.

Stalking to her end of the bar, he sat on the stool next to her. "Someone once told me you're not drunk if you can lie on the floor without holding on." He leaned close. "Don't you have something you're supposed to be doing in, oh," he glanced at his watch, "about half an hour?"

Her guilty gaze swung to his. "I'm sorry," she whispered.

"For what?" His gut clenched, he held his breath waiting for her reply.

"For being such a terrible person." She sniffed and wiped her eyes on a cocktail napkin. "You deserve so much better."

"I deserve you. Hey, I'm no prize, either. Just ask my brother." He touched her cheek. "But I will love you and honor you until my dying breath. So . . . what do you say? Are you ready to make an honest man out of me?"

Her smile lit up her face. Well, maybe the tequila helped a little. "I'm not sure marrying you will do that, but I'm willing, if you are."

He stood and tugged her to her feet. "Elvis has left the building, and is waiting to perform our ceremony. C'mon, little darlin'."